PaperQuake

Kathryn Reiss

Paper

Quake

A PUZZLE

HARCOURT, INC.

San Diego / New York / London

Requests for permission to make copies of
any part of the work should be mailed to:
the following address: Permissions Department,
Harcourt, Inc., 6277 Sea Harbor Drive,
Orlando, Florida 32887-6777.

www.harcourtbooks.com

Library of Congress Cataloging-in-Publication Data
Reiss, Kathryn.
PaperQuake: a puzzle/by Kathryn Reiss.
p. cm.
Summary: Certain that she is being drawn by more than
coincidences into the lives of people living nearly 100 years ago,
Violet, who feels like the odd sister in a set of triplets,
searches for clues to help her avert an imminent tragedy.
ISBN 0-15-204707-7
[1. Triplets—Fiction. 2. Sisters—Fiction. 3. Earthquakes—
Fiction. 4. San Francisco (Calif.)—Fiction.] I. Title
PZ7.R2776Pap 1998
[Fic]—dc21 97-33217

Text set in Galliard
Designed by Camilla Filancia

Printed in the United States of America

K J I H G F E D C B A

For MARILYN CHANDLER MCENTYRE,
who introduced me to earthquakes

and in memory of my mother-in-law,
VIOLET STRYCHACZ,
no shrinking violet, either

One generation passeth away,
and another generation cometh:
but the earth abideth for ever.

—ECCLESIASTES 1:4

March 25, 1906

Dear Diary,
    Truly, V frightens me now. She says such strange things and twitches while she speaks. What started as an ordinary job is turning into a nightmare. I know V needs me and, goodness knows, I need the work—but when she gets that odd look in her eyes, she seems like a different person from the sweet, frail girl I came to take care of. She turns cold and hard and seems quite as ancient as the earth itself—the earth she keeps going on about—and I want to leave here. There are other positions where I can earn my living. There <u>must</u> be! Perhaps I shall start looking on my afternoon off.
    It makes me feel better to have this plan to look for something new. Some normal sort of job with normal people. When V has one of her spells, she carries on and on about the earth as if it is something <u>alive.</u> That cannot be called normal. "Stretching," she muttered tonight, and I hurried to her side. "The earth needs to stretch."
    "Do you need to stretch?" I asked. These days she is sometimes too weak to do this herself. "Shall I help you turn over in bed?"
    "Stretching out," she said, pushing my hands away. And I saw that her eyes were wide open, staring at nothing. "It's going to happen soon! Very soon! The earth . . . deep inside . . . People running—over the bridge—oh, there's no time—the bridge!"
    "You're ill," I told her. "Just lie back in bed and relax. Close your eyes."
    But her eyes stayed open. They glared hard into mine,

lit with fiery intensity. "We cannot stop it, no one can," she hissed. "We can only try to help. Help the children. Help the little girl! We must help!"

"I'm trying to help you," I said. "I'm trying to take care of you."

"The earth takes care of itself," she moaned, tossing her head back and forth on her pillow. "But who will help the people?"

I patted her hand where it lay limp on the white sheet and touched my palm to her damp forehead. I felt so tired suddenly. I wanted to crawl onto the bed next to her and collapse. She drains me when she goes on like this. "Go to sleep now."

"Sleep?" V laughed, but it was a dark, unpleasant sound. "Don't you understand what I'm telling you? The earth *never* sleeps."

Finally she grew quiet. Finally she slept. But her words seemed to hover in the room; and as I sit here in my chair in the corner, writing in my diary, they hover over me still:

The earth never sleeps.

CHAPTER 1

Violet Jackstone was doodling in her science notebook when her desk seemed to jump an inch to the right. She dropped her pen and turned to look at Beth, but her best friend was still taking notes as Mr. Koch lectured about rock formations. All around the classroom the other eighth graders rustled at their desks, shuffled papers, and whispered, waiting for the bell to release them for the weekend. No one else's desk had moved.

But then the entire room gave one great shake, like a shaggy dog after a bath. Mr. Koch stopped talking about rocks. The class held its breath, but then the room was still again, as rooms tend to be.

"Whoa!" cried Beth, breaking the tension.

"Was that an earthquake?" someone else called out.

"Cool!"

"We haven't had one in ages!"

Everyone started talking at once. Everyone except Violet,

who sat with closed eyes, trying to breathe. *It's all right, it's over now,* she told herself. *Don't panic.*

"All right, all right," Mr. Koch said, trying to quiet the class. "That was just a temblor—probably hardly registered on the Richter scale. But what perfect timing!"

Violet's eyes flew open. Perfect timing?

"What was I just telling you about rocks?" Mr. Koch smiled as if he had personally arranged the earthquake. "I couldn't have come up with a better example. Rocks are not just dead bits and pieces. They are part of the whole—part of the whole living earth." Mr. Koch threw his arms wide. "Look out the windows!"

Everyone obediently swiveled to look. There wasn't much to see from where Violet sat. Tops of trees, leaves turning brown, squares of blue autumn sky. How could Mr. Koch just keep on teaching as if nothing had happened? What if the tremor was only a taste of another quake yet to come? How could everyone keep sitting calmly, taking notes? Violet clenched her hands into fists. She wanted to leap up and run out of the room.

"What do you see out there?" Mr. Koch walked over to the windows to look down. "What do you see? It's the earth! The earth we live on! Houses, shops, parks, streets, people. Once there were forests and rivers, wild animals, native tribes living off the land. Now we're here instead. It's like layers of paint, one layer painted over another over another."

"What's he talking about?" muttered someone in the back of the room. "Art?"

"No, geology, I think," someone else whispered back. "But you know how he runs on."

"Scrape off the layers of our present culture and you're in another time. Dig into the earth, and it's the same. Layers of soil and rock, telling the earth's story—just as all of you will be telling part of the earth's story in your science papers." Mr. Koch glared at the class. "Now, how many of you have chosen your topics?" His booming voice made Violet flinch. "I hope *all* of you, because—guess what, folks?—time's up."

Violet slumped in her seat, the earthquake anxiety receding to the back of her mind as the more immediate worry about her science topic took over. She liked Mr. Koch, who both fascinated and frightened her with his intensity. But she hadn't come up with a topic for this month's project on some aspect of science especially relevant to their state of California. She hadn't even started to think about it.

Hands shot up. "Beth?" asked Mr. Koch.

"How logging in northern California destroys ancient forests," Beth told him, and Violet sighed. Beth was a good student. Everything seemed to come easily to her.

Mr. Koch noted her topic on a pad of paper. "Good," he said. "Dina? What about you?"

"Um—like, something about the Gold Rush? About, like, the process of mining for silver and gold?"

"Like, fine." He noted her topic on his pad while the class giggled. "Jack?"

"Soil erosion in the hills."

"Excellent. Melanie?"

"Water pollution control in the bay."

"Super. How about you, Violet?"

Violet looked at her desktop as if a topic might appear there in magic writing. Nothing happened. "I—I'm not sure yet," she said quietly.

"Not sure?" Mr. Koch left the windows and walked over to frown down at her. "Then I will have to choose for you. A shame, really, because we tend to be more interested in subjects we select for ourselves. But, let me see . . ." He tapped his fingers on her desk. She could feel heat color her face. "How about earthquakes? We've just been reminded that California is no stranger to earthquakes—but do we know what causes them? You will do some research and write about what you discover." He scribbled her topic on his pad. "In fact, I have some books I can give you about the big earthquake back in 1906. San Francisco was all but destroyed then—by fire as well as from the quake itself. You may as well focus on that quake for your paper."

Violet slumped lower as he walked away. She hated even *thinking* about earthquakes. But she wouldn't dare ask Mr Koch to change her topic to another one now.

And then the teacher was at her desk again, holding out some books. "Take these," he ordered. "You may find them useful."

Violet accepted his books with a weak smile.

"In many ways, history and science are not separate subjects at all," Mr. Koch said, throwing his arms wide to encompass the whole class. "Both are the dust under our feet and the air we breathe. Sometimes things happen that we attribute to coincidence, but historians look for patterns. Scientists look for *reasons*."

The students sat back, listening. They were used to Mr. Koch's ramblings. Sometimes the lectures were interesting, sometimes not, but his loud, gravelly voice compelled them to listen. "There are layers and layers of history all around us," he intoned, "just as the earth is made of layers of rock and soil. Mostly the different layers are hidden from us. But sometimes cracks form and we can see what came before."

"I think *he's* cracked!" whispered the boy behind Violet, and Beth snickered.

"Both scientists and historians delve into the cracks—"

Mr. Koch broke off with a gasp as the room was lifted and dropped as though by a giant hand. "Not again!" someone shouted, and Violet screamed as the floor began dipping and the walls shook. The teacher yelled, "Duck and cover, people! Duck and cover!" He ran around the back of his desk and tried to fit his lanky form into the small space meant for the chair.

This was no mild shaking. This time the earth meant business. There was a grinding roar miles beneath the surface of the earth, and then the crash of books as they tumbled from the shelf in the back of the classroom. In half a second Violet was crouched under her desk, covering her head with her arms. Belatedly, a buzzer went off in the hallways, adding its noisy warning to the tumult. The floor rolled and the lights went out. Violet squeezed her eyes shut and saw—*flames?* She saw three shadowy figures—children—moving out from flaming wreckage, two taller figures and a little girl in tattered clothes, holding out her arms. The children's screams and Violet's merged into one desperate howl that seemed to go on forever.

"Hey, Vi, it's okay now," someone was saying, but it *wasn't* okay, it *couldn't* be until that little girl was safe, until all three of those children were safe— Someone's arms wound tightly around Violet, and she shut her mouth abruptly. She uncovered her head and looked into Beth's eyes.

Beth crouched in the aisle, holding Violet. "Major panic attack," Beth said.

Violet took a shuddering breath. The room was silent for a long moment. Was she the only one who had screamed?

"That was a big one!" the girl in front of Violet said with a nervous giggle.

"I bet it was only a three," a boy called from across the room.

Violet drew a shaky breath and edged cautiously out of Beth's grip, out from beneath her desk.

Around the room kids began joking and talking. Violet didn't see how they could laugh.

"Whoa! That was like a roller coaster—"

"I was just thinking the other day that it's been a long time since we felt a quake, and now we've had two in one day—"

"I thought for a second I was going to barf—"

Mr. Koch walked down the aisles, checking on everybody. He looked pretty shaky himself. "Are we all okay?"

The door to the classroom opened cautiously, and a girl stepped inside. "Vi! Oh, Vi, are you okay?" It was Jasmine, one of Violet's two sisters. Violet groaned.

It was bad enough that she'd been the only one screaming her head off, but having her sister come to check on her was even worse.

The nervous tension that gripped the class during the quake evaporated into laughter as Jasmine hurried over to Violet's desk.

"I'm fine," Violet said stiffly. She wiped her sweaty palms on her jeans. Her heart was still pounding so hard she could hardly hear what anybody was saying. *Who were those children in the fire? Wasn't anybody helping them?*

Then she thought: *What fire?*

"She's fine," echoed Mr. Koch. "But it was nice of you to come see for yourself." He looked at Jasmine curiously.

Jasmine's face still wore an expression of concern, but she smiled at the teacher and waggled her fingers at Beth. "Well, um, I guess I'd better get back to English. If Vi doesn't need me—"

"I don't," muttered Violet, her voice tight with embarrassment. "You can go now."

"I was just trying to help," Jasmine murmured. She turned and left the room.

"Hey, can I go check on my brother?" a boy called out from the back row. And then other kids chimed in, all insisting they wanted to roam the halls, looking for siblings and friends. This excited chatter gave way to further speculation about the quake's magnitude and location.

Violet wanted to be able to laugh off all the things that scared her—like ghost stories, airplanes, and earthquakes, especially earthquakes—the way her sisters and friends did. She sometimes thought she was still getting over the quake they'd had a year ago. She'd been soaking in the tub when that one hit, rolling the bathwater into waves that splashed out onto the floor. She still dreamed of that quake and remembered it every single time she took a bath. Usually she took showers now, trying to keep the memory of her terror at bay. The only time she'd screamed more loudly was when she was four or five and a big earthquake sent books tumbling off the shelves in the public library where she had been listening to story time. That time she thought she was going to be killed. Some people had been, though not in the library.

"Enough now," said Mr. Koch, as the loudspeaker sputtered on the wall. "Let's hear what the official word is."

The lights flickered on again. The principal's voice came crackling over the loudspeaker, informing everyone that the first news reports were measuring the earthquake at 3.8 on the Richter scale. That wasn't particularly large, but it seemed to have been on the Hayward fault, Ms. Lynch told them, the one running right through Berkeley, quite near their school. There were no signs of damage, but the students could leave for home right now.

The eighth graders cheered.

"I think Mother Nature just paid a visit to remind us of her own role in California's history," Mr. Koch joked uneasily. "Maybe Violet should ask for an interview for her report."

The class chuckled obligingly, but Violet sat silent. She was remembering what Mr. Koch had said about cracks. Did bits of the past crack through more easily in California than elsewhere because of all the fault lines? The thought made her feel shivery. She pushed it out of her head and started packing her notebook into her backpack. The extra books from Mr. Koch made a bulge.

Mr. Koch picked up an eraser and swept away the writing from the chalkboard. Then the bell rang and the students rushed toward the door. "Don't forget, we're going to the Academy of Sciences in San Francisco on Monday," he reminded them as they filed out into the hallway. "Be here on time." Then he added, "You kids go straight home now. There could be aftershocks."

Violet's sisters, Jasmine and Rose, were already waiting by the lockers when Violet and Beth arrived. "Hey, what's shakin'?" Rose greeted them.

Violet was taking deep breaths, trying to calm her fluttering heart. She didn't answer.

"It *is* a pretty cool start to the weekend," said Beth. "You have to admit."

"Yeah," said Rose. "But are you okay, Vi? You look like you're going to faint."

Immediately Jasmine reached for Violet's backpack. "Here, I'd better carry this."

"I can do it!"

But Jasmine held tight to the backpack. "I'm sorry if you're mad that I came to check on you," she said earnestly. "But our classroom was just next door, and I thought I could hear you screaming though the wall. I was scared."

"I thought about checking on you, too," Rose chimed in. "I was trying to tell Mr. Yarris that you are really terrified of quakes and have a weak heart, and that you might have an attack or something, but everybody else was talking, too, and he wasn't even listening. Brett Hudson agreed with me, though. He said he'd come with me to check on you—"

"I'm fine!" Violet crossed her arms and glared at her sisters. They were wearing nearly identical outfits, as they always did since entering junior high—jeans and baggy red sweaters. But Rose wore low black boots and Jasmine had on red high-tops so people who needed to could tell them apart. Their gold-flecked brown hair flowed to their shoulders and their blue eyes sparkled. Violet was wearing jeans and a red sweater, too, but it didn't help much.

She reached out and plucked her backpack off Jasmine's shoulder. "I'm fine, and I can carry my own stuff!"

Jasmine still looked worried. But Rose just shrugged.

Beth tried to smooth things over, as she often did. "So what's this about Brett Hudson, Rosy? Do you like him?"

"Brett is cool," Rose said, closing her locker. "In fact, he and I decided we're going to hang out at the Halloween Ball."

"Then I'll see if Casey Banks wants to go, too," said Jasmine.

"You mean you guys are going with boys to the dance?" asked Beth. "With *dates*?"

"Oh, nobody dates," said Jasmine, flipping back her long hair with a sophisticated gesture Violet had tried before to emulate. "We just, you know, *hang*."

"Like Vi, hanging on to the legs of her desk during the quake," Rose added with a smirk. *"Tight."*

Violet gritted her teeth.

"What?" demanded Jasmine.

"Why are you looking at us like that?" asked Rose.

Violet pushed ahead of them down the hall. They drove her crazy with their combination of teasing and overzealous protection. Her parents weren't much better. Her father joked that she was the favorite vacation spot for every flu and virus bug on the continent, and both her parents were always feeling her forehead for fevers and making comments about her appearance—discussing whether she looked flushed or pale or somehow *wrong*. But at least that was only at home. They didn't come barging into her classroom.

She would die of embarrassment if they didn't leave her alone.

The problem was her sisters meant well. They really did. They always wanted to help her—their poor baby sister who had nearly died at birth. Beneath their teasing was their worry, and Violet knew it. But it had to stop.

"Mr. Yarris just stood there, holding the chalk and waiting for the room to stop shaking so he could finish talking about calculating the frequency of genetic mutation or something," Rose was saying as the other girls reached Violet. "He's one cool guy—he barely missed a beat."

"You can always tell the people who grew up around earthquakes from those who didn't," agreed Jasmine. "Poor Ms. Martuscelli looked terrified. She tried to get under her desk but didn't quite fit."

Violet fell into step with her sisters and Beth.

"She must not have lived in California very long, then," said Beth. The girls headed outside and started walking home. "Everybody here knows that these small quakes are nothing to worry about, that they just, you know, relieve the pressure."

"Yeah?" Jasmine grinned. "Tell poor Vi." She reached over and squeezed Violet's arm.

Violet pulled away.

Two boys from the ninth grade coasted by on bikes and howled like wolves.

"Look, it's Brett and Casey," squealed Rose, and she and Jasmine waved hello.

"Hey, it's Jazzy and Rosy, the gorgeous twins!" shouted Casey as the boys sped past.

But they *weren't* twins! Violet stamped along the sidewalk, resentment flaring up more fiery than ever. They weren't twins at all. They were *triplets,* and she was their third, invisible member.

As she walked, resentment turned to remembering. Three shadowy children, flames behind them, had cried out from the ruins. They, too, had been nearly invisible.

CHAPTER 2

Violet and Beth walked together behind Jasmine and Rose, Beth chattering on about her mom's latest boyfriend, Rose and Jasmine discussing boys. Their voices were muted by traffic and the rustling leaves of the trees, but Violet wasn't really listening anyway. In her head she heard again the screams of the shadow children and her own scream merging with theirs. It had only been her imagination, she reminded herself. A scary vision brought on by the earthquake.

The Berkeley streets were crowded with children on bikes and with people walking dogs. Beth waved good-bye at the corner of North Street, and the triplets continued on with Violet still lagging behind. The Jackstones' brown-shingled house stood back from the street, shaded by oak trees. Hanging baskets of colorful nasturtiums, left over from summer, dotted the porch. Violet saw with surprise that their mother's car was parked in the driveway.

Lily and Greg Jackstone owned two busy florist shops, one

in Berkeley and one in Oakland. Lily worked in Oakland and Greg in Berkeley, and the girls sometimes helped out by filling orders on weekends or during holidays when flowers were in great demand. The shops were open until five o'clock, but neither parent arrived home before six.

Violet hurried ahead of her sisters now. She ran into the house, dumped her backpack by the stairs, and went straight to the kitchen, where her mother was arranging a huge bouquet of autumn flowers in a ceramic vase.

"You're home early, Mom," she said. "Because of the quake? Are the shops all right?"

"Hello, Baby," her mother greeted her. "Everything's fine. I came home early to celebrate—but I can't tell you the good news until your sisters and Dad are all here. Come tell me all about your day. Were you scared in the quake, darling? I thought of you, poor little one."

"I was okay." Violet pulled out a stool at the counter.

"It knocked over the fern in the dining room—I just finished vacuuming up the dirt. Only 3.8, I heard on TV. But still enough to make a mess."

"It's been a long time since we had a quake," said Jasmine, coming into the kitchen.

"Yeah, really," agreed Rose. "About time, I'd say." She perched on a stool next to Violet.

Violet watched their mother pour out tall cups of cider—Jasmine's in the yellow cup, Rose's in the pink, Violet's in the purple.

Lily Jackstone was long-boned and fine-featured like Jasmine and Rose. She had the same gold-streaked light brown hair (her streaks came from a bottle, but the effect was the same) and happy blue eyes. *Mom looks more like the third triplet than I do myself,* Violet thought sadly. And the resemblance only became stronger as the girls grew older. Violet looked like her father, Greg: dark and small, with frizzy brown hair and brown eyes. *It's not fair,* she thought.

"Now tell me about school," Lily invited, joining the girls at the counter with her own cup of cider.

"I was in English when the quake hit," said Jasmine. "Poor Vi was in science. She was roaring like a lion, and I rushed in to see if she had been swallowed up in a huge crack."

"I was fine!" snapped Violet. "Mom, tell her to stop doing things like that. I mean it. I'm going to die of embarrassment before I'm ever killed in an earthquake."

Maybe, said a little voice inside. *Maybe not.*

Rose laughed. "And just listen to our little cub snarl!"

"Now don't tease," said Lily. "Poor Baby needs her sisters on her side."

"We were interrupted by the quake right in the middle of a really neat assignment," Jasmine told them. "Ms. Martuscelli was talking about logic—we're supposed to write logical arguments in our essays. But she was teaching us these really cool puzzles, called—um, what was it?—*lateral thinking,* that's what she said. It's when you're thinking along certain lines, trying to solve a problem, and you just can't get anywhere, and nothing makes sense. And then suddenly something shifts in your brain, and you can think about the problem in a whole new way—and then everything makes sense!"

"You mean, sort of like hidden pictures?" asked Rose. "You know, where you stare at a picture and it's of a beautiful young woman, and then you blink and—bingo!—she somehow looks like an old hag?"

"Yeah," nodded Jasmine. "Like—here's one we did in class. Rosy, see if you can do this. Mom, you try, too."

Violet sipped her cider and listened resentfully. She wasn't very good at doing puzzles, but it was typical of the others to leave her out.

"Here's the situation," began Jasmine. "A man lies dead in a cabin on the side of a mountain."

"Okay," said Rose. "So?"

"You have to ask yes and no questions about the situation," Jasmine explained, "trying to figure out what happened to the man."

"You mean how he died?" queried their mother.

"Yeah." Jasmine tilted her stool back and regarded the others with bright, amused eyes.

Violet pictured a cozy wooden cabin built of logs, nestled back among pine trees atop a mountain. A man lay dead inside the cabin, sprawled on top of his bed near the hearth. "Did the man have a heart attack?" she asked Jasmine.

"Nope," said Jasmine.

"Liver failure?" suggested Rose.

"Nope."

"Was he embarrassed to death by his sister?" Violet asked slyly. Jasmine frowned at her.

"It was probably some sudden illness," diagnosed Lily. "He wouldn't wear his jacket when his mother told him to?"

"Nope," giggled Jasmine.

"Was the man murdered?" asked Rose.

"Nope and nope," smiled Jasmine. "All wrong. No illness. No murder. The man was in perfect health. Ask about something else."

"Like what?" Violet couldn't think what else there was to ask. "People in perfect health don't die."

"Ask about the cabin," instructed Jasmine.

"What about it?" What was there to say about a cabin? "Was it a log cabin?" Violet asked.

"Nope!" cried Jasmine. "But that's good, Baby. Go on! You're getting close. Ask more about the cabin."

But Violet couldn't think of anything else to ask. She pictured the poor man dead in his bed, poor guy, and that was all there was to it. "Don't call me Baby," she snapped. It was one thing for her parents to call her Baby, but she didn't have to take it from her sisters.

When the phone rang, Lily left to answer it, but the three girls remained at the counter. Violet was sulking. Jasmine and Rose faced each other with twin looks of concentration.

"Was the cabin built in the woods?" asked Rose.

"No," grinned Jasmine. "It wasn't."

Rose narrowed her eyes. "Aha," she said. "And is the cabin a house? Can you live in it?"

"No," said Jasmine.

"So the man didn't live in the cabin. Did anyone? No? And was the man alone?" Rose was firing questions fast now. "Is he the only one dead?"

Violet sighed and stopped listening. Her sisters were always together in things like this, tuned to the same wavelength. They enjoyed puzzles and games of skill; they were good at sports and contests. She wasn't especially good at anything.

"I've got it!" squealed Rose, and Violet tuned in again. "Is the cabin made of metal?"

Now why in the world would Rose ask that? wondered Violet. But Jasmine laughed and cheered. "Yes! Oh, you're so close now, Rosy!"

"I know I am," exulted Rose. "It's a plane, isn't it? The cabin of an airplane. Because there was a crash on a mountain, right? And the dead man is the pilot—or I suppose he could be a dead passenger."

"Got it!" Jasmine crowed. "You're brilliant, Rosy."

"What?" Violet was completely bewildered. "I don't get it."

Jasmine looked at her pityingly. "Listen, Vi, it's simple. A man lies dead in a cabin on the side of a mountain! And first you picture a little log house and a man lying dead in his bed. Illness or something, right? But it's a plane crash. See? Something switches in your brain, and then it all makes sense."

"Totally," Rose agreed.

Violet sat looking from sister to sister as if she were watching a tennis match. She had no idea how Rose managed the leaps to airplane cabin, to dead pilot, to plane crash. She felt lost as her two sisters chortled together like conspirators and Rose begged, "Come on, test me again."

"Okay," said Jasmine. "Here's another good one. Ready?"

Rose nodded, brow furrowed already in concentration. Violet sighed. But she listened.

"The man was afraid to come home because of the man in the mask," announced Jasmine.

Violet immediately envisioned a man wearing a gorilla mask on his face, waiting at the door of another man's house. The other man stood outside in the driveway, afraid to enter. "Is it a gorilla mask?" she asked Jasmine tentatively.

Jasmine giggled. "Nope."

"Is it a scary mask?" asked Rose. "Like for the Halloween Ball?"

"Nope," said Jasmine.

"*Hmmm,*" murmured Rose, deep in thought. "Well then, is 'home' really a house? A house you could live in?"

"Nope!" squealed Jasmine. "But, *ooh,* Rosy, you're getting closer..."

Completely baffled, Violet shoved back her stool and left the kitchen. She stomped up the stairs to her room. Her sisters shared the big bedroom on the left. The walls were papered in yellow and pink flowers. Jasmine's bed had a yellow quilt and Rose's had a pink quilt. Her own room down the hall was really just an alcove off the master bedroom. In fact, it didn't even have its own door. To get to it, she had to cross through her parents' room. The room had been perfect for her when she was a baby, they had told her, because she was so frail and tiny. They needed to be close by to check her heart monitor. The other two girls, always robust, roomed together right from the start.

But I don't need anyone checking on me in the night anymore, Violet fumed as she entered her small room and sagged down on the lavender quilt. *And I haven't for years.* She should be able to share the big bedroom with Rosy and Jazzy and have a bedroom door to close. *Three's a crowd,* Violet thought dourly. *Not that I ever was really part of the threesome anyway.*

Once she hadn't minded being set apart—it had made her feel special to be fussed over. But lately she hated being so different. And the scene with Jasmine flying in to check on her in school was the last straw. It was time for a change.

She got off her bed and went to the phone in her parents' room. She pressed Beth's number, the only one besides her own that she knew by heart. "I need your help," she said when Beth answered.

"With what? Your science paper? You're the lucky one—getting Mr. Koch's books to help you."

The last thing on Violet's mind was her science paper. "But I need help with *me*," she said, "not with school stuff. You're an artistic type. You ought to be able to manage a little transformation. Make me tall and blond."

"You know I don't do plastic surgery." Beth giggled. "But how about platform shoes?"

If you knew how awful I feel, you wouldn't laugh, Violet thought miserably. But she had tried before without success to make Beth understand how it felt to be so different from her sisters. "I'm nothing like my brother, and yet I don't care a bit," Beth had argued. "So what's the big deal?" The big deal was that Beth and her younger brother, Tom, were *supposed* to look different. They were different ages and different genders. They had never shared their mother's womb. Beth had not been born the odd-one-out of a matching set.

But there was no sense explaining to Beth anymore. Better just to make plans.

"How about dyeing my hair?" Violet suggested. "You know. Kind of golden."

"Well, my mom dyes her hair and it looks pretty good," Beth mused. "But on you—"

"Let's try it," said Violet impatiently.

Beth agreed that they could try it at her house while her mom and brother were out. "Come tomorrow," she said. "After lunch. Tom's soccer game starts then. He and Mom will both be gone for a couple hours. We can go to the drugstore first to get the color. That's where my mom gets hers."

After Violet hung up, she sat on her parents' bed staring at her reflection in their big wall mirror. She tried to imagine her dark hair as light as her sisters'. She hoped the drugstore would have the exact right color. She'd have to get a sample to take along to the shop.

She jumped off the bed and went across the hall to her sisters' pink-and-yellow bedroom. It was empty. She crossed to the long dresser her sisters shared and picked up a hairbrush. It was clean and hairless; it must belong to Rose. Jasmine wasn't such a neatnik. Violet looked all around and finally located Jasmine's brush under her yellow-quilted bed. It was full of hair, but also of dust, and the wad that Violet pulled from the bristles looked more like a bird's nest than hair from her sister's head. It was dark and matted. Sighing, Violet looked around the room for inspiration. Her gaze fell on the red-handled scissors in the pencil mug on Rose's desk. Smiling, she stuck the dirty mat of hair back into the bristles and dropped the brush back on the floor where she'd found it. Rose's voice called up the stairs and Violet jumped guiltily. It was Violet's night to set the table. She would have to come back later.

At dinner the family sat in the dining room. The triplets' father, Greg Jackstone, who had been fairly beaming ever since he'd walked in the door, stood at the head of the table and poured his wife a glass of wine. Then he poured each daughter a quarter inch as well.

"Hey, all right!" said Jasmine, accepting the tiny drink. Normally Greg Jackstone allowed his daughters a sip of wine only during holidays or on birthdays. "Which holiday have I forgotten?"

"It's not a holiday," said Rose. "We haven't forgotten someone's birthday, have we? Or your anniversary?"

Violet sniffed her wine. "It's because nothing was damaged in the quake, isn't it, Daddy?"

"You're all way off base," their father said genially. "This is just a little family celebration in honor of the expanded business of Jackstone Gardens."

Lily beamed at him across the table. "I'll drink to that!"

Violet sipped her wine; it tasted sharp and clean.

"Mom and I closed the sale today on the new shop in San Francisco." Greg grinned at his girls. "You girls all know how long we've been trying to buy it. There were loads of glitches, but now we've got it. It has been empty for years so it needs some work. But once it's fixed up, it'll be great. And it's in a neighborhood where there isn't any competition."

"Pretty cool, Dad," said Jasmine. "Three Jackstone Gardens in the Bay Area."

"It'll be one for each of you to inherit someday," said Lily. Her eyes rested on Violet, and Violet imagined she could read her mother's thoughts: *If only poor Baby lives that long!* Her mom never seemed to notice that Violet had grown nearly as tall as the other girls and was just about as strong. And she'd hardly been sick all last winter.

"Oh, Mom. You're so morbid." Rose drained her wine and held the glass out for more.

"That's not morbid, Rosy. It's called planning for the future." Greg waved away her glass. "Anyway, we'll need to work fast to get the shop in shape for business."

"I'm so glad you girls promised to help with cleaning," Lily said, passing the salad. "We're counting on you."

"When did we promise that?" squealed Rose.

"A few weeks ago," their mother said calmly. "I remember it perfectly."

"Weeks ago? I'm sure it was *months* ago," Jasmine objected. "And you have to give us a warning, Dad."

"We weren't in our right minds then, Dad," Rose protested.

"Nonetheless, you did promise, and I'm giving you fair warning right now. I need you tomorrow, and I'm counting on you."

Violet picked at her salad, barely listening. She dug into the rice pilaf her mother had prepared. It was fragrant with herbs and fresh vegetables. She had no special interest in her parents' business and was thinking instead about the transformation she and Beth would bring about with hair dye. Her sisters' outraged voices broke into her reverie. "Dad! That isn't fair!" cried Rose. "We already have plans for tomorrow!"

"Any day but tomorrow, Dad," begged Jasmine. "Casey

and Brett are coming over. Coming *here*! We just arranged everything."

Their father frowned. "Well, I'm afraid you'll just have to *rearrange* everything."

And their mother's gentle voice seconded him. "Really, girls, we were counting on your help. You did offer, and we took your offer seriously."

"Yeah, but not tomorrow," said Rose coldly. "We have a life, too, you know."

"We can't just drop everything, Dad," explained Jasmine in a more wheedling tone. She was the best negotiator of the three girls. "How about if we go on Sunday instead?"

Greg frowned. "Your mother and I are planning to go on Sunday as well. But tomorrow, as you all well know, we'll be busy in the other two shops. I don't want you having guests over to the house when we're not at home, anyway. Now, you kids promised your help, and I'm going to hold you to your promise."

"Oh, Dad!" wailed Jasmine.

"You can meet with your friends just about any other time," said Lily comfortingly. "You can make new plans."

Jasmine and Rose looked at their father's implacable face, then at each other across the table. "Oh, all right," said Rose ungraciously.

And Jasmine added, "Plans? Who had any plans?"

"All right then," said their father. "That's the old Jackstone spirit! Now, I'm going to give the two of you all the supplies you need, and I'll drive you right after breakfast to the BART station. You won't be afraid to take the BART alone?"

"Actually we will, Dad," said Rose. "We'll be terrified. It's cruel to make us go."

Greg fixed her with a stern eye. "Enough, young lady."

"Of course, we can go," said Jasmine brightly. "We *are* fourteen, after all." The look she gave Rose across the table was one that held a message. Violet, although she wasn't included in what she privately called their "twinspeak," was nonetheless able to interpret that Jasmine had a plan up her sleeve—something that would make having to go to San Francisco more fun.

"I'll go, too," Violet announced.

Rose groaned.

Jasmine tossed back her mane of hair. She looked over at Violet and spoke earnestly. "You don't want to come, Vi. We'll be cleaning for hours. It'll be hard work."

"No, not you, Baby," agreed their father, smiling indulgently. "Your sisters will do a fine job." He winked at them. Rose glowered back. But Jasmine nodded.

"That's right. We'll be fine."

"I'm going with them. I want to work, too." Violet folded her arms across her chest. She felt fierce. Jasmine had a plan for fun—fun that once again excluded her. She was determined not to miss out.

"We've got zillions of orders to fill at the other shops," Lily explained. "But Dad and I will go over on Sunday, and you can come with us then, sweetheart."

Violet smacked her hand down on the tabletop, making everyone jump. "I'm going with Jazzy and Rosy tomorrow!" she cried. "You have to let me! It's not fair if they get to do everything and I don't get to do anything! I'm fourteen, too, remember! And if they're going, I'm going. It's going to be all three of us together—from now on." She felt tears on her cheeks and brushed them away angrily.

She met the amazed stares of Jasmine and Rose with a fierce glare, then felt a burst of happiness when Jasmine grinned and gave her the thumbs-up signal.

"Sure, Dad, we'll all go together," Jasmine said. "We'll keep Vi safe, don't worry."

Rose just sat there, frowning.

Violet sat back and blew her nose into her paper napkin. Then she polished off her dinner while they discussed her plan. But eventually Lily and Greg gave in. "I guess you can't turn away a willing worker, eh, girls?"

"You got it, Dad," said Jasmine.

Rose snorted. "If Vi wants to be a drudge, who are we to stop her?"

Of course, her sisters wouldn't understand in a million years, Violet thought. They had each other, and always had. They were almost always together at school. And they were busy together on weekends, with girlfriends or boyfriends, at club meetings or sporting events, always leaving her behind. This time she'd be with them. The hair-dyeing date with Beth would have to be rescheduled and a full day of cleaning lay ahead, but that was a small price to pay for the chance to turn twins into triplets once and for all.

CHAPTER 3

Violet dreamed she was lying on her bed, stabbing a needle in and out of a piece of fabric stretched onto a round wooden frame that she held on her lap. She chose among different colors of yarn from the bag next to her on the bed, and worked them into the picture she was needlepointing. It was nearly done—a portrait of a handsome dark-haired man with bright blue eyes, his face made up completely of tiny stitches.

She was working in the beige stitches of his rather large nose when the bed began shaking violently from side to side. She clutched the needlepoint frame tightly and squeezed her eyes shut.

Stretching. It's just the earth, stretching.

When Violet opened her eyes, it took her a moment to realize that the bed had stopped shaking. Was she still in the dream? She could feel the weight of the needle in her hand and the silky strand of yarn against her skin. That was especially weird because she'd never done any sort of sewing in her life. The man's face seemed familiar, but she couldn't think where she'd ever seen him before.

She slipped out of bed and dressed in her jeans and a gray sweatshirt, still feeling tense from the dream. Her body was alert, ready for the earth to move.

The idea that the earth could move was something she would never get used to, even though she'd been born right here in California and lived on top of fault lines all her life. Her father had tried to soothe her with tales of how people in other parts of the country lived with the threat of hurricanes and tornadoes—both of which could be as devastating as earthquakes, or even worse. But Violet didn't think hurricanes and tornadoes were in the same league as earthquakes. They were weather conditions, and you could see them coming. In most cases, you had time to prepare, to take cover, even to evacuate if necessary. With earthquakes there was no warning. No preparation time. The only completely safe place to be was *off* the earth—up in the sky. People in airplanes didn't feel earthquakes. But what if you weren't in an airplane? Where could you go when the very earth beneath your feet turned deadly?

She took a deep breath. She would ask her parents to check their earthquake supplies again. Make sure the first-aid kit was in an easy-to-find spot, that there was extra drinking water stored away. Was their house bolted securely to the foundations?

As she hurried down the hall to find her parents, a gentle snore from her sisters' room made her stop at their door.

Jasmine and Rose were still asleep. Violet recalled the plan she'd made the evening before. This was the perfect opportunity. Pushing her fears about earthquakes to the back of her mind for the moment, Violet went to her sisters' long dresser and opened the bottom drawer. She pulled out two plain gray sweatshirts, identical to the one she wore. Then she found the jeans they had worn yesterday—Rose's lay folded neatly on her desk chair; Jasmine's lay in a wrinkled heap on the floor next to her yellow-quilted bed. Violet put the clothes she'd chosen for them at the foot of each bed.

She stood quietly for a long moment, watching her sisters sleep. Strange to think that once they'd all been curled up together, sleeping, swimming, waiting to be born. Slowly she moved to Rose's desk and lifted a pair of scissors from the pencil mug—it would have been impossible to locate anything on Jasmine's paper-strewn desk—then walked to the head of the beds.

Jasmine slept on her back with her arm thrown up over her eyes. Rose slept on her stomach, her long hair fanning out over the pink quilt. Violet cautiously lifted a lock of Rose's hair and snipped off a good two inches from the end. Holding her breath, she turned to the other bed and considered Jasmine.

"Come any closer with those scissors, Vi, and you'll be dead meat." Jasmine spoke softly, her eyes still covered. "And not from a weak heart, either."

Violet jumped back, bumping Rose's bed. *"Mmmphh,"* objected Rose.

Jasmine uncovered her eyes and sat up. "What in the world are you doing?"

Violet's face was flushed. She crossed to the windows and pulled back the pink-and-yellow curtains. "Rise and shine. It's time to get up."

Rose groaned and turned her head away from the sunlight. "But what are you doing in here, Baby? It's the middle of the night."

"She's come to kill us," Jasmine said.

"I told you, stop calling me Baby," Violet told Rose automatically, clenching her fist around the lock of hair she'd removed from Rose's head. Good thing both sisters had the same hair color. "Come on, we have to get going. Dad wants us to take the nine o'clock BART. Here are your clothes." She threw the jeans and sweatshirt to Jasmine, then flung the other set at Rose.

Rose and Jasmine exchanged a look, eyebrows raised. Violet hated their wordless code. It was yet another facet of their twinship—and proof of her exclusion.

"Thank you, Jeeves. You may go now," Rose said haughtily. She tossed her hair over her shoulders. Violet was glad Rose couldn't see the missing chunk from the back.

"You may return the scissors now, Jeeves," added Jasmine. "We won't require any further services."

Violet dropped the scissors onto Rose's desk with a clatter, then stomped out of the room. Their laughter followed her down the stairs and into the kitchen, where she slipped the lock of Rose's hair inside a plastic sandwich bag and tucked it into her pocket. Already the day seemed sour.

It seemed even more sour when Lily came in and switched on the radio. A news announcer was talking about earthquakes, giving a summary of all the precautions families should take to protect their homes from damage. Violet listened carefully, then started quizzing her mom about their own family's level of preparedness. Lily brushed away her worries. "We've got everything we need, dear. Extra cans of food, lots of bottled water, a first-aid kit—everything." She kissed Violet on the top of her head. "And yes, the house is bolted to the foundations, the big bookcase in the living room is bolted to the wall, and none of us has pictures in heavy frames hanging over our beds. We've covered all the bases. We even have a fire extinguisher."

The memory of three shadowy figures, outlined by flames, flickered in Violet's head.

Then Jasmine and Rose came into the kitchen, ready for breakfast and dressed identically—but not in the gray sweatshirts and jeans that Violet had chosen for them and that matched her own. Instead they wore overalls and green cotton sweaters. Their golden hair swung in identical ponytails. Violet spread jam on a muffin and sipped her orange juice. She pushed the vision of the children out of her mind and told herself it didn't matter about her sisters' clothes. There would be other days, other outfits, other chances.

The triplets had been three tiny babies at first—two bald healthy babies with blue eyes, one frighteningly tiny baby with a thatch of dark hair to match her darker eyes. "Once I almost mixed Jazzy and Rosy in the bath," Lily would confide to people who looked into the triple stroller in astonishment. "But then I put a dab of pink nail polish on one of Rosy's toes, and after that we always knew the difference. Of course, there was never any question of mixing up Vi. I keep her with me every second. We're so afraid she won't make it."

Then they were three little girls—two bold, mischievous girls with golden curls, and one very sickly girl with brown frizz. Their mother dressed them all differently right from the beginning, believing from the first that each girl should forge her own identity. Only on holidays would they be dressed in identical outfits. Lily and Greg's favorite photo was one taken on the triplets' third birthday: three girls in matching flowered dresses, with yellow hair ribbons for Jasmine's braids, pink for Rose's, and purple for Violet's. Whenever Violet looked at photos of herself flanked by her sisters, she thought of the kindergarten worksheets that directed: "Cross out the one that doesn't belong."

When people commented, as they always did, Lily readily launched into her Triplet Talk. "You know how identical twins are formed, don't you?" she'd ask. "How the sperm from the father fertilizes a single egg from the mother, and then the fertilized egg splits into two parts? Well that's what happened with Jazzy and Rosy here. But Vi, now, she's different. She's from a separate egg and sperm entirely. But they all grew in here together." (Lily would pat her belly at this point to illustrate.) "Amazing, isn't it? Three babies at once—though poor Violet was the teensiest thing you ever saw. The doctors didn't think she'd live. She's our miracle."

When the girls started school, their father insisted on separate classrooms. "It's important for each to develop her own personality," Greg maintained. Violet remembered feeling lost without her sisters in kindergarten. She looked so completely different, most of the kids didn't even know she belonged in the same family, much less was one of triplets. In first grade, Violet's heart, never strong, began pumping erratically, and she needed an operation to fix things. She missed so much school that she had to repeat the entire year. After that, Rose and Jasmine were always a grade ahead of Violet. They were a boisterous pair who made friends easily. Often they would bring friends home after school. They formed clubs in the backyard, holding meetings high in the old oak. Violet rested after school, reading in the living room under Lily's watchful eye.

Although the doctors assured the family that Violet was fully recovered from her heart surgery, it wasn't until Violet was in third grade that Lily could bear to leave the house to work. Violet was glad when she did, though it seemed strange at first to come home to a housekeeper who urged all three girls to play outside instead of to her cautious mother who kept her safe indoors. Jasmine and Rose allowed Violet into their after-school clubs, but only as their little mascot. They never let her climb up to the highest level of the tree house. She might get dizzy the way she used to before the operation, they worried, and fall. When Violet and Beth became friends, Jasmine and Rose took Beth aside on the playground and warned her always to look after poor Vi. They were afraid she would die young.

In fourth grade three kids in Violet's class took to walking with their arms around each other, telling everyone they were triplets, too. So what, they said, that one girl was African American, one was visiting for a year from Japan and didn't even speak English yet, and one was a red-haired, freckle-faced boy? Other kids laughed—even the teacher laughed—but Violet was mortified. She tried to ignore them the way Beth said she should, but no one knew how she cried at night over their teasing.

When Jasmine and Rose entered junior high, they began taking special pleasure in their identical appearance and started dressing alike to enhance it. "It's just a phase they're going through," Lily murmured to Greg when he complained about living with "a couple of clones." But when Violet joined them at junior high a year later, she felt more left out than ever. Jasmine and Rose were a special club unto themselves—in which Violet could never be anything more than a charter member.

For her science project in September, Violet had written a report about triplets. She learned that fraternal triplets were no more closely related to each other than to any other siblings in the same family. Each fraternal triplet grew from her (or his) own fertilized egg. Fraternal triplets were the most commonly occurring type—not that triplets could ever be called common. She learned that identical triplets, all three children growing from one fertilized egg, happened most infrequently. Their own case—a combination of identical and fraternal—was the middle ground. Violet wished fervently that theirs had been one of the other combinations. Life would be so much easier if all three were identical or different.

Dyed hair would help. And identical clothes. *If only Jazzy and Rosy would cooperate.* Violet took her plate and glass to the sink, glancing resentfully over her shoulder at her sisters in their overalls, their matching heads bent together over the comic section of the newspaper.

Greg entered the kitchen, buttoning his shirt. "Ready, girls?" He blinked exaggeratedly and put his hand to his eyes. "Am I still seeing double, or what? I thought the eye doctor corrected my prescription."

"We like it this way, Daddy," said Jasmine, looking up.

"It's fun," said Rose. "Some people can't even tell us apart."

"Hmm." Greg glanced over at Violet, who was drying her hands on a towel, then back to Jasmine and Rose. "Well, I can tell you apart no matter what, and don't you forget it."

"Greg, dear," said Lily softly. "I think it's just something twins go through."

"Well, I don't like it. They look like one of those old ads for Doublemint gum."

Jasmine and Rose had their heads together again. They were whispering. Violet edged closer to hear. She caught the name "Brett" and then the name "Casey," and realized that Jasmine's big idea the night before was that they would invite the boys to come along to San Francisco.

But Violet didn't want to share her sisters with Brett and Casey. She didn't want any boys around at all. This was going to be a day for the triplets to work together—alone.

"Mom?" she asked brightly. "Can we invite friends to go along to help us?"

"No, I don't think so, dear," said Lily, switching off the radio news. "I don't want any of your friends there until the place is in better order."

Jasmine and Rose glared at Violet. "But, Mom," protested Rose, " 'Many hands make light work.' That's your favorite proverb!"

"Well, I suppose you might ask Beth to go," said Lily. "She'd be a big help."

"How about Brett and Casey?" asked Violet innocently.

"No way," said Greg, thumping his fist on the counter. "No boys. Not alone over there with my girls all day."

"Dad!" shrieked Rose. "We'd be *working*. We'd be cleaning! You have a filthy mind."

"Let's not have any more discussion," he said, sitting down at the counter and pouring himself some coffee. "Wait till you see the amount of cleaning there is. There won't be time for socializing."

"But Dad—," cried Jasmine.

"Call them and invite them over for some other time, girls," said Lily soothingly. She handed Rose a shopping bag full of cleaning supplies and loaded others into Jasmine's backpack. "Here are most of the things you'll need, but there will still be more. There's a hardware store on the same street as the shop. I'm going to give you money to buy a broom and a mop. You'll also need money for your BART tickets and lunch."

Greg finished his coffee and reached for his jacket on a peg by the door. "I can drop you girls off at the station now." He hesitated, looking over at his wife. "Is Vi really going? Maybe it'll be too much for her after all."

"I'm thinking the same thing. Vi, darling, why don't you stay home? You and Beth can get together as you'd planned, and your sisters will go to San Francisco on their own."

"Good idea," said Rose. "After all, it's the big bad city out there. And there could be another earthquake."

"Yeah," said Jasmine. "And don't you have a science paper to write or something?"

Violet ignored her sisters. "I'm going. You can't always make me stay home like some invalid."

Greg reached over and gave Violet a hug. "All right, Lil," he said to his wife. "I guess she'd better go."

"Well, I want you to call me as soon as you get there. There's no phone yet, but you can call from the hardware store. Or from the café down the street."

"And when you're on your way home," instructed Greg, "call from the BART station and tell me which train you're taking. I'll be there to pick you up."

"Be sure to stay together," cautioned Lily. "And Jazzy and Rosy, you take care of Vi."

"We always do," said Jasmine.

And Rose added under her breath, "We always have to."

"Everybody stop acting like I'm two years old!" Violet poked the towel through the handle on the refrigerator door. "I'm exactly the same age as Jazzy and Rosy!"

"You are not," Rose corrected her. "You're forty minutes younger than me, and a whole hour younger than Jazzy." She stomped down the hall after their father.

Jasmine laughed. "You're the runt of the litter, Vi, and there's no getting around it." She hugged their mother good-bye and headed out the door.

Violet flounced out after her without saying another word.

CHAPTER 4

The girls rode the BART train under the San Francisco Bay and got off at the Powell Street Station. Jasmine shouldered the backpack, and Rose carried the shopping bag of cleaning supplies. They trudged to the cable car terminus. Tourists milled around waiting for the famous trolleys to take them up and down San Francisco's steep hills. Vendors sold sweatshirts and flowers and ice-cream cones, even this early in the day. Violet felt excited to be in the city—on their own. She hopped up onto the back of a packed cable car behind Rose and hung on tight, waving away Jasmine's offer of the only available seat. She could hear people around them talking about yesterday's earthquake.

Several blocks past Union Square, enough tourists had disembarked so that the three girls found seats together on a bench across from a thin woman reading a Chinese newspaper and a heavyset man chewing an unlit cigar. The man regarded them curiously.

"Twins, eh? Fred and Ed, eh?" He chuckled.

Rose and Jasmine just smiled at the man, but Violet spoke right up. "We're triplets, actually," she corrected him, ignoring Jasmine's jab to her ribs.

"Fred, Ed, and Ned, eh?" asked the man. He looked skeptical, but Violet felt mollified.

"Don't talk to strangers," hissed Jasmine in her ear.

"I'm not, I'm just telling him."

Rose and Jasmine exchanged one of their looks. After another several blocks up a steep hill, the girls got off, hauling the cleaning supplies. Violet carried the slip of paper on which Greg had scrawled directions to the shop. Walking four blocks up and down even steeper hills brought them to Chance Street.

Chance was long and narrow, with skinny Victorian houses on both sides. Some had been turned into shops, but most were still private residences. They stopped in front of their parents' new property. It had a front stoop facing right onto the sidewalk. Peeling gray paint and loose green shutters framed the windows. The big bay window in what once must have been the front parlor had been replaced by large shopwindow-sized plates of glass. The windows were soaped over now, and the house had a desolate air.

Violet thought about what Mr. Koch had said about layers of history being all around them. Once this old house had been a bustling shop, bright with new paint and sparkling glass, with a display of something or other in the front window. With some hard work and new layers of paint, it would once more come to life.

Rose set down the shopping bag and fished in her pocket for the envelope their father had entrusted to her. She tipped the key into her palm. The keys to their parents' other shops were small and shiny, no bigger than their own house key.

But this one was old, ornate, and dark with tarnish. Nonetheless, it fit into the lock on the carved wooden front door without a hitch. Rose turned the key smoothly and pushed open the wide door.

It was dark and chilly inside. The door swung shut with a thud, immediately silencing the sound of traffic from the street. There was a smell of dust and mildew. Violet looked around in the dim light through the soap-filmed windows, then reached toward the wall for the light switch. The single bulb above the long wooden sales counter cast a tepid glow. Jasmine set the backpack down on the sloping countertop with a groan.

"How can we clean up such a dump?" she asked. "I'm tired already."

"You haven't had much practice with your side of the bedroom," Rose said with a smirk.

It didn't look anything like the bright, airy, flower-filled shops their parents owned in Oakland and Berkeley. Those were part of new, elegant malls. Violet walked around the sales counter, noting the sagging wooden doors hanging on broken hinges. Behind the counter was a wooden ladder-back chair with a few rungs missing. The walls were a dingy non-color; the floor was scuffed wood and littered with stacks of old newspapers. In one corner a bundle of gray rags overflowed from a metal bucket. A matted broom with a broken handle lay in the cobwebs along one wall. It would take a whole lot more than cleaning, she decided, to make this place into a florist shop.

A door at the back of the room led into a hallway. Violet wandered on, flicking on lights as she went. There was a little kitchen—at least Violet supposed it had once been a kitchen. It had no refrigerator and no stove, but cupboards along the wall and a chipped iron sink testified to the room's long-ago function. At the end of the hallway a narrow staircase led to the second floor.

"Careful," called Jasmine, hurrying down the hall after Violet. "Let me go first."

But Violet stamped straight up the steps.

"Some of the steps look rotten!" Jasmine climbed right behind her. "This place is horrible."

"Ugh," called Rose. "I'm not going up. Baby, you'd better stay down here."

Violet ignored them both. Upstairs were four small empty rooms and a bathroom the same size. Maybe the bathroom had been a bedroom once, Violet thought, back when people had outhouses in their gardens and chamber pots under their beds. The bathtub stood high on clawed feet.

The upstairs rooms were brighter because their windows were not soaped, but that made it all the easier to see how filthy the rooms were, empty and covered with dust and mouse droppings. In the bedroom at the back of the house, Violet stopped. Her heart gave a funny thump in her chest, just the way it used to do before the operation. She wandered farther into the room, over to the long windows along the back wall.

"Let's go down," said Jasmine. "There's nothing here."

But there *was* something. Violet could feel it. A lingering sadness. As if someone had cried here, long ago, and left a shadow of that sorrow behind.

"I'm going down," said Jasmine. "Come on, Vi."

But Violet looked out the windows. There was no garden, just a paved yard where two metal trash cans stood by a sagging wooden stoop. She stared outside a long moment, trying to see what wasn't there. Then she followed Jasmine out of the room, but the sensation of the shadow followed.

They clattered downstairs and returned to the front room,

where Rose was pulling bottles of bleach and pine cleaner and abrasive cleanser from the shopping bag and backpack. Violet leaned against the sales counter, and it wobbled under her weight. She moved hastily away again. No wonder she felt sad here. It was hard to be cheerful in such a dump. Better get to work and brighten things up.

"So, where do we start?" she asked, gathering her dark hair back into a ponytail like her sisters'. She saw a dirty rubber band on the floor and used it to secure the stubby tail of hair. It would do for now. She'd have to let her hair grow, like theirs. She could buy some of those pretty elastic scrunchies at the drugstore when she bought the hair dye.

"The windows, I guess." Rose opened a pack of rubber gloves. "Here, Vi, you work on the lower sections. Jazzy, you and I can trade off climbing up on that old chair to reach the top."

Violet started dragging the chair across the room, but Jasmine stopped her. "Don't strain yourself. We can't let anything happen to you."

"What a stupid waste of a Saturday," observed Rose.

"I could just kill Mom and Dad." Jasmine sighed. "Not to mention *you*, Vi. We should have brought Brett and Casey along. They'd be good helpers, and it would be a lot more fun."

"Yeah," Rose agreed.

Violet didn't argue. But she was happy just to be there, just the three of them, just the way it was supposed to be. She opened the heavy front door to let in more light and some fresh air. She tipped the old rags out of the metal pail in the corner, then took it back to the kitchen, hoping—but not really expecting—there would be running water. And there was. She filled the pail, added pine cleaner, and opened one of the packages of scouring pads. Then she lugged it all back to the front room, water sloshing. "Okay," she announced. "Let's get going."

But the room was empty and the front door stood open. Rose and Jasmine were sitting out on the front stoop giggling at some boys showing off with skateboards. The girls didn't even turn when Violet stepped out behind them. One of the boys looked like a younger version of the man in the needle-point dream—with a large nose and dark curls spilling over his forehead. The boy looked up and pointed at her now.

"Hey, it's the Maid-of-All-Work!" *He has a voice like a bulldozer,* Violet thought. *Loud and grating.* He nudged his companion, and both broke into catcalls.

Violet frowned. What was it about her that set boys jeering, while Rose and Jasmine set them flirting and bantering?

Rose glanced over her shoulder. "Oh, there you are. This is Sam—and his friend David. Guys, this is our sister, Vi."

"You shouldn't be carrying that pail," Jasmine cautioned her. "It's too heavy."

"It is not!" But it was heavy, so Violet set it down in the doorway. "You're supposed to be working, not socializing," she reminded her sisters. Then she gave the boys a tentative look. She felt awkward, as usual.

She tried to turn the tentative look into the same sort of grin Rosy and Jazzy used on boys and flashed it down the steps at Sam and David. She hoped to dazzle them.

The boy named Sam backed down the curb into the street, his skateboard tight under his arm. *Stunned him,* thought Violet.

"We'll get started in a second." Jasmine looked irritated. "There's nothing wrong with meeting our neighbors." She appealed to the two boys. "She may look little, but believe me, she's the boss."

"You can say that again," muttered Rose.

The boys across the street laughed some more. Jasmine bowed to them, blew kisses. Then Rose remembered they needed to buy a new broom and a mop. And they'd never called their mother to say they'd arrived safely.

"We'll just go on over to that hardware store and be back in a few minutes," Rose said. "Hang in there, okay?"

Violet went back inside and slammed the door. There they were already, off without her. She donned the yellow rubber gloves, dragged the pail over to the big plate-glass window, and started scrubbing. With each swipe of her sponge, the front room grew brighter. Outside in the street, cars passed and people walked by. She watched the boys roll off on their boards, tipping up and down the curb effortlessly, Jasmine and Rose striding along at their side. The only time Violet had tried skateboarding, she'd fallen off and sprained her wrist. Jasmine and Rose, of course, had no trouble soaring along on skateboards, Rollerblades, or bikes. Violet didn't ride her bike very often. She seemed to fall as easily as her sisters balanced. They loved flying in airplanes, too, while Violet worried about birds being sucked into the engines or terrorist bombs going off and blowing the plane to smithereens.

When the big window was clean, Violet began washing off the grimy sales counter. Then, using the broken old broom, she energetically swept the cobwebs out of the corners of the room, stirring up dust.

When she was satisfied that most of the dirt had been banished, she bundled up the old newspapers. They were so yellowed and damp from mildew, it would be a chore even to read the headlines. She hauled the papers down the hall to the back door, turned the bolt to unlock it, then hefted her stinking bundles down the rickety steps to the back fence by the trash cans. There was no recycling bin yet. She'd have to tell her parents to see about getting one. She turned to go back in and grimaced with distaste as a spider ran across her arm and sailed off on a strand of web into the bushes. Once inside, she gathered up the grimy rags from the corner and wrapped them in the last sheets of newspaper. These she carried back to the garbage cans and dumped them in.

When she turned to go back up the steps, something held her. She looked around the backyard at the cracked concrete, the broken fence, the single bush, the walls of the buildings next door and directly behind. Why did she feel sad that there were no flowers in this small space? If she knew how to needlepoint, she would work a picture of flowers cascading over a gray concrete wall. *You can tell I'm the florists' daughter, that's for sure.*

Then she went back to the front room. Her sisters had returned with the new broom and mop. They were standing by the sales counter, taking in the changes in the room. Jasmine had the grace to look ashamed.

"Really, you should have waited. You've done all the work yourself."

"No one made her do it," said Rose. She sounded angry. "And she *shouldn't* have. What if something had happened? She could have hurt herself doing it, and it would be our fault."

"It's so changed now," said Jasmine in wonderment, turning to look. "There's more light than I thought there'd be—and now that the cobwebs are gone, you can see the walls have textured wallpaper on them. And all those gross newspapers—Vi, you didn't lift them yourself, did you?"

"Who was here to help?" asked Violet. Her voice was cool, but she felt an inner warm glow. *At last!* she was thinking. At last she had shown them she wasn't a useless baby anymore.

"Give us a break, Baby," snapped Rose. "We were gone ten minutes, tops." She shook back her long ponytail and put her hands on her hips.

"I must *really* be fast, then, if that's how long you were gone." Violet tried to shake back her nub of a ponytail in the same manner, but it was too short. "And don't call me Baby!" She put her hands on her hips, mirroring Rose's stance. "I hope you had a nice chat with those boys while you were buying the broom and the mop. But what would Brett Hudson think?"

"Look, don't you two fight," said Jasmine, handing Rose the mop. "It's not good for Vi to get all upset. She *has* done all this work, Rosy, so we must have been gone longer than we thought." She turned to Violet. "We really didn't mean to be gone so long. I guess we sort of lost track—"

"Oh, it's okay." Violet wasn't used to having her sisters apologize to her. Or even one sister. Rose's face was still thundery.

Jasmine picked up the pail and opened the front door. "I'll just empty this dirty water outside into the gutter. Then we can start on the floor, Rosy. Okay?"

"At least Vi has left us *something* to do!" snapped Rose.

"Listen, don't tell Dad." Jasmine looked anxiously at Violet. "That you did all this work, I mean. You're not supposed to, you know, exert yourself."

"Yeah," spat Rose resentfully. "We'll get in trouble if you look even the teensiest bit tired out." She frowned at Violet. "I don't know how you get away with it."

"I won't tell." The small glow inside Violet brightened.

While Rose wielded the mop and Jasmine scrubbed the floor on hands and knees, Violet returned to the begrimed cupboards and countertops. They would need repair before her parents could install their top-of-the-line computerized cash registers. She stooped behind the counter and tried to close the sagging cupboard doors, but the hinges had pulled away from the old wood. "We'll need to buy hinges at the hardware store," she said, reaching gingerly inside and rolling up the brittle, stained shelf paper. It shredded in her hands. She gathered all the scraps, actually enjoying the work now that she had impressed her sisters.

She was just standing to carry the scraps out to the trash when another piece of paper caught her eye. It was different from the shelf paper—a thicker rectangle, stuck along the back of the shelf. She reached inside again to pull out this last offending bit of rubbish, then stopped and looked closely at what was in her hand. It was an envelope of thick white paper, yellowed at the corners. The back flap was tucked in. On the front, in elegant brown ink, was a single initial: *V*.

Violet sat back on her heels, turning the envelope over in her hands. She stood up to show her sisters what she'd found, but they were heading back toward the kitchen to refill the pail with clean water. Violet hesitated, then opened the envelope and removed the folded sheet. It was a short note written in the same brown ink, in a strange, hard-to-read handwriting, all unfamiliar angles and curlicues. The salutation read: *Poor Baby V.*

Violet's heart thumped hard. *That's me,* she thought in astonishment. But how could it be? Then she heard Rose's and Jazzy's laughter from the kitchen and sighed. She sank onto the floor and read the letter.

> *Poor Baby V,*
> *I look at the flowers in the garden and think how wrong it is that they soak up the sun and rain while you are kept indoors. You must pull yourself together and prove to your parents that you will be well and*

*can work as hard as anyone. Ah, wild V! Remember
the quarrel in the restaurant? You were most
wonderfully vibrant. Your response to those
abominable twins proved to me—if I ever needed
proof!—that you are as strong and capable as anyone.
One day you will make an excellent mother—though,
of course, our children will never test your patience to
such a degree! I think about you all the time and
long to save you from your family. Though they say
they want to keep you safe, they are only stifling
you. My darling, for now you remain their hothouse
flower, but someday soon, dear girl, we shall be
together in a real garden, in a house we share, and
you shall be strong and fresh and free. I am working
on a plan.*

    Your Hal

Violet read the letter again, then folded it, and inserted it
back in the envelope. She stood up and dusted off her jeans.
Rose and Jasmine came sloshing down the hall with the pail
of water. "Ha-ha, you guys," Violet said, flapping the envelope at them. "Getting me back for the hair?"

"Nothing funny about spilling water all over the floor,"
said Jasmine. "Be a good sister and wipe it up, will you, Vi?
Here's a towel." Jasmine threw her a cloth.

"What hair?" asked Rose.

Violet figured they'd probably written the note at the
hardware store and hidden it when they returned while she
was still out back dumping the old newspapers. It really
wasn't very funny at all. She frowned, watching Rose dip the
mop into the pail and sluice a path of fresh water across the
floorboards. Jasmine followed behind on hands and knees,
rubbing with a towel. Violet dropped the cloth on the sales

counter and walked over. "I don't like it—and I want to know what it's supposed to mean."

"Mean what?" asked Rose, depositing another spray of water on the floor.

"Not so much, Rosy!" cautioned Jasmine. She looked up at Violet. "Don't walk there. It's still damp and you might slip."

"And break your leg or something," muttered Rose. "And we'd be to blame, of course."

Violet held out the envelope. "Are you trying to say you didn't write this?"

Now Jasmine stood up, looking intrigued. "Write what? What is it?"

"This letter—to me. To 'Poor Baby V.' It's not funny. So what's the point?"

Rosy leaned the mop against the wall and came to look. "We didn't write that. At least *I* didn't. Look, you can see it's ancient. Did *you* write it, Jazzy?"

"What's it say? Let me see?" Jasmine held out her hand.

But Violet stuck her hands behind her back, shielding the letter. She looked around the room as if seeing it for the first time. She felt stiff and chilled, as if the dirty water in the pail ran through her veins. How could this letter be waiting here for her if her sisters hadn't hidden it? And even more important to know, who in the world was Hal?

CHAPTER 5

"Look, I'm starving." Violet wedged the letter into her back pocket. "Mom said there was a café on this street. I'm going to go get a sandwich or something." As much as she'd earlier wanted her sisters close by, now she wanted privacy. She wanted to sit and read her letter again, all alone.

But her plan was dashed as Jasmine kicked her towel into a corner. "Sounds good."

"I want to see that letter," said Rose. "Where'd you find it?"

Violet led the way out of the old house, carefully locking the door behind them. She would have said earlier there was nothing inside anybody could possibly want to steal, but the letter had changed her mind. What other secrets might be hidden in the house for her?

They found the café half a block away, a cheerful place with plants hanging from the ceiling and a smell of roasted coffee beans. None of the girls drank coffee, but they appreciated the aroma. They sat at a booth near the window and ordered hamburgers and fries. Rose and Jasmine ordered chocolate shakes and Violet, her mind so preoccupied with the mysterious letter, nearly ordered vanilla. But she kicked herself mentally. *Pay attention!* How could she be like her sisters if she didn't watch them carefully?

She ordered chocolate.

Rose demanded again to see the letter, and Violet handed it over. Jasmine edged closer to see. They sat on the vinyl bench across from her, their identical gold heads bowed together over the table as they read. On the opposite bench, Violet watched, thoughtful. They were doing an excellent job of acting surprised.

"This is really cool," said Jasmine. She looked up and grinned.

"It's weird, if you ask me." Rose looked across at Violet suspiciously.

The waitress, her dry, pink hair spiked high with gel, brought their meal. She scrutinized Jasmine and Rose as she haphazardly dealt them the platters of burgers and fries. "Twins run in my family, too," she said. "Always thought I shoulda been one myself. Is it fun?"

"Heaps of fun," Jasmine assured her. "Except—when we get ourselves mixed up."

"Like today," added Rose, her face serious. "I'm still not sure whether I'm me or her."

The waitress just stared at them until Violet snorted in disgust. Then she laughed. "Oh," she said. "It's a joke, right? Heh-heh. I get it." She walked away, glancing back at them over her shoulder.

Rose tucked the letter carefully under the edge of her plate, as if to be certain no wind would blow the mystery away. "So, tell us about Hal," she urged, picking up a fry and popping it into her mouth. "Where'd you meet him?"

"And we thought you couldn't get a boyfriend!" exclaimed Jasmine. "You sly old thing. Does he go to our school?"

Violet just stared at them.

"I don't think the letter sounds like it's from a kid . . ." Rose's voice trailed off.

Jasmine stared at Violet. "Don't tell me you're hanging out with *an older man*! Some guy in high school? If that's true, we'll *all* get in trouble. You know Mom and Dad will be angriest at me and Rosy for not watching out for you better."

"As if we're your *keepers* or something," Rose added sourly. "Dad goes on about Brett and Casey already as it is. He'll freak out if you're involved with somebody he doesn't even know!"

Violet took a big bite of her hamburger and chewed slowly. "It really does sound as if you guys don't have the faintest idea who wrote me the letter," she said finally. "But I don't know who Hal is, either."

"It's weird that the letter wasn't actually mailed," said Jasmine. She sipped her shake. "Just addressed to you—well, not really you, but somebody with your initial." She reached for the letter and turned it over in her hands. She looked excited. "It's a real mystery!"

"The mystery is how come some old guy named Hal would hide a letter in the first place," said Rose, polishing off her fries.

"Do Mom and Dad know anybody called Hal?" wondered Jasmine. "Maybe they mentioned we'd be here cleaning, and someone overheard and snuck in earlier and left the letter."

Rose looked doubtful. "Why would anybody do that?"

Jasmine shrugged. "It was just an idea."

"But the paper is old," observed Rose. "Look how dry and yellowed it is."

Jasmine nodded. "You're right. The ink is old, too—look how dry and faded."

"You know what I think?" Violet's voice trembled with the thrill of what she was about to say. "I think it was written a long, long time ago. It's a letter from the past—meant for me."

"Hmm," said Jasmine. She ate a few more fries, regarding Violet with wide eyes. "Where was it?"

"In the cupboard. It must have been there for years and years, waiting."

"That is totally too weird to be true," said Rose dismissively. She crossed her arms. "You know what occurs to me, Jazzy? This just might be a case of our own little—what was it?—our own little *hothouse flower,* drawing attention to herself. As if she doesn't get all the attention already."

"What do you mean?" asked Violet. She had finished her hamburger and was working on her milk shake. The chocolate had a bitter taste. She wished she'd ordered vanilla after all.

"I mean maybe you hid the letter there yourself," Rose said.

"Why would I do that?"

"So you could find it and make a big deal over nothing. To make us notice you," snapped Rose. "Because you're jealous of us, or something."

"I never hid the letter! I never even saw it until I was cleaning out the cupboard. And how would I write it? I couldn't make those weird curlicues even if I tried. And what about the old paper? And the old ink?" *And what do you mean I'm jealous of you?* she wanted to cry. *How dare you think I want your attention?* But she pressed her lips together.

"I bet you found the letter somewhere else and brought it along today and just pretended to find it," Rose insisted. "Nothing else makes any sense."

"Look, let's pay for this stuff and get out of here," said Jasmine. She stood up and went to the counter. The spike-haired waitress took the money, glancing from one girl's face to the other.

"You twins look even more alike when you're mad," she said with interest. "Cool!"

"They're not twins," Violet said through clenched teeth. "They're *triplets*." She stamped out of the restaurant, leaving the waitress staring after her in amazement. Jasmine and Rose followed.

Back inside the shop, the girls worked in tense silence. Rose and Jasmine finished scrubbing the floor. Violet dusted the window ledges and washed out the cupboards. From time to time she reached back and fingered the folded letter in her back pocket. After a while, she put down her dust cloth and wandered upstairs.

As before, she felt drawn to the back bedroom. She stood there now in the center of the floor, looking around carefully. The wallpaper was so faded and tattered, she could barely make out the pattern of lavender flowers. The paper hung in strips, the old paste exhausted. Should she bring the pail of water and the mop up here? If she scrubbed hard, the old floorboards might gleam again, the way she was certain, suddenly, they once had gleamed. Early afternoon light filtered in through the murky windows. Violet pulled down the sleeve of her gray sweatshirt, spat on the cuff, and used it to polish a clean place on one long window. She peered down into the concrete yard. Maybe once there had been flowers growing out there. Long ago.

Violet took out the letter and reread it.

I look at the flowers in the garden and think how wrong it is that they soak up the sun and rain while you are kept indoors....

She would pull herself together as the mysterious Hal advised. She would prove to Jazzy and Rosy, as she had by working so hard today, that she was healthy and well. She wouldn't be Baby anymore. She would be one of the triplets, part of their club, somebody just like they were. *I'm trying, Hal,* she thought.

Then she screamed as the room dipped and the windowpanes rattled in their frames. She screamed as the floor rolled like the heaving deck of a ship at sea. Downstairs she heard Jasmine and Rose call her name. But she couldn't stop screaming, and she huddled in a corner of the room as old plaster rained down on her from the tattered walls.

Flames—and three shadowy figures running out of the rubble behind them with outstretched arms, howling for help . . .

Her sisters found her there when the quake ended. "Oh, Vi!" cried Jasmine, hugging her.

Violet blinked up at them. *That little girl—who would help her?*

"We heard you and we tried to come," babbled Rose, her anger forgotten. She joined the hug. "But we could hardly walk, so we stood in the doorway, you know, the way you're supposed to do if there's no big table to duck under. We came up as fast as we could. You're not hurt, are you?"

"We couldn't bear it if anything happened to you," moaned Jasmine. "It only lasted a few seconds, but it seemed like forever. We were so worried." She laughed shakily, brushing plaster dust off Violet's shoulders. "Look, you're covered in snow!"

Violet stood up and took a deep breath. Two quakes in two days. Two visions, as well. Her muscles tensed, bracing for aftershocks. She looked around the little bedroom at the damage. So much plaster had shaken down that the wooden lathes inside the wall were exposed. In one place, near the windows, the sill had cracked through and fallen to the floor. Violet caught her breath and stared, the shadow children momentarily forgotten.

There was a piece of paper sticking out from the crevice beneath the window where the sill had been. "Look," she whispered.

Jasmine and Rose stopped jabbering about the Richter scale and looked, but Violet was already across the room. She tugged the paper free. It was an envelope like the other, yellow and brittle with age. Violet felt giddy when she saw the same curlicued *V* on the front. "See?" she demanded. "You don't think I managed to hide this inside the window ledge somehow, do you? Just to get your attention? Do you?"

Jasmine shook her head, her eyes wide.

Rose reached for the envelope. "Well, let's open it!"

"I'm the only one here whose name starts with a *V*," said Violet, grabbing the envelope back. "The letter is for me."

"Don't be crazy. It can't really be for you if it was inside the wall." Rose shook her head.

"Oh yeah? Listen to this!" And Violet read the letter aloud, her voice triumphant and wondering at the same time.

"My own beloved Baby V,

"Is your heart still aching? I ache myself when I think of the pain you have been in. It is dreadful that the twins should be so difficult and demanding when they know you are poorly. It seems to me they need a caretaker even more than you do! I long to be able to comfort you in person during your illness, yet your parents forbid me to come near. The frustration of it is enough to cause me to collapse as you have! There are your parents, going about their work as ever,

*bristling with health, and pitying my Poor Lamb, but
they don't seem to realize the best medicine for you
would be to let us be together. I can see you only
outside the window, yet even at that distance you look
like heaven to me. Darling, you must grow well
again. You have the purest heart and the strongest
will of us all. You also have the love of one who will
give you his eternal devotion.*

*"Be brave, my love. Remember the time you were
lost in the crowds—how frightened you were? Yet you
overcame that fear and prevailed. I see you as lost in
the bosom of a family that tries to control you. They
simply do not understand you as I do. But soon, very
soon, you will prevail once more. We will be together
as we are meant, I know it. Be of strong heart.*

"Your Hal"

"That is *so* cool," breathed Jasmine.

"Well, it's a real mystery, I'll grant you that." Rose looked
baffled. "I wish there were a date on these letters. I wonder
who put them in these hiding places? Oh, you guys, won't it
be fun to try to find out who these people were?"

"We do know who V is," said Violet softly. "But I'd give
anything to find Hal."

Her sisters stared at her in silence for a long moment. "Oh
no," said Jasmine finally.

"You can't really think these letters are meant for you!"
Rose snorted.

"Well, look at what he said in the first letter about 'abominable twins.' Who was being so unsupportive and disbeliev-
ing in the restaurant? And now? Look what it says about my
heart. Who else do you know who has had open-heart surgery?" Violet reread the letter and felt that same heart thump-

ing steadily in her chest. "And parents going about their work?"

"Parents always do that. And the letter is old. Much older than you," objected Rose.

"Bring the letters home," said Jasmine. "We can study them later. But we'd better get going. Mom and Dad will be worried about us."

"Yeah," said Rose. "There might be aftershocks. And we've done more than enough cleaning for one day."

"For a week at least," agreed Jasmine. "For maybe a whole month." They left the room together. At the top of the stairs, Rose turned back.

"Come on, Baby. We can't leave you behind."

The adrenaline surge from the earthquake still filled Violet's blood. Suddenly she wanted to dance and sing and jump around. She clutched the letter, staring at her sisters through the doorway. *Be of strong heart,* she remembered.

"Don't ever call me Baby again!" she shouted at the top of her voice, and smiled when they flinched. Then she stuck the second letter into her back pocket with the first. Her sisters stood silently aside when she came out into the hallway, and they followed behind her as she led the way downstairs.

CHAPTER **6**

The girls rode a cable car, then walked to the Powell Street Station, where they disembarked into a carnival atmosphere. People swarmed everywhere. Music blared. Delicious smells of Thai, Chinese, Polish, Mexican, Italian, and Greek food mingled with the everyday smells of hot dogs and french fries, wafting with the music through the brisk October air. *"Mmm."* Rose sniffed. She pointed. "Look, they've blocked off the streets. It's a street fair."

"It makes me hungry again," commented Jasmine.

"Wish we had time to stay and check it out," said Rose, glancing wistfully at the booths lining the streets, tables of earrings and necklaces, essential oils, carved wooden pipes and animals, puzzles and games, used toys stacked in cardboard cartons, T-shirts with slogans piled on wooden crates.

The minor earthquake did not seem to have disrupted the festivities in the least, though there was an air of heightened excitement around a group of people repairing a booth of scarves and jewelry that had toppled in the quake. Violet couldn't understand how people could just continue with their day almost as if nothing had happened.

She had been strong and buoyed up back at the shop, but now she felt shivery and strange. Deep in her stomach a cold lump of fear was growing, and she felt queasy, as if she might be sick. She stood with her feet apart, firmly planted on the sidewalk. Was that a shudder she felt beneath her? "We'd better get home," she said.

"No, let's stay," begged Jasmine. "Just for a few minutes."

"Well, let me check when the BART leaves," said Rose, ever practical. She pulled the schedule for the trains from the front pocket of her overalls and scanned it, then checked her watch. Around them the tumult rose as the musicians playing the accordion and fiddle on the corner gave their spot over to a new group of rap singers. "We have twenty minutes."

"Perfect," said Jasmine. "Just enough time to get a snack."

How could anyone even think of eating when the earth might start heaving again at any time? Violet shook her head, trying to muster some of the confidence she'd felt back at the shop, but her sisters started off down the steep street.

She had no choice but to follow them. The street was closed to traffic but teemed with people of every size and color, of all ages, speaking half a dozen different languages. Violet stayed close to Jasmine and Rose. Every few yards, it seemed, another band was playing, and the varied types of music merged as one loud song in Violet's head, thumping along with her heart. *This* was the sort of Saturday she'd longed for—a day in her sisters' company, working and playing together—but now she was too uneasy to enjoy it.

They walked single file, picking their way along the

crowded sidewalk, with Rose leading the way, Violet safe in the middle, and Jasmine bringing up the rear. Violet found herself scanning the faces of people they passed. Was she looking for the shadow children—or for the man named Hal? She didn't know. *I wouldn't know Hal, anyway,* she thought. *Unless he wore a name tag.*

Rose stopped by a stall of feathered earrings. "Oh, look at these!" The other girls stopped to admire the jewelry.

Jasmine sniffed the air. "Anybody want a burrito?"

"Sure," said Rose, lifting a large dangly pair of pink feathers with silver beads to her ears. The man tending the stall held out a small mirror, and she stooped to peer into it.

"We'll be back in a sec," Violet said, trailing after Jasmine.

There was a long line at the Mexican food stall. Jasmine grew restless as they waited.

"I wanted to check out the used books over there," Jasmine told Violet, pointing. "Can you wait alone?"

"Yes," said Violet. "And I'll buy the burritos, too." The letters from Hal in her pocket made her feel generous, and the delectable smells of Mexican food banished her queasiness.

Jasmine grinned her thanks and disappeared into the throng of people. Violet moved closer to the Mexican food stall. The line moved quickly. In moments, Violet was holding three chicken burritos wrapped in white butcher paper. She scanned the crowd but could not see either of her sisters. So she headed down the street, where Jasmine had gone to look at books. She reached the corner without finding a used book stall, and stood in consternation, trying to peer through the crowds to the next block. Maybe Jasmine had gone farther?

Violet crossed the intersection and wandered down the next block. Sure enough, there was a stall of used books. But no sign of Jasmine. Violet stopped to ask the vendor if he'd seen a girl with long brownish gold hair, wearing a green sweater and blue-jean overalls.

"Seen a hundred girls like that today," the old man said. "See a couple hundred more before I close. You want to buy a book? You like to cook? We got cookbooks. We got thrillers. You into history? We got boxes of old stuff, some of it real valuable. Just take a look around."

Violet shook her head. "No, I have to find my sisters."

"Sisters, you say? What's the other one look like?"

"The same. Same hair. Green sweater and overalls."

"That the uniform or something?" He chortled. "Or are they twins?"

Violet sighed. "Triplets." She craned her neck, seeing one of her sisters' gold heads at the next stall. Hurriedly she headed away. There! There was Jasmine—or was it Rose?—just up ahead.

Violet pushed past a couple with two children in a double stroller and stumbled into a cluster of elderly women. "Sorry. Sorry. Oh, wait up, Jazzy! Rosy!"

But when she reached the golden-haired girl, she found it was neither Jasmine nor Rose—not even a girl. The golden-haired figure was a grown woman, hugely pregnant, walking a tiny spotted dog on the end of a leash.

Violet wasn't wearing a watch, but she felt certain more than twenty minutes had passed. The burritos were dripping salsa through the white paper onto her hands. She pressed forward, crossed the street, and walked back up the steep hill to the stall where she'd left Rose.

The stall was crowded with potential customers, all oohing and aahing over the feathered-and-beaded jewelry. But Rose wasn't there. Violet rushed across the street, dodging a group of high-spirited boys, to check the Mexican food stall once again. No Jasmine.

The next stall was selling needlework kits. Violet hesitated, for a moment distracted from her search. She gazed with admiration at the display of intricately stitched tapestries. The feeling of holding a needle in her fingers returned. Maybe she'd be good at needlework. Maybe she should buy a kit and make a pillow—just as she'd been doing in the dream....

Someone shoved a piece of paper into Violet's hand and she glanced down in surprise. It was a leaflet printed in large green letters: THE EARTH TAKES CARE OF ITSELF! read the headline. Needlework pillows forgotten, Violet read the text in smaller print:

> The Gaian Principle teaches that our Earth is an entity who will not let itself die. It cannot be destroyed by mankind's folly, ignorance, and malice. The Earth gets even. It keeps itself healthy and balanced by changing conditions to counterbalance the man-made influences that weaken it. Killer diseases, plagues, hurricanes, tornadoes, floods, and earthquakes are all simply the Earth's attempts to readjust itself after mankind has wreaked havoc. Our job is to live in harmony with the Earth.

Violet felt a chill pounce up her spine. *The Earth gets even,* she thought. *Is that what's going on with all these quakes?* She shoved the leaflet into her pocket with the two letters from Hal. This was her day for receiving all sorts of strange messages. She turned away from the needlework stall and stood in the middle of the street. There was still no sign of her sisters.

Back at the shop on Chance Street she had felt powerful and strong. Now she felt weak again, and alone. What was the best thing to do? Go ahead to the BART station and see if her sisters were there? Call her parents? *But Dad will never let us come to the city alone again, if I call and tell him what happened,* Violet thought. Should she keep searching? *But I've already wandered all over the place. If I go off to check the book stall again, then Jazzy and Rosy might come back here, and we'll just keep going in circles.*

She stood by the needlepoint stall and opened one of the burritos. She ate with nervous bites, looking down the street. People jostled against her as they passed. The music from half a dozen different bands engulfed her. She felt smaller than ever. Smaller—and more vulnerable.

The aromas from the different food stalls merged into one overpowering stench. The groups of people on the street were too loud, too large. What had, moments before, seemed a good-humored crowd of San Franciscans enjoying a weekend street fair now seemed a threatening mob. A man stumbled against her, and Violet gasped as if the contact had been an assault. *I'm lost,* she thought in sudden panic.

The fluttering in her chest made her feel weak, and she stepped back up on the curb and crossed the sidewalk to lean against a building. She glanced at the sign above the door: UNITED STATES POST OFFICE. Her thoughts were muddled. She wished she could just go inside the post office, slap on a stamp, and mail herself home to Berkeley. If only she were a letter . . .

A letter. Violet reached into her back pocket and drew out the two letters from Hal and the leaflet. She unfolded them and read each one through.

Remember the time you were lost in the crowds—how frightened you were? Yet you overcame that fear and prevailed.

"I will prevail," she whispered.

The Earth takes care of itself! . . . The Earth gets even. . . .

She scanned the street. Then she laid the two uneaten burritos on the ground next to the blue mailboxes. Straining, she hauled herself up onto one of the mailboxes by gripping the top of the mailbox and using her knees to shinny up far enough to lodge one knee on the shelf. Then, with extra effort, she was able to pull the other knee up.

She crouched there atop the blue box for a moment, then slowly raised herself to stand, one foot on the little shelf in front of the metal door, one foot on the rounded top of the mailbox. She could see above the heads of all the people in the street. She could see Sam, the dark-haired boy from Chance Street, walking toward her with a grin.

"Hey, it's the Maid-of-All-Work! What are you doing up there?"

She knew Jazzy and Rosy would have jumped down and chatted to him in an easy, friendly, grown-up way. But she didn't care anymore. She looked out over the crowd.

She drew a deep breath. "Jazzy!" she shouted at the top of her lungs. "Rosy? Where are you? Jazzy! Rosy!"

And then suddenly Sam was climbing up on top of the mailbox next to her. He steadied himself by placing one hand on her shoulder, and added his own voice to hers. "Jazzy!" he bellowed, his foghorn voice sounding out over the noise and music of the street fair. "Rosy! Come to the post office on the corner!" He looked down at Violet. "How am I doing?"

"Great," she said, nearly crying with relief as she saw the two golden heads of her sisters turn toward her. She pointed, laughing now. "There they are!"

Sam jumped down and reached up his arms to swing her down after him. When her sisters ran across the street to her, she embraced them, exultant, then turned to thank Sam. He was already disappearing down the hill on his skateboard.

Jasmine and Rose were furious. "Where *were* you?" wailed Jasmine. "I came back right away to the Mexican food place and you were gone. So I went back to the earring stall, but you weren't there, either!"

Violet scooped up her sisters' burritos from the sidewalk. "Here," she said, holding them out as a peace offering.

"We were frantic," hissed Rose, shaking Violet's arm as she pulled her toward the BART station. "Can't you be trusted not to wander off like a toddler?"

"We promised Mom and Dad we'd take care of you," cried Jasmine. Her face was streaked with tears. "And then we couldn't find you anywhere. All those people—they might have been murderers or kidnappers."

"And it would be our fault if anything happened to you," said Rose, unwrapping her burrito and taking a huge bite. "No one would ever forgive us," she continued, spewing out bits of lettuce. "*Dad* will never forgive us for not calling sooner. He's probably worried sick."

"I was fine—," Violet began helplessly, but Rose stalked ahead to a phone booth.

"Don't tell Dad we lost Vi, Rosy," cautioned Jasmine. "We'll be in total disgrace."

"Vi's the disgrace," said Rose. "She made a complete fool of herself with that boy on top of the mailbox." Rose glared back at Violet. "Anyway, you'll probably tell Dad and Mom everything, won't you?"

"I won't tell," Violet said quietly, "—*if* you don't tell anyone about the letters I found."

Rose swallowed her mouthful of burrito and then spoke into the phone receiver in a bright voice, telling their dad they were fine, the quake hadn't scared them. They'd worked hard and were taking the four o'clock train home.

The girls waited for the BART in silence. The train service had been delayed as the cars and rails needed to be checked for safety after the earthquake. Violet could see that her sisters were so upset they would not listen to a word she said. Inside the train, she sat in the seat in front of them—"Where we can keep an eye on you," Rose growled—and read through the letters from Hal again and again until she had them nearly memorized.

His was a voice speaking out to her, promising rescue. How was that possible? How could he help her? Violet glanced over her shoulder at the identical stony faces of her sisters and felt her heart tighten.

I see you as lost in the bosom of a family that tries to control you. They simply do not understand you as I do.

If only Hal could be with her now. She could use someone who understood.

The quake that day had measured 3.3 on the Richter scale. Lily and Greg were relieved to have their girls back home safely and asked for a full report of their day in the city. All three girls kept their promises. Violet did not say a word about being lost at the street fair. And Jasmine and Rose did not mention the letters. Instead all three of them regaled their parents with details of the cleaning up and told them how the quake had knocked plaster off the walls. Violet tried hard to keep her account of the quake as breezy and matter-of-fact as her sisters'.

Greg and Lily would be going to the new shop the next day to inspect the damage. Violet was eager to go with them, and asked if Beth could come along, too. Jasmine and Rose begged off, convincing their parents they needed to stay home on Sunday to meet with the Halloween Ball committee at Brett Hudson's house. Violet was glad they wouldn't be coming back to the shop, since they were still so annoyed with her, keeping out of her way and tossing their hair in irritation when she looked in their direction.

It turned out that Beth could not come to San Francisco on Sunday. Her mother's newest boyfriend had decided to take them all sailing on the bay. "It means we can't dye your hair till after school on Monday," Beth said. "But my mom says I have to go along. I'll probably get seasick! At least this guy seems nice—but then, all of them do, at first. Anyway, I'll fill you in on all new developments tomorrow at school."

"I have some new developments to tell you about, too," said Violet mysteriously, and only laughed when Beth pressed for details. That night Violet dreamed she was dancing with that boy, Sam, on top of the blue mailbox. They held each other tightly and seemed to be waltzing. Even in the dream, she thought it was odd that they didn't topple off. When she woke up, she thought how nice it was to dream about something other than earthquakes for a change.

Back in the new shop on Sunday morning, her father put his arm around Violet's shoulders. "I'm truly impressed," said Greg. He wandered around the front room, exclaiming over all the work they'd done the day before.

"The place is really beginning to sparkle," Lily added. "I'm proud of my girls."

"Jazzy and Rose helped a little," Violet said modestly. "And it was even cleaner before that last quake." She led the way upstairs. She showed them the back bedroom walls and plaster dust everywhere. Would they notice the niche under the windowsill where the second letter had been waiting for her?

But they were more interested in sweeping up the plaster and mopping the floors. "We want this place clean from cellar to attic," Lily said, rolling up her sleeves.

"What cellar? What attic?" asked Violet.

"Well, the attic is only a crawl space." Greg pointed to the ceiling in the hallway, where Violet could see a small square trapdoor. "Nothing up there but mice. I'm going to put in some insulation, though."

"What about the cellar? We didn't see a cellar."

"The entrance is out back," her father said. "I've only peeked in there, and it's as big a mess as the rest of the place. We'll have to clean it out. We'll need all the storage room we can find."

"Why don't you go open it now, dear," said Lily. "We might as well know the worst. I'll stay up here and do the floors."

"I'm coming with you," said Violet, following her father down the stairs, along the narrow hallway, and out the back door. He rooted in his pocket, finally withdrawing another large old key like the one for the front door. "Here we go," said Greg, and turned it in the lock. He had to shove hard to get the door open. Then he stepped down and, with a grunt of surprise, tumbled away into blackness.

"Dad?" Violet stepped inside after him.

"Careful!" he called, but too late—Violet found herself falling through nothingness and landing with a teeth-jarring thud on hard-packed earth. She sat, stunned, peering into the dark.

"Baby!" In a flash her father was at her side, lifting her into his arms. "Oh, Vi, I'm sorry. I tried to warn you." Her father put his hands on her shoulders and drew her toward him. "Are you all in one piece?"

"I–I'm okay, Dad. I think." Violet flexed her arms and legs. "What about you?"

"Thought I twisted my ankle, but it seems to be all right." He shook his head. "I should have remembered it was a steep drop."

Violet peered into the windowless space. In the light from the open door, she could make out vague humps and shadows but nothing more definite. She stood up and took a tentative step back toward the door, a full three feet above ground level. "There aren't any steps!"

"There were once, though." Her father kicked the old

pieces of wood at his feet. "I'll go back up for a flashlight, and we'll check out what's in here." He hauled himself out of the cellar and looked back at her with concern.

"Go on. I'm fine." Violet waited by the doorway in the rectangle of light from the little yard. She looked out at the trash cans and imagined instead a low stone bench. She looked at the cracked concrete and imagined instead green grass dotted with daisies. It could be such a beautiful garden, given a little love and a lot of time. A birdbath would look nice in the center, surrounded by rosebushes. She would sit out here and work on her needlepoint—

Then her father returned with the flashlight. He jumped down into the cellar next to her and beamed the light into the corners. Immediately Violet could see that the large humps were piles of planks and bricks. The small humps were stacks of newspapers, yellowed and brittle, tied with string. A brown leather suitcase, sticky with cobwebs, leaned against one stack. Everything was covered with the grime of years. As Greg swung the flashlight's beam in an arc, Violet caught her breath. There, to the left of the doorway they had fallen through, stood a stone garden bench. Fallen onto its side and covered with cobwebs was an ornate birdbath, intricately carved of stone.

Violet could only stare in wonder. Then the light moved and the bench and birdbath vanished into darkness. Greg walked over and picked up one of the bundles of old papers.

"Here, Baby. Will you hold the light while I toss this junk outside?" He passed her the flashlight and started heaving the newspapers up and out the door. "It's a fire hazard, having them down here. Hand me that old suitcase, too, will you? Wait—is it heavy? Don't strain yourself."

The suitcase *was* heavy. "I want to look inside, Dad," Violet said.

"Well, let's get it outside, first." Greg lugged the suitcase to the door and lifted it outside. "We can leave the bricks and boards for now, I guess," he said, flashing the light all around the small space again. Then he boosted Violet out of the cellar and climbed after her.

Violet knelt on the concrete to examine the battered brown suitcase. Her heart was thumping rapidly in her chest. She knew, she just absolutely, positively knew for certain, there was something for her inside. She hesitated, wondering how to get rid of her father. She didn't want to share Hal more than she already had.

But her father was kneeling by her side. He lifted the suitcase by its handle, fumbled with his fingers for the clasp, and the metal tabs popped open. "So much for stolen pirate booty, huh?" Greg laughed, lifting the lid. "It's not even locked."

Violet leaned forward to see. Packets of old sales receipts held together with rubber bands filled the suitcase. Beneath them were ledgers—bound books full of handwritten numbers and lists. Greg removed one of the ledgers and flipped through the pages. "And I was hoping for gold and rubies! This is an account book for an old shop." He showed her the first page on which someone long ago had neatly penned *Albert Stowe, Milliner.*

"What's a milliner, Dad?"

"Someone who makes hats. So this was a hat shop. And look at the date. 1903."

"Wow, that's old." Violet reached for another ledger and opened it. *"Fourteenth June 1904,"* she read. *"Eighteen yards red silk ribbon. One-quarter inch, twelve bolts green satin cord. Twenty feathered birds in brown, ten in blue."*

"Why would a hat shop need birds?" she asked.

"For the hats. You have no idea how elaborate fashionable women's hats were at the turn of the century." Her father laughed. "Feathers and ribbon and lace, little baskets of fruit and berries—and little stuffed birds galore. All piled a mile high."

He stood up and dusted off his pants. "These things might be of interest to a historical society or maybe the library archives. I'll look into it later. But now, let's close it all up and get back inside to help your mother."

"I'll be in in a few minutes," murmured Violet, leafing through the account book.

"It's chilly out here."

"No, really. I like it out here in the garden."

"Garden? You have better eyes than I have, Baby." But her father left her with an indulgent smile. As soon as he'd gone back inside, Violet tipped the entire contents of the suitcase onto the concrete.

There *had* to be a letter!

She shook each of the ledgers, looking for an envelope tucked inside. Several loose sheets sailed out and her heart thumped in anticipation. But each time she was disappointed when the page proved to be only another sales receipt or list of hat-making goods needed by Albert Stowe, Milliner. The last ledger had been torn in half, right down the middle. The stiff cardboard cover with Albert Stowe's now-familiar label was the same as on all the other ledgers. But the whole second half of the book, including the stiff cardboard back cover, had been ripped away. Violet pawed through the last few packets of receipts but found no trace of it. She flipped through the torn ledger. It, just like the others, listed fabrics, laces, and decorative baubles (birds, gold leaves, beads, bunches of cherries—even a banana). It listed the amounts of various materials, and in some cases the prices as well. But just as she was about to toss the book back into the case with the others, Violet stopped in surprise. The last page was not a list of goods for the hat shop. It was a letter written in brown ink, the handwriting full of curlicues and flourishes.

Hadn't she known it would be here?

But on closer inspection she saw it was not written by Hal at all. This handwriting was in a similar style, but the words were smaller, tighter on the page, and more neatly formed. And it wasn't really a letter at all. Violet read it eagerly nonetheless.

May 10, 1906

Oh, Diary—

For so long I have been wounded by the irony of it all. Small wonder, then, that I have been driven to desperate measures. My daily agonies were truly enough to drive anyone mad. Do you think perhaps that is what happened? Would madness provide the excuse I need if ever I am brought to task? The facts remain unalterable. I have done a terrible thing. She is dead and I am wracked with guilt. She is dead, and all her prophecies of doom are gone with her to the grave.

She is dead, but I am not. And Hal must never know how we have come together. Indeed, I shall endeavor all my life to ensure he never discovers the truth

Violet sat there on the concrete, staring down at the strange diary entry. Hal's name jumped off the page at her. The person who wrote this knew Hal. Had *"come together"* with him. What did that mean? Who had written these words?

The October wind gusted between the houses, fluttering the pages of the ledger. The ragged edges of torn paper attested to the fact that whoever ripped out the other pages had been in a hurry. This page had been left behind by mistake.

She shivered as she read the diary entry again, her eyes freezing on a sentence they had glided over before: *She is dead and I am wracked with guilt.* Who had died? *I have done a terrible thing.* Had the person who wrote this killed someone and then regretted it? Written about everything—and then tried to destroy the evidence?

And where did Hal fit in? *May 10, 1906.* That was just after the huge earthquake, the one she was supposed to be researching for her science paper. Violet couldn't remember the date of the 1906 quake but thought it had been sometime in April.

As Violet sat there lost in thought, she started trembling. Gradually she realized that *she* wasn't trembling, but the earth itself was. She leaped up, clutching the ledger, just as her mother ran out onto the back step.

"Baby!"

The trembling subsided. Violet and Lily stared at each other in silence across the yard, as if speaking might set off another quake. Then the fear in the pit of her stomach welled up, and Violet covered her face. "Mom—help—" The words came out as a groan. Behind her closed eyes she saw the flicker of flame, the shadow children moving away from twisted ruins—

"Come inside now." Lily's voice was sharp with anxiety. "Put that filthy old book down and hurry. Dad's ready to leave."

Violet lifted her head and swallowed, hard. She replaced the ledger carefully with all the other ledgers and receipts in the suitcase.

"Leave that old case. It's too heavy for you, darling. Dad will deal with it."

Violet obediently rose to her feet. Then, her back turned so her mother wouldn't see, she crouched back down and ripped the diary entry right out of the torn ledger and stuffed it into her pocket. She followed her mother into the shop, her thoughts tumbling around in her own private quake.

CHAPTER 7

"Listen, did you get the hair sample?" Beth asked on Monday morning when the two girls met as usual at the corner of North Street to walk to school together.

Violet nodded wearily. She had lain awake the night before for what seemed like hours, tensing against imaginary earthquakes. Then, having finally fallen asleep, she'd woken several times, sure she'd felt her bed moving. Now she pulled the plastic bag containing the lock of Rose's hair out of her backpack and showed it to Beth. "I've only got Rosy's. But Jazzy's hair is exactly the same." Her urgency to look more like her sisters had been overshadowed by her unease. She tried to inject her smile with some of her earlier enthusiasm as they walked along.

Inside the drugstore on the next block, Violet's attention was immediately caught by the headlines of the newspapers lined up in racks by the door:

SWARM OF QUAKES RATTLES BAY AREA

SCIENTISTS PREDICT BIG ONE STILL TO COME

BAY AREA ON EDGE

She tried to push the stark words out of her head as she and Beth hurried to the aisle of shampoos and cream rinses, gels and mousses, sprays and perms. At the far end were the boxes of hair color. Swatches of artificial hair hung from a plastic rack with tags identifying the color. Violet removed the chunk of Rose's hair and held it up to the samples. "What do you think?" she asked Beth. "Golden Cornhusk?"

"Too blond," said Beth. "How about Wheatberry Sunset?"

Violet compared colors. "That's closer," she agreed. "But kind of red."

They examined the other swatches and finally agreed that Medium Honey Ash was the closest match. Violet paid for the box of hair color out of her allowance, then she and Beth hurried on their way.

"We'll go to my house and do it right after school," Beth said. "Maybe I should go back and get some for myself."

"You have gorgeous hair." Beth's hair was vibrant red and curled naturally into corkscrew ringlets on hot days.

"I don't think so. But I'll wait to see how yours turns out before I do anything drastic." Beth looked both ways before starting across the busy intersection. "Anyway," she said, looking back over her shoulder at Violet, "let's hear about the 'mysterious developments' you mentioned on the phone."

Violet hesitated. Before she'd found the diary entry, she had been looking forward to showing Beth Hal's letter. But she hadn't told even her sisters about the latest find. She felt almost as if the diary entry and Hal's two letters were secret messages from the past, seeping inexplicably through layers of time, just for her.

And yet Beth was her best friend. She always told Beth everything.

"Well," she said slowly now, "I have something to show you."

"Come on then!"

Again she hesitated. "Not now, it'll take too long and we're almost late." She ran across the street and jogged along toward school, Beth panting at her side.

"Tell me!"

"After school, at your house. Promise!"

Violet had no inkling then that by the time she was at Beth's house after school, there would be something even more compelling to show.

"Listen up, people, we're here!" boomed Mr. Koch as the school bus stopped in front of the California Academy of Sciences in San Francisco's Golden Gate Park. He looked at his watch. "I want you all on your very best behavior. Have your notebooks open at all times and your pens working. Now we'll walk quietly inside and wait for the docent to lead us on our tour." He bounded out of the bus ahead of everyone else and led the line of students inside the Academy.

Violet and Beth hurried to catch up with him.

The museum was crowded, but their guide, a poised, fair-haired woman in a blue suit, was waiting for them. She led them away from the lobby and into the darkness of the first exhibit hall. Violet had been to the Academy before with her parents and sisters, but several new exhibits had been opened to the public since she'd last come. She wandered, her interest engaged, listening to the guide talk about rocks. There were semiprecious gems and geodes to look at. There were fragments of meteorites and even some moon rocks.

When they came to the earthquake simulator, the guide stopped. "This should be of special interest to those of you who might have felt our own big rock—our earth—move these past few days," she said.

"Who *wouldn't* have felt the quakes?" whispered Beth to Violet. "You'd have to be dead not to notice them."

Violet nodded, a shiver prickling the hairs at the back of her neck. She could do without seeing this exhibit.

The guide showed them the delicate instruments that measured seismic activity, and pointed to the computer print-out for the last few quakes. "You can see how steady the stylus was, then how it veered sharply up and down here."

Violet was pushed to the front of the crowd to look into the glass case. Reluctantly, she gazed down. Sure enough, there were the abrupt dips, up and down on the page, for Friday's quake and for Saturday's. The tremble on Sunday morning was recorded only as a small blip in the lines. The lines reminded her of the EKG machine she'd been connected to in the hospital for her heart surgery. It had measured the delicate variations in her heartbeat just as this instrument measured the movements of the earth.

Violet stepped away so Beth could see, and watched the guide lead several of her classmates onto the earthquake simulator—a raised walkway with waist-high railings along both sides. A brief film flickered on a large screen and informed them that they would be experiencing a 5.0 earthquake, with lateral ground movement only. In a real quake, the man in the film explained, the ground would move up and down as well as back and forth. But for safety reasons, the museum exhibit would reduce actual shaking by using only one movement.

"Cool," said Beth. "I want to try it out." But there wasn't enough space for her on the platform. The guide told her to wait for the next group.

Violet held her breath and watched the platform shake. Her classmates clutched the railings and laughed. Noises boomed from loudspeakers to simulate the roar of the tectonic plates grinding against each other below the surface of earth.

"Come on, Vi, we're next!" Beth tugged Violet to the platform.

"No, thanks. I take my quakes real or not at all." She gave a short, carefree laugh, but her palms were sweating. No way was she going on that platform.

Violet darted away before Beth could say another word. She headed for the exhibits about outer space. But before she reached them, a soft light from a special display alcove caught her eye. The alcove was sectioned off with a twisted red velvet rope. She stopped to peek inside and found herself looking in on what seemed to be an old-fashioned sitting room, with a wing chair in the corner next to a round-topped wooden table. A cut-glass bottle of amber liquid—was it supposed to be brandy?—sat atop the table, along with an ashtray and carved pipe. The soft glow in the alcove was cast by a flickering lightbulb in the lamp fastened to the wall above the desk. Violet guessed it was supposed to be gaslight. A calendar, askew on its nail in the wall above the desk, read "April 1906," with the eighteenth circled in red. An ornate clock lay on its side on the mantel, its hands pointing to 5:12. On the desk lay an uncorked inkwell, tipped out over a piece of creamy paper, yellowed at the edges, half of the message obliterated with a large brown inkblot. The impression was that someone had been writing a letter right when an earthquake struck. The impression was heightened by the jagged pen line careening off the page. As a special touch, the pen lay on the floor next to the overturned chair.

Violet leaned forward to read the sign: "AN INTERRUPTION." SAN FRANCISCO EARTHQUAKE, 1906.

Too neat, thought Violet. *Wouldn't there be fallen plaster? Wouldn't the gaslight have gone out? What about the sounds of screams from the street?* There had been fire after that earthquake, Mr. Koch had said—a horrible fire that raced through the city and destroyed much of San Francisco.

To Violet the past had meant nothing. The people were black-and-white images from old photographs. Just thin paper impressions. But now, after she'd read Hal's letters and found the diary entry in the old ledger, the past was taking shape in a less nebulous way. Real people had lived then—had worked in the shop. Had received letters full of promises. Had written in a diary. Had killed someone?

An Interruption, she thought, and leaned forward to see if she could read the letter displayed on the desk.

She caught her breath.

My sweet Baby V, it began.

She glanced wildly over her shoulder. Her classmates were still shrieking on the earthquake simulator. The docent was speaking to Mr. Koch. No one was watching. Lifting the red twisted rope, she slipped beneath and reached for the letter on the desk. She *had* to read it, *had* to know. Stepping back behind the rope, she scanned the page quickly, hunching over with her back to the class.

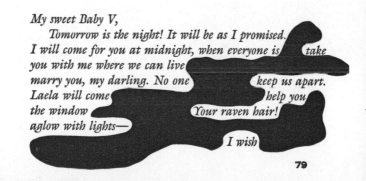

My sweet Baby V,

Tomorrow is the night! It will be as I promised. I will come for you at midnight, when everyone is take *you with me where we can live* marry you, my darling. No one *keep us apart. Laela will come* help you *the window* Your raven hair! *aglow with lights—*

I wish

There was no signature, but Violet knew.

"Violet, come on!" Beth's loud whisper summoned her back to the tour. "We're going to the Fish Roundabout now."

Violet stood, still holding the letter from Hal, the sound of her heartbeat pounding in her ears. Of course she must put it back. It was part of the museum exhibit.

But wasn't she Baby V?

She took a deep breath and smiled at Beth, hoping her face would not betray her. She waved her hand casually. "Be right there." Then she knelt down and fumbled with the zipper on her backpack. She slid the sheet of paper neatly into her history notebook, then followed the class without a backward look.

CHAPTER 8

On the bus ride back to school and again on the walk home to Beth's apartment, Violet was silent. She knew she needed to talk to Beth about Hal's mysterious letters and the diary page—but she was afraid. She couldn't believe she had really stolen the ink-stained letter from the exhibit, and her guilty secret chafed like a hidden sore. So she waited, silent and tense, until Beth unlocked her apartment door with the key she always wore on a ribbon around her neck. The giddy barking of Beth's small schnauzer, Romps, greeted them.

"We'll have the place to ourselves till Tom gets home from soccer practice at five," Beth said as she tossed her schoolbag down in the small hallway and knelt to scratch the excited dog's ears. "So let's get started."

It took a moment for Violet to remember why they were here. Having the same hair color as her sisters seemed less important now than it had before she'd found the letters from Hal. But she rummaged in her backpack and brought out the packet of Medium Honey Ash. Beth took it from her and headed down the hall to the bathroom. She started reading the instructions.

"Better take off your shirt. Sounds like this could be messy."

Violet removed her sweater and T-shirt. She was wearing the bra her mother had bought after Violet insisted that if Jasmine and Rose wore bras, she would, too. So what if she didn't really need one yet? The bra helped to hide the thin pink scar that ran from her breastbone all around the left side of her ribs to her back. That was where the doctors had cut her open for the operation. The scar had faded from red to pink over the years and the doctors promised it would one day be white and barely visible. Sometimes she thought of her scar as a sort of badge—proof that she was perfectly healthy now. But other times she hated her scar. It was a symbol of what kept her parents hovering over her and why Lily insisted she be excused from gym classes. The scar was another way she looked different from her sisters.

Normally Violet was self-conscious about having other people—even Beth—see her scar. But now when she looked down at her chest she didn't even notice it. Instead she thought she could see her heart thumping extra hard. *Stress*, she told herself. *Guilt*.

Romps edged his way into the room and sat watching, tongue lolling, as Beth motioned Violet over to the side of the bathtub. "First we have to wash your hair," Beth said. "Let's use my mom's shampoo—it's another Rich Woman's Special."

Beth's mother worked hard to support Beth and her brother. They didn't have money for a lot of luxuries, but Mrs. Madigan didn't skimp on luxurious bath oils, fragrant hair products, and little designer soaps shaped like stars and hearts. Violet shut her eyes and enjoyed the scrubbing as Beth lathered her hair with scented shampoo and rinsed it with warm water. She thought about the claw-footed bathtub upstairs in the Chance Street shop. Had Hal's beloved V washed her hair in that tub? Had she used scented soap?

"That was great," she sighed after Beth rinsed away the suds. "You should open a spa."

"No way. I'm going to be a famous artist."

Beth was the only kid Violet knew who already had decided what she'd be. Violet flicked some suds out of her eyes. "I guess I'll have to wait and see what Jazzy and Rosy want to be."

"What—you mean you'll just become whatever they do?" Beth snorted. "I don't know what's wrong with you these days, Vi. You never used to care so much about being like your sisters. They aren't *so* special, you know. They just think they are."

Violet bit her lip. Beth didn't understand. Violet wasn't sure *she* understood, either.

Beth wrapped a blue towel around Violet's head. "Blot excess moisture," she read from the package insert. "Okay? Are you blotted?"

"Mmm." Violet pictured the blot of ink across the stolen letter. She looked at the two bottles on the ledge by the sink. "Are you sure that's the right color? It's so red."

"The box says Medium Honey Ash," said Beth. "So here goes."

"What am I supposed to do, just pour it on?"

Beth consulted the directions. "Well, first I need to put on these plastic gloves." Violet bent over the bathtub again while Beth worked the thick solution into a lather on her hair. "Oh no," Beth exclaimed suddenly. "I forgot I was supposed to mix the two bottles of stuff together first. Well, it shouldn't matter." She reached for the second bottle and unscrewed the top. "Yuck."

"Shouldn't matter?" squealed Violet as a terrible smell filled the bathroom. It was enough to banish all thoughts of the mysterious letters and her crime. She squeezed her eyes shut.

"Keep your head down, you're dripping everywhere. Look, I'll just pour this clear stuff on now and mix it together right on your hair. What's the difference?" Beth pressed Violet back over the tub and poured the other liquid onto her head. "You get used to the smell after a while."

Violet felt the cold oozing right down her back. "This better work."

"You'll be gorgeous," Beth said cheerfully.

Violet kept the image of her sisters' long, shining hair in her mind. *Please*, she thought.

When the mixtures had been thoroughly worked into Violet's hair, Beth wrapped her head in the plastic turban provided in the box and clipped the plastic in place with a bobby pin. Slowly Violet raised her head and glanced into the mirror.

"I look like a monster from the deep!" she wailed.

"True, but not for long." Beth consulted the instructions again. "You just have to wait twenty minutes before we can rinse it out. Then you'll look like a princess."

"Forget princesses. I want to look like—"

"Like Rosy and Jazzy, as you've said about a million times! And you will, you will." Beth's voice was confident, but her expression betrayed some nervousness. "Hold still—there's goop running down your cheek." She dabbed at Violet's face with the towel. "Don't let it drip on the dog."

Violet wondered what she'd do if there was another quake while she had the dye on her head. What if it were a big one and she had to leave the building wearing the plastic bag over her hair? What if she had to leave the goo on longer than the prescribed twenty minutes? Would her hair fall out?

They went across the hall to Beth's tiny bedroom, followed by the dog. The room was the same size as Violet's alcove at home, but at least Beth could have privacy when she wanted it. Her door closed and locked.

Romps lay down by the door and seemed to fall asleep. Beth flopped across the bed. "You don't have to look so scared. It'll be fine. Come on, get your mind off it. Tell me the big deal about what you found in San Francisco."

How could Beth know about the stolen letter? Violet stared at her with wide, guilty eyes, then remembered she had promised only that morning to tell Beth about the other letters from Hal and the diary entry. The morning already seemed an eternity ago.

Violet sat stiffly on the edge of Beth's bed, holding her neck straight so the dye wouldn't run, and tried to think where to start. She described the shop on Chance Street, how hard she and her sisters had worked to clean it up, and how she'd found the first envelope in the back of the cupboard. She sent Beth to fetch her backpack by the front door, then pulled the wad of letters out and handed the first one to Beth. She watched while her friend read Hal's letter.

Beth looked gratifyingly intrigued. "It almost sounds like he's talking to *you*, did you notice that?"

"Exactly. I thought so, too. And then I found this second one."

Beth grabbed the second envelope and read the letter. "How weird. Look—did you see what it says about the family—the twin sisters? And about V's weakness? It sounds like her family hovered over her the way yours does over you."

"Isn't it amazing?"

"You can tell these letters are really old, though." Beth looked delighted. "It's just like mysteries in books. You never think anything can happen that way in real life. But then it does."

"And there's more. Yesterday when I went back to the shop with my parents, I found something else." Violet explained about the cellar, about the suitcase. Sharing the strange story with Beth made the letters even more special. She felt more certain than ever that she had been singled out to receive them. She reached up with her towel and dabbed a trickle of hair dye from her forehead. "I found this one at the back of an old account book." She handed the ledger page to Beth. "It's spooky—and different from the others."

"This is a diary entry!" Beth exclaimed.

"I know." Beth's excitement pleased Violet. Maybe Beth would understand, after all, why she'd had to take the letter from the museum.

"Is it Hal's?"

"No—but whoever wrote it knew Hal. It's kind of creepy."

Beth read it through, looking shocked. "This sounds like she killed somebody!"

"That's what I think, too."

"But who wrote it? It says she and Hal got together. Could that be V?"

"We don't know for sure that a woman wrote it at all," Violet pointed out hastily. She identified too strongly with Hal's V to want her to be a murderer. "Maybe a man wrote it."

"It sounds like a woman to me," said Beth.

It sounded like a woman to Violet, too, but how could some woman's diary fit with the letters from Hal? And who had been a prophet of doom? "I know it sounds impossible," she said quietly, "but I keep wondering if the letters could be meant for me. Somehow."

"What are you talking about? These letters are almost a hundred years old!"

Violet scanned Hal's letters, frowning. "I know, I know. But look how V has something wrong with her heart."

"That's just a coincidence," said Beth.

"Maybe," said Violet slowly, "but maybe not. Mr. Koch says scientists don't believe in coincidence—and I don't think I do, either." An elusive thought tickled. What was it about the letters that bothered her?

"You're giving me the creeps, Vi. Come on. I mean, look at the date! My grandparents weren't even born when Hal wrote those letters."

Violet was silent. Just as she couldn't fully explain—even to herself—why she'd stolen part of a museum exhibit, she couldn't explain her strange certainty that the letters were meant for her. She shuffled through the pages, rereading.

Long ago V had argued with her sisters in a restaurant. And then Violet argued with Jazzy and Rosy at the café on Chance Street. V had been lost in San Francisco. Hadn't Violet herself been separated from her sisters at the street fair?

"Beth," she whispered. "Look at this . . ."

Beth leaned toward her. "What?"

"The letters. I just realized—I can't imagine why I didn't see this before."

"What? What do you mean?"

"It isn't that the letters were written *to* me—they're *about* me. Somehow what happened in the past—" The letters trembled in Violet's hand—"What happened to Hal's poor V in the past is happening to me in my life *now*!"

Beth's eyes widened. "But how can that be, Vi?"

Violet hurried to point out the passages in the letter that had come true. The quarrel in the restaurant with her sisters. Getting lost in the crowd.

Beth looked skeptical, then slanted Violet a grin. "If that's true, then some handsome guy like Hal is going to fall in love with you. And won't Jazzy and Rosy freak out?"

"*I'll* freak out if that happens!" Violet looked at her in wonderment. "I've never had a boyfriend." She hadn't thought about what Hal's plan might mean to her. "But it might happen soon—look at this!" She jumped off the bed and dug her history notebook out of her backpack. With eager fingers she extracted the third letter from Hal and handed it to Beth.

"Hal spilled his ink," Beth said. "Hey—it sounds like he planned to take V away somewhere—the very next night, he says. That might mean someone will come for you, too—" Beth broke off. "Wow, Vi—the date on this letter is April 18, 1906. Wasn't that the date of the San Francisco earthquake?" She looked puzzled. "Hey, wait a minute—where did you get this letter, anyway?"

"Well..." Violet hesitated. Then she confessed. "From the Academy of Sciences. You know, the earthquake exhibit with the desk and everything?"

"You *stole* it?"

Violet shook her plastic-wrapped head. "I didn't *exactly* steal it..."

"Yes, you did! That's *exactly* what you did. I can't believe you, Vi. You must be crazy."

"But it was from Hal!" Violet tried to defend herself. "I need to find out about V and what happened to her. Because, well, because maybe it's going to happen to me, too. Don't you see? Hal must be sending me these letters—okay, not really sending them, but putting them in my path. A sort of paper trail!"

"You mean you really think Hal is trying to—like—*warn* you of something?" Beth's eyes were very round. "A warning from the past? That's totally weird. But, hey—I've got a warning from the *present*. What if the police are looking for this letter? Have you thought about that?"

Violet flushed. Of course the museum officials would have discovered the missing letter by now. They would be searching all the visitors before letting anyone out of the museum. The police would have been called. There might even be roadblocks set up all through Golden Gate Park to detain people while detectives searched their cars.

Outside Beth's apartment, a siren whined. Romps scrambled to his feet and barked. Beth grabbed Violet's arm. "Hide!" she whispered. "I'll tell them I'm alone here."

Violet jumped to her feet. The closet? Under the bed? But wouldn't the hair dye drip on Beth's white rug?

The siren vanished into the distance. The girls looked at each other and laughed shakily. "I guess I'd better return the letter," mumbled Violet. "And fast."

"But how?"

Violet sank back onto the bed. Her knees felt like taffy. Too much was happening all at once. As if diary entries from murderers and letters that foretold the future weren't enough to deal with—now she had to worry about breaking the law as well. What happened to people who stole things from museum exhibits? Would pleading momentary insanity help her case?

Would madness provide the excuse I need if ever I am brought to task?

Would she go to jail? Reform school? "Maybe—maybe I can just mail it back to them?"

"Anonymously," stressed Beth. "And maybe you should

send the diary page to the police at the same time, so that they can get busy trying to track down the murderer."

"But we don't know who wrote it or who was murdered or anything! And it's so old I don't see how the police could solve the crime anyway. I found these things, and I want to solve the mystery myself. And don't you go telling people about any of this," she added. "Please."

"I won't," Beth promised. "As long as you send the letter back to the museum."

"I will, I will. First thing tomorrow." Violet took a deep breath of relief. She would send it back on the way to school. *But not until I photocopy it,* she decided, looking guiltily over at her friend.

It will be as I promised. I will come for you at midnight.

The words echoed in her head across the decades. Would she still be here tomorrow morning? She glanced down at the letter in her hand. A drop of reddish dye plopped onto the inkblot and she mopped it up hastily with the corner of her towel. "Hasn't it been twenty minutes yet?" she asked in a plaintive voice.

"Close enough," answered Beth with a quick glance at her watch. "Come on."

They left the letters on Beth's bed and returned to the bathroom. Violet knelt over the bathtub again while Beth rinsed her hair. Rivers of muddy dye streamed from Violet's head and swirled down the drain. Beth shoved Violet's head directly beneath the tap for a final rinse. When the pounding water finally ran clear, she wrapped Violet's head in a clean towel.

Violet hurried to the mirror, trying to push all thoughts of letters and crime from her soon-to-be-revealed golden head. Both girls leaned toward the mirror above the sink. *"Ta-dah!"* Beth cried, and the towel fell away.

Violet started into the mirror. A bubble of disappointment rose into her throat. As far as she could tell, her hair looked the same as always. Wet, but the same dark brown, nearly black frizz. "Nothing happened, Beth!"

"Wait," said Beth, and reached under the sink for her mother's hair dryer. "Let's see what happens when we dry it."

Violet stood still, trying not to cry, while Beth blew hot air on her hair.

"I think there are highlights," Beth said encouragingly. "Golden highlights, coming through. Hang on. They're just like Jazzy's and Rosy's."

Violet tilted her head. Golden? In the fluorescent bathroom light her hair now seemed to have an odd-colored cast, like the skin of an overripe plum. "They look like *purple* highlights to me, Beth." And now tears coursed down her cheeks. "Now I don't look like Jazzy and Rosy, and I don't even look like *me* anymore."

Beth consulted the package insert. "It wears off in four to six weeks, anyway. That won't be so bad."

But Violet could only stare in the mirror, shaking her head.

Your raven hair!

Oh, Hal, Violet thought sadly. *You would have liked me better just the way I was.*

CHAPTER 9

When she returned home from Beth's, Violet went straight to her little alcove bedroom and tied a red bandanna over her hair. She went down for dinner, relieved to find that her sisters had been invited to eat pizza with Casey and Brett at Brett's house and wouldn't be home until bedtime. Although she was eager to tell them about the letters' ability to foretell her future, she did not want to hear comments about her purple hair. And she did not want them to know about the stolen letter but couldn't quite trust herself not to tell.

Over dinner Lily and Greg asked whether she was coming down with something—her face looked a little flushed. And why was she wearing that scarf on her head? Violet pushed back her chair and said she thought she'd do her homework and go to bed early.

She lay across her bed, poring over the letters from the past, looking for more clues to her own life. There were connections she hadn't caught at first that leaped out at her now.

I look at the flowers in the garden...

Flowers. And Violet had imagined flowers in the back concrete yard so clearly she could almost *see* them. Not to mention the fact that her parents were florists. And the very garden bench and birdbath she'd envisioned turned up in the cellar.

Is your heart still aching? I ache myself when I think of the pain you have been in....

This was clearly a reference to her open-heart surgery.

No one...keep us apart....help you...the window...

She glanced at her bedroom window. It gave her delicious shivers down her back to think that Hal—no, how could it be Hal?—that *someone* might come for her. She'd never thought to try it, but a person probably could climb up the front porch pillars, right up onto the porch roof and over to her window.

And what about the earthquake? Hal had been writing the letter to V when he was interrupted. Violet shivered and slipped under her quilt. Could all the quakes they'd been having recently somehow be tied to the letters? She quickly pushed that thought away.

Your raven hair! aglow with lights—

Aglow now with highlights. Purple highlights.

Violet pulled another pillow under her head and lay back, thinking. Could it really be just as Mr. Koch kept saying in class? That nothing is coincidence, that there is a reason for everything that happens. That history and science are connected. That the past leaves clues for the present, and the role of scientists is to decipher those messages to better understand how the world works.

She tossed and turned until she heard her sisters come up to bed, and then her parents. Still sleep wouldn't come. The glow of the street lamps outside shone through her windows like a beacon from the past on which, she imagined dreamily, someone might fly in to take her away with him. . . .

When the wind rattled the panes of her window, she sat bolt upright in bed. Was Hal here for her now? At last she slept, dreaming first of the face in the needlepoint portrait and then, as the mournful *whoooo* of the wind insinuated itself into her dreams, of howling shadow children. She slept fitfully, jerking awake whenever the clock chimed on the mantel downstairs.

At breakfast the next morning, Violet glanced across the table at Jasmine and Rose and her tired muscles relaxed with a small glow of satisfaction. *Too bad we don't wear school uniforms,* she thought. That would make looking alike much easier. But at least today her sisters had put on the clothes she'd selected and laid out on their beds. They were all three of them wearing jeans, blue sweatshirts, and white running shoes. They were all wearing their hair in ponytails tied back with blue elastic scrunchies. She was the only one, however, who wore the blue hood of the sweatshirt pulled up over her head and tied tightly under her chin.

"I knew it was true about our poor sweet Baby," Jasmine said to Rose as she poured herself a glass of orange juice from the carton, "but I didn't think it would manifest itself until she was older."

"All the signs have been there a long time." Rose shook her head sadly and reached for the carton. "Poor attention span, poor ambulatory skills—" She poured herself a glass of juice, too.

"What's *that* mean?" interrupted Jasmine.

"You know—moving around. Walking. She always crashes

into things or trips over her own feet—and her feet aren't even as big as ours. It's poor ambulatory skills. It's because her gravitational force is different from ours."

"She's trying to adapt," said Jasmine solemnly. "But it's an uphill battle. Her true origins keep betraying her no matter how she tries to fit in."

"What are you talking about?" asked Violet in irritation. This was twinspeak in full force.

Rose sipped her orange juice. "The hood. It's because your antennae have started to sprout, right?"

"Now girls," protested Lily, coming in from the kitchen with a platter of scrambled eggs.

"It's because she's an alien," Jasmine said kindly. "She can't help it."

Violet bit back a snide retort and adjusted the hood of her sweatshirt. All desire to tell them of her amazing discovery about the letters disappeared. They didn't deserve to know anything. Just let them find her gone—rescued from this family by a handsome boyfriend.

Jasmine winked at her. "It's elementary, my dear Baby. On your planet, girls' antennas—or do I mean *antennae?*— usually don't sprout until they're about eighteen. You're pretty young to have this happen to you. It's perfectly understandable that you'd want to hide them."

The teakettle whistled in the kitchen, and Violet waited until Lily left the room. Then Violet leaned across the table and hissed at her sisters, "I had something totally important I wanted to tell you. It's to do with the letters from Hal. But forget it."

Jasmine and Rose exchanged one of their maddening twin looks. Then Jasmine said, "Pretty please with sugar on it?" And Rose said, "If you don't tell us, I'll tell Mom you ran off at the street fair!"

Violet drained her juice and set the purple plastic cup

down with a bang. "No way. You don't deserve to know. I'm leaving early—I have an important science project to work on." She pushed back her chair. Really she was leaving early to have time to photocopy the stolen letter before she mailed it back.

She'd been hiding it under her sweatshirt all the time she ate breakfast. It crackled against her chest. As she stood up, the manila envelope with the letter inside slid to the floor. She knelt to retrieve it, but Rose was faster.

"What are you sending to the Academy of Sciences?" Rose asked, looking at the address. "Are you offering them your alien body for display?"

"Give it back!" Violet grabbed for the letter, but Rose smiled in a supercilious way and held it above her head.

"Don't give it back until she tells us," directed Jasmine.

Violet prayed that Rose would not open the envelope. She hadn't sealed it yet, merely tucked in the flap. She grabbed again for the letter and knocked a fork off the table. It clattered on the wooden floor. When she bent to pick it up, she had to restrain herself from reaching under the table with it to stab Rose in the leg. Their mother returned with her cup of tea.

"Mom! Tell Rosy to give me back my letter!"

"Rose, dear," chided Lily, sitting down in her chair.

"It's to the Academy of Sciences," Rose reported.

"It's for my science project!" Violet snapped.

"You've written to the museum for information?" exclaimed Lily. "Baby, I'm proud of you. Your schoolwork will be hugely improved if you apply yourself this way from now on. What's your topic?"

"The 1906 earthquake," muttered Violet.

"Push your hood back, dear, I can hardly hear you," said

Lily. "Really, it's very unbecoming, sitting around indoors with your face half covered like that."

"My head's cold," said Violet.

"Oh my, I did think last night you looked like you were getting sick. Let me check." In a flash, Lily was up and at Violet's side. She placed one hand on Violet's forehead, then—before Violet could stop her—pulled back the hood to feel the temperature at the back of Violet's neck and revealed the dark curls with their odd sheen.

"Baby! What have you done to your hair?" demanded Lily.

"It's a mistake, Mom—it was supposed to be *golden*. Like Jazzy's and Rosy's. But don't worry, it'll wash out." Violet spoke quickly, her head down. She couldn't bear to look at her sisters, couldn't bear to see the contemptuous amusement on their faces.

She was surprised when no one laughed and no one suggested she was already in costume for the Halloween Ball. She raised her head a little when Jasmine's voice broke the silence. "It's cool—sort of. Sort of, um, eggplant-colored."

"Probably no one will notice," added Rose in an uncharacteristically gentle voice. "Much."

Violet dragged the hood back up to cover her hair, her face flushed with humiliation. She held out her hand for the envelope, and Rose returned it without another word.

Violet said a hasty good-bye to her mother, then went to the kitchen for her coat. She was just going out the door when Jasmine and Rose came after her.

"We can walk together, if you want," Jasmine offered.

Rose shouldered her backpack. "I'm ready, too. Let's all go."

"Now that's what I like to see," said Lily approvingly as the girls left the house together.

"Vi's hair gives me an idea," Rose said. "We can dress as aliens for the dance!"

"All three of us," said Jasmine. "With antennae and purple hair. It'll be cool. Okay, Vi?"

Violet didn't answer. The letter in her hand seemed to be burning a hole into her skin. Its guilty weight was heavier than all the books she carried.

Rose narrowed her eyes. "So, what were you going to tell us about Hal, Baby?"

"Don't call me Baby," Violet said automatically. She walked faster.

"Then stop acting like one." Rose hurried after her. "What's going on?"

"We're all in this together," insisted Jasmine. "We were there when you found the letters, after all. So if you've learned something new, we have a right to know, too!"

Violet stopped and faced her sisters. If they were all in this together, then Jazzy and Rosy would help rather than condemn her. She glanced left and right, checking to see who might overhear. Two women walked in front of them, high heels clicking on the pavement. Behind them a raucous group of high school students was surging forward, all cackling like Halloween witches. Violet waited until they had passed. "Will you swear to keep this a secret?"

"You don't have secrets," scoffed Rose.

"Sshh!" snapped Jasmine. "Of course we will. At least I will."

"I will, too," vowed Rose. "Cross my heart and hope to die."

After a moment's hesitation, Violet told them about finding the diary entry in the old suitcase. She pulled it from her backpack, watching their expressions with satisfaction as they read.

"It mentions Hal!" exclaimed Jasmine. "Did V write it? I bet she did—"

"But there's something terrible—it sounds like murder," said Rose. "Do you really think V murdered someone?"

"No, I'm sure she didn't. I don't think this is her diary at all," Violet told them. "It's too creepy and weird. Hal wouldn't love somebody who was creepy and weird. But there's something more—" and she told them about the letter from Hal she had discovered in the museum exhibit.

They listened with identical expressions of fascination. Then Violet held up the large manila envelope.

"That's it?" asked Rose, wide-eyed.

"You stole it?" gasped Jasmine, horrified.

"*Borrowed* it," Violet said firmly. "And I'm returning it this morning."

They couldn't believe she'd done it, of course. They snatched the letter back and forth, reading it and exclaiming over it until Violet rescued it, afraid it would be torn. Jasmine and Rose shrieked and carried on so loudly that two old men with shopping bags who passed them on the sidewalk frowned darkly and muttered about "kids today."

Jasmine and Rose walked on either side of Violet, shaking their heads at her. "What nerve," said Jasmine. "I just can't *believe* you."

"I can't believe you, either," said Rose. "You really are an alien after all."

But when Violet glanced from side to side and saw their faces, she felt a little thrill inside as she realized that her sisters' appalled reactions masked a very real envy. *They* had never stolen something from a museum. *They* had never found mysterious letters from the past addressed with *their* initials. Did she imagine it, or were they looking at her now with awe?

"It's amazing," Rose said finally. "I think you're crazy to

have taken it, Vi, but now that you have it, you can't send it back without keeping a copy. It's—I don't know—*evidence,* or something."

"Yeah," concurred Jasmine. "It belongs with the other letters."

Violet stopped, a little smile playing about the corners of her mouth. "And so, *voilà,*" she said, pointing to the Copy Shop in front of them. "Great minds think alike."

She led the way inside, glancing back over her shoulder, noting with satisfaction the twin looks of grudging respect on their identical faces.

But after they made the copy and stowed it inside Violet's science notebook, after they sealed the original letter in the envelope and ran all the way to the mailbox on the corner, Jasmine put her hand on Violet's arm to stop her from dropping the letter inside.

"Wait—the postmark," Jasmine said. "We didn't think of that!"

"Oh, you're right," agreed Rose, panting slightly. "It's a dead giveaway."

Violet paused with her hand on the mailbox door. "What do you mean?" She longed to send the letter back where it belonged and have it off her conscience.

"A Berkeley postmark will show that the stolen letter was mailed from Berkeley," explained Jasmine. "If the San Francisco police are looking for the thief—that's *you,* Vi—then they'll know to look here."

"And the museum can check which schools came to the museum the day the letter was stolen," added Rose. "It will be only a matter of time before they track the thief to your class. And they'll be able to tell just by looking at your face who took the letter."

Violet put her hands to her face. She could feel the heat.

She felt the thud of her heart as she pictured the police pouring into her classroom. Mr. Koch would try to hide under the desk the way he had during the earthquake. When the police wrestled her out of her seat, the hood of her sweatshirt would fall back, revealing her hair. . . . There would be no living it down. Any of it. Ever.

"But what do I do?" wailed Violet. "Go back to San Francisco to mail it from there?"

Rose nodded. "I think that would be better. Throw them off the track."

"Wait, I have a better idea," said Jasmine. "What if the letter just reappeared?"

"You mean, like magic?" asked Rose.

Violet broke in excitedly. "That *would* be the best way! Oh, Jazzy, how will we do it?"

"We'll go back to the museum and create a diversion and slip the letter back where it belongs. Easy as pie."

Rose looked from Jasmine to Violet and back again. "Jazzy, I can't believe you're going to get involved in this. You'll just make things worse if you get caught."

Jasmine linked her arm in Violet's. "But we are in this together," she said softly. "Aren't you with us, Rosy?"

Violet held her breath.

After a long moment, Rose linked her arm through Violet's free arm. "I think you're *both* aliens," she muttered. "I don't know how I managed to get mixed up with you."

Violet squeezed both her sisters' arms. *Mixed up right from the start,* she thought, and relief flooded through her—relief, and something more. It was the last outcome she would have expected from her foray into the world of crime. But here they were, triplets all together, united in purpose and plan. "So let's go today" was all Violet said. "Right after school."

CHAPTER **10**

Violet nibbled her thumbnail nervously. She had never gone anywhere without telling her parents. "But if we call the shop to ask permission," explained Rose as the triplets left their lockers after school, "Mom will ask questions."

"We could tell her I'm working on my science project," Violet suggested uneasily.

"She'll say it's too late now and we'll have to wait till the weekend," objected Jasmine.

"But I can't wait that long to return the letter!"

"Exactly," said Rose. "You've already embarked on a life of crime, so why should stretching the truth bother you now? Besides, Mom and Dad don't need to know exactly where we are every second. It isn't as if we're babies."

"But if we don't go right now," added Jasmine, "we might as well forget it for today."

They compromised by calling their house and leaving a message on the answering machine. Rose spoke in a firm, grown-up voice, explaining that Violet had to do some research for her science class, and that she and Jasmine were helping her, and that they would all be home for dinner. She was careful not to say where they were going. "That way," she told her sisters as she hung up, "they'll probably just think we're at the library."

The bus to the BART station seemed to take forever, stopping at nearly every street corner along the way. At the station, Rose bought a map of BART and bus routes, then they jumped onto the BART train just as it was leaving. It sped under the bay to San Francisco, where they had to walk to a bus stop, where, Rose's map promised, another bus would take them on to Golden Gate Park.

But the bus didn't come, and didn't come, and Violet kept glancing nervously at her watch. The drive to the museum by school bus had seemed so quick. And the days were getting shorter. It might be dark by the time they rode home again. Their parents would be frantic if they didn't come back in time for dinner. Violet started feeling frantic herself. What if there was another quake while she and her sisters were in San Francisco? What if they couldn't get home and the phone lines were dead so they couldn't even call to tell their parents they were safe? And what if they *weren't* safe?

"Well, *finally*," said Jasmine, and Violet looked up to see the big bus lumbering toward them down the steep hill. The triplets climbed aboard the crowded bus and showed the driver their transfer ticket. Then they stood near the front, hanging on to the metal poles. Other school kids jumped on and off at the next stops, laughing and shouting, and dropping books and papers in the aisle. Slowly, too slowly for Violet's liking, the crowded bus made its way toward Golden Gate Park. She felt hot and exhausted and was no longer worrying what her parents would say if they knew about the trip to San Francisco. She worried instead what the police would do if they found out who stole the letter.

Finally the girls disembarked. Violet broke out in a sweat. She imagined she could feel the envelope with the stolen letter in it growing warm against her back through the canvas backpack. It grew so hot, it seemed to burn. She sucked in cool air and slipped the pack off her shoulder, holding it tightly by one strap as they neared the Academy.

Violet and her sisters paid admission with their lunch money, which they'd saved. Then they walked down the hall toward the earthquake exhibit. Though their footsteps made no sound on the carpet, it seemed to Violet everyone was looking at them. *Don't be paranoid,* she told herself. But it was true. Heads turned as they walked by. *It's probably my hair!* She pulled up the hood of her sweatshirt even though she was already feeling overheated.

But the eyes of other museum patrons continued to turn their way. People smiled at them. Violet hunched her shoulders and trailed behind her sisters, trying to look inconspicuous. One little girl pointed and tugged at her mother's arm. "Look, Mommy. It's three twins!" And, belatedly, Violet realized their identical outfits were creating the stir.

For once she wished she had not dressed to match her sisters. They were all three of them far too visible at the very time they needed not to be seen. Violet longed for a cloak of invisibility. She would fold it around herself, drop the letter back on the table from which she'd taken it, and run out of the museum.

"Okay," she whispered, reaching out to pull her sisters to a stop. She nodded in the direction of the exhibit. "That's it." From where she stood, the exhibit appeared to be the same. There was even a piece of paper on the writing table. "It looks like they've put some other letter there."

"I don't see any cops," Jasmine whispered.

"Maybe they're undercover cops," muttered Rose darkly. "Take off your hood, Baby. It makes you look suspicious."

Violet didn't have to be told twice. She wished she could take off the whole sweatshirt—but that would leave her wearing only her bra. She walked swiftly away from the exhibit and collapsed on a bench across the big room. "I feel dizzy."

Jasmine and Rose bent over her in concern. "It's probably just stress," said Jasmine.

"Take deep breaths," advised Rose. She reached for the backpack. "Here, give me the letter." Her eyes met Jasmine's. "If Vi faints, there will be people all around her. I don't want the letter to fall into their hands."

"If Vi faints . . . ," murmured Jasmine. "Baby? Are you really going to faint?"

"I'm just hot. Aren't you?"

"Nope." Rose pulled out the large envelope. "But, you know, it might be a good idea now if you *do* faint. You know, fall on the floor and gasp for breath."

"Thanks a lot, Rosy. What a great sister."

"No, don't you see?"

Violet peered up at Rose, frowning. Suddenly she did see. "Oh!"

"It'll be a totally perfect diversion," said Jasmine. "And while you're flopping around, people will be looking at you, and one of us can slip the letter back onto the table in the exhibit."

"I'll do it," said Rose. She removed the letter from the envelope. It was funny, thought Violet, watching her sister square her shoulders and prepare herself for action, that at first Rosy had been reluctant to join this adventure at all. And yet here she was now, as usual, taking charge.

"Baby? Are you ready to faint?" Rose glanced over her shoulder.

Violet squared her shoulders, ready for action. "Don't call me Baby or I really will faint." She took a deep breath.

Be of strong heart!

Jasmine touched her shoulder lightly. "Okay. Ready, Rosy?"

"Ready." Rose flipped her hair back and looked casually around to the left and right.

"Okay then. Ready..." Jasmine sat down next to Violet on the bench. "Aim..." Violet sagged against her and moaned. Rose darted off across the big room.

"Fire!" whispered Jasmine.

Violet moaned more loudly and slumped forward.

Jasmine jumped to her feet. "Help, somebody! My sister's fainted. What should I do?"

Two elderly men hurried over. "Get a doctor," one called. "A girl here needs some help."

"Lean over, dear, with your head down between your legs, that's the way." A large woman with a bleached crew cut and half a dozen dangling silver earrings placed her hand on Violet's back and forced her to bend over. "There! Get some blood flowing to the old brain."

Violet gasped for breath and moaned.

"Move aside, everyone, please," said a firm voice, and Violet saw a pair of feet in sensible gray pumps pressing through the crowd.

Violet looked up to see a tall, dark, stern-faced woman in a gray suit. The badge of a museum official was clipped to her tailored jacket. She wore large pearl earrings, and her hair in a short Afro style. Her museum badge read: MS. JAMES. She reeked of authority, and Violet's heart thrummed with fear.

Had Rosy been caught?

"The girl fainted," one of the onlookers explained, standing to one side so the museum official could have a closer look at Violet.

"Looks like you're coming around now, though," Ms. James said. "Were you with a school group?"

"She's here with me," said Jasmine quickly.

"Is there someone who can drive you home?"

"No . . ." Jasmine hesitated a moment. "We came on the bus."

Ms. James put her hand on Violet's arm. When Violet dared to meet her eyes, she saw the woman's severe expression soften. "Can you stand up now? Would you like to rest in my office for a few minutes? We can call your parents from there."

"No! I mean, I'll be all right." Violet scanned the room for Rose and located her standing by the earthquake simulator. Rose flicked a surreptitious victory V with her fingers. Violet sighed with relief. They had done it! They were almost safe. *But we can't let Ms. James call Mom and Dad!* She shot an urgent look at Jasmine.

"Our parents are at work," Jasmine said swiftly. "But I'm her sister, and I can get her home, no problem."

"On the bus? During rush-hour traffic? I'm not so sure that's a good idea at all."

"Oh, um, it's not really so far at all. We can walk. The fresh air will be good for her."

Ms. James frowned. "Well, come to my office," she said to Violet. "I want to be sure that you're fully recovered."

The crowd began to move away. Violet and Jasmine had no choice but to let Ms. James lead them across the large room and down the hall to the lobby. Violet darted a look behind them just before they turned into a small office. She saw Rose sauntering along some distance behind them and felt reassured. Rose would rescue them.

The office was filled with plants and cardboard boxes stacked along the walls. "It's a mess in here, I'm afraid, since all these boxes haven't been sorted through. But here"—Ms. James hefted one box off a chair—"have a seat. And some water."

Violet sank down and accepted the paper cup Ms. James brought her from the water cooler. "Thanks a lot. I feel fine now." She sipped the cold water, wondering how she and Jasmine and Rose would ever make it home before dinnertime.

"I'll go look for our other sister," Jasmine said brightly. "Between the two of us, we'll have Vi home in no time."

"Oh, there's another sister? Well, good. Go find her then." Ms. James nodded approvingly, and Violet sighed in relief.

Violet finished her water and tossed the paper cup into the wastebasket. The museum official looked at Violet as if she didn't quite know what to do with her until her sisters returned. She seemed grateful when the phone rang, and she perched on her desk to answer. Violet noticed the nameplate on the desk: AUDREY JAMES, DIRECTOR OF ARCHIVES.

While Ms. James spoke on the phone, Violet looked at the posters of sharks and starfish mounted on the walls. She wished Rosy and Jazzy would hurry up. What in the world was taking them so long?

She shifted restlessly on her seat. Her gaze fell on the stack of boxes crowding the small room. They were all labeled in scrawled handwriting from a thick black marking pen. MISC. LETTERS—1940S, one label read. And underneath, another read: INVERTEBRATES—FIELD REPORTS.

"I see you're interested in our boxes."

Violet looked up, startled. Ms. James was off the phone.

"They're new acquisitions for the museum—donations, really," explained the director. "It's part of my job to sort through and decide which documents we'll keep for our archives, and which have no value to us."

Violet's thoughts were whirling. Had the letter from Hal been a donation? "Who donates old stuff like this? Old letters, I mean."

"Oh, we get all sorts of things when someone dies and the relatives clear out the attic or basement." Ms. James pursed her lips. "Most of it is complete junk, but the families don't want to hear about it. They want to think that Great-uncle Frank has been hoarding treasure up there all these years."

"Treasure!"

"Historical treasure, my dear. Or scientific treasure. To some of us it's finer than gold. We catalog it for our collection. Scholars come to use our archives. And we occasionally use an item in the exhibits."

Violet chose her words carefully. "And—um—what do you do with the junk? I mean, the stuff the museum doesn't want? Do you just throw it out?"

"It depends. Sometimes old letters and photographs are valuable to other institutions, even if we can't use them here at the Academy of Sciences. We send such things on to one of the historical societies. And they're very good about sending us things, as well, when they know we can use them. If the donations have no historical or scientific value, we try to give them back to the people who donated them in the first place—but usually they refuse to take them back!" Ms. James glanced at her watch. "Now, I wonder what is keeping your sisters."

Then, Violet heard Rose's laugh from out in the lobby—

or was it Jasmine's?—and knew she had to make a last-ditch effort. "Ms. James, I'm doing a report for school, and I wonder if you have any old—uh—letters or photos or stuff about the 1906 earthquake in your archives? That people donated, I mean."

Ms. James nodded. "There's a lot of public interest, these days—probably due to all the recent quakes. So we're setting up some new exhibits." She walked to her bookshelf and lifted out a box. "This was given to us recently. We found a couple items of interest and have cataloged them for use in our exhibits. The rest is just junk, but you might enjoy looking through it. There's nothing about the earthquake left, but it's fun to see the old newspapers. Take a peek at the prices listed in the ads—those were the days!" Then the phone rang again and Ms. James turned away.

Violet had a shivery feeling along the back of her neck as she reached into the box. She glanced over at Ms. James, but the director had her back turned and was deep in conversation, making notes on a pad of paper.

The first thing Violet lifted from the box was a leaflet about planting window gardens. Then there was a newspaper clipping about the latest spring fashions in ladies' hats and accessories. The page was yellow and brittle, and Violet handled it carefully. There were drawings of elaborate hats, festooned with ribbons, pieces of artificial fruit—and even, in one, a small bird. Violet checked the date at the top of the page. March 16, 1906.

1906 again.

Violet quickly removed the next layer from the box: several old cookbooks. One opened, and she caught sight of an inscription on the inside cover. *Jane Stowe.*

Stowe again.

She didn't even feel particularly surprised. The year and

the family name were familiar to her now. The sense that something was waiting for her here was very strong. *Getting closer,* she thought.

She leafed through the books, but there was nothing else. Beneath them were loose sheets of newspaper. The dates were all from 1906. Violet scanned them quickly, but they seemed mostly to be advertising pages featuring sketches of ladies wearing large hats. She looked closer and discovered that the ads all mentioned Stowe's Millinery Shop on Chance Street. It was as if clues were just dropping into her lap.

But clues to what?

As she lifted the next layer of papers, Jasmine and Rose peeked through the doorway.

"Twins!" exclaimed Ms. James, hanging up the phone as the girls came into the room. "Identical, I believe? I'm a twin myself."

Ordinarily Violet would have piped up with the information that they were triplets, but now she was busy searching through the box. Cookbooks, leaflets about gardens, ads for hats—clearly all these things had come from someone in the Stowe family. But who had donated the box to the museum?

"I'm sorry we took so long," Jasmine was saying. "But I couldn't find Rosy. She'd gone to get a snack. Anyway, we're ready now."

But Violet wasn't quite ready. She was sorting through the last newspapers from the box, and there at the bottom was a ledger—identical to the ones she had found in the suitcase. ALBERT STOWE, MILLINER read the label. She caught her breath and flipped through the pages. Inside were the lists of expenses, each page dated neatly at the top. March 10, 1905. June 4, 1905. Then more pages, all blank. At the very back of the ledger, beyond the clean sheets of paper, more writing—in handwriting familiar to Violet. *Dear Diary,* she read, and the writing was the same as on the other diary entry.

She closed the ledger quickly and a folded sheet of paper sailed out, landing on the floor. She reached down and slipped it into the ledger again, then hugged the book to her chest.

"Your sister is just going through a box of things that came to us," said Ms. James. "I doubt she'll find anything for her school project, but you never know." She smiled at Violet. "Any luck?"

Violet looked up, flushed. "Well, sort of. This old book is, um, interesting."

"Oh?" Ms. James looked amused.

"Yes!" Violet saw the amazed expressions on her sisters' faces. "I mean, well, it seems to have belonged to someone whose house we own now."

"Oh?" inquired Ms. James again, and reached for the book. "A house?" Quickly Violet opened the cover to show her Albert Stowe's label. She didn't want to hand over the ledger, didn't want Ms. James to see the diary entries at the back, or the folded paper tucked loosely inside. She looked at her sisters beseechingly.

Rose frowned, perplexed, but Jasmine gave her a little smile. "Vi means our parents' new place on Chance Street," Jasmine said.

"Right," Violet clarified. "Our parents are opening a florist shop, and the house they bought used to belong to the Stowes. I think this ledger belonged to the same family."

"There could be a lot of families named Stowe," Ms. James pointed out.

"Yes, but the advertisements are for hats—see?" Violet pointed to the newspapers. "And we already know that Albert Stowe was a milliner."

"Well, what a coincidence!" Ms. James smiled. "It doesn't

help with your research project, of course, but it's certainly interesting."

"Is there—is there any chance I could, um, maybe buy this book from you? I'm sure my parents would like it," said Violet quickly. "Or if it's a lot of money, well, could I borrow it?"

"I don't mind if you just take it," said Ms. James. "We won't be using it. As I said, anything useful to the Academy has already been removed from the box and cataloged."

"Thanks a lot," Violet said, trying not to sound too excited. Then she took a deep breath, surprised at her own daring. "Um, do you remember what you *did* find that was useful?" she asked. "Stuff from the time of the 1906 earthquake, maybe? Any, um, old letters?"

Ms. James glanced at her sharply. "No, there were no letters in that box. But it's funny you should mention letters written at the time of the 1906 quake." She frowned. "Because we did in fact have a wonderful old letter on display recently that was actually written during the quake—you could even see where the ink spilled when the shaking started."

"Oh!" cried Violet, her face flushing. "How amazing!" She felt her sisters' eyes boring into her but didn't dare to look at them.

"That letter was on loan from the historical society," continued Ms. James. "They often send us things people have donated, if they look useful for public viewing. But," she added with a shake of her head, "that letter was stolen from our new exhibit just yesterday—can you believe it?" Ms. James pressed her lips together.

"Stolen—" Jasmine coughed. "That's awful."

"What a shame," murmured Rose, then turned to Violet. "Hey, are you ready to go now?"

Violet stood up. "I'm, um, sorry about the stolen letter," she murmured.

"You never know when just such a theft will happen," Ms. James said. "No doubt the thief hoped the letter was valuable and wanted to try to sell it to an antiques dealer."

"And is it—*was* it valuable?" pressed Violet. She felt her sisters' eyes on her, warning her to stop talking. But she couldn't help herself.

Ms. James smiled grimly. "It is indeed. And impossible to replace—*if* the thief had got hold of the original. Fortunately we used a facsimile in the exhibit—as we do in many of our exhibits—to guard against the very sort of thing that did, in fact, happen."

"You mean the letter was just a copy?" Violet couldn't believe they'd gone to all this trouble to replace a fake. The letter hadn't looked like a simple photocopy.

"Well, a very artful, professionally done reproduction. The original is safe in our archival vault." Ms. James looked at her watch. "Now, are you girls sure you can get home on your own? The museum will be closing soon. Perhaps I should drive you myself."

"Oh, no—," began Violet. She slipped the ledger into her backpack.

"We'll be fine on our own—," said Jasmine.

"Thank you," said Rose firmly. "But we'll be home in no time."

The girls walked decorously through the lobby, past the gift shop, and out through the exit doors into the early evening dusk. They moved sedately out onto the sidewalk and across the street. Then, out of sight of the museum, they clutched each other, shrieking with laughter and outrage and relief.

"We did it!" Jasmine exulted.

"But it was just a copy all the time!" cried Rose. "As I found out as soon as I was trying to slip your stolen letter back on the desk. A letter was already there—and it looked exactly like the first one! Another copy. Baby, we should kill you for this."

"Well, how could I have known?" Violet hugged herself defensively. "And don't call me Baby or *I'll* kill *you*. Anyway, it didn't look like a copy, did it? I mean, it looked old. The ink spill was real. And it was in Hal's own handwriting—you saw that for yourself." She hugged herself again to ward off the chill. It was quickly growing dark. The nighttime fog was settling over the bay, enshrouding San Francisco's hills. "Come on," she said, filled with an urgency to be home. "Let's hurry."

They ran to the bus stop and were just in time to catch the bus. As they climbed aboard, Rose turned to Violet with a smirk. "Copy or not, you should have seen how cool I was. Like I'd been a master spy for years. I just crept right up and slid the letter under the desk, up against the wall. It looked like it had just fallen off, somehow."

"They'll know it wasn't really there all the time, though," Jasmine said. "I just hope that Ms. James doesn't put two and two together. You know, the letter reappearing the very same afternoon a girl who nearly fainted—causing a convenient distraction—starts asking questions about old letters!"

"I had to find out where they got Hal's letter from," Violet said defensively. "There may be more."

"Yeah—but what if that historical society place has a whole trunkful of letters from your darling Hal—only off-limits to the public?" teased Jasmine. "What then? Will you go back to your life of crime?"

"Her life of crime and deception," Rose pronounced with relish. "But I'll admit I was impressed with your performance,

Vi. You were great, too, Jazz," she added generously. "When I heard the moaning and looked over and saw you propping up Vi with all those people crowding around, well, it seemed, sort of *too* real. Like playing with fire, if you know what I mean."

She and Jasmine exchanged one of their twin looks. "I know," murmured Jasmine. "I thought so, too."

"What?" asked Violet. "What do you know?"

"Oh—" Jasmine tossed back her hair. "Well, pretending like that . . . Tempting fate."

Rose frowned at Violet. "You *do* feel all right now, don't you?"

"I'm *fine*. But I'm never going to be a criminal again."

"Even if there are dozens of letters from Hal at the historical society?" pressed Rose.

"Well . . . don't tempt me." Violet grinned. "No, my life of crime is over. Well—nearly." She patted her backpack. "Wait till you see what's in the back of this ledger!"

Jasmine and Rose groaned aloud. "Oh no, don't tell me—," began Rose.

"Is it another letter from Hal?" squealed Jasmine.

"No. It looks like more diary entries." She met their incredulous looks triumphantly.

"Well, come on!" cried Rose. "Let's see them."

"Wait a minute. We have to get off here." Violet led them off the bus.

The three girls huddled together while they waited for the train. Violet opened the ledger and leafed through the pages to the first diary entry. Before she could begin reading, the folded paper slipped out and fluttered to the concrete.

"Grab it!" yelled Violet as it drifted toward the BART tracks. Jasmine stepped on it, halting its flight. "Watch out, don't tear it!"

Jasmine unfolded it and studied the page. "It's just an old sketch. Not bad, really. In fact, it looks sort of like that kid we met—Sam. But why would the artist draw lines through his face?"

Rose peered over Jasmine's shoulder as Violet's heart began to pound harder. "Yeah, it makes the guy look like he's standing inside a fence or something. Like he's in a cage."

Violet reached with trembling fingers for the paper. "It's not Sam, and it's not a fence," she whispered, gazing down at the familiar face in wonderment. "It's a grid for a needlepoint pattern."

"How do you know that?" demanded Rose.

"I've seen it before," Violet said. "In a dream." She smoothed the page with her palm and looked up at her sisters. Excitement coursed through her, and a tingle of jubilation. "You know what? I have a feeling this must be Hal."

"That's totally *weird*!" Jasmine squealed.

"Come on, quick," ordered Rose. "Let's read the entries. Maybe they'll explain everything."

Violet tucked the needlepoint pattern into the ledger, then turned the pages until she came to the diary entries at the back. The faded script that at first looked so difficult to decipher seemed to unfold as she went along, as if it were eager to be read.

"January 4, 1906

"Dear Diary,

 "Well, this is a fine kettle of fish!

 "As my Christmas gift to Hal, I agreed to apply for the position he'd been after me about, though I did it only to please him, not because I really thought to land the job. But shortly after applying, I had word that I would be hired

and must start immediately. Hal was beside himself with excitement for he wants me here so badly. This is not the sort of work I ever had in mind to do, but I will do it for Hal. With my dear parents gone in last winter's influenza epidemic and no other family to speak of, I am all alone in the world and have to earn my living—at least until I marry. _If_ I ever marry. I packed my bags and moved here to Chance Street in time to see in the new year, since I do long to help Hal out in every way I can. It seems my poor charge fell down the cellar stairs before Christmas, and her injuries, along with her weak heart, make her unfit to work in the shop or do housework, and she needs the most tender care. I don't know how well I will suit in the long run, though, never having done this sort of work, and I cannot teach Jane and Rachel, the little sisters, piano as the last companion, a Miss Abigail Chandler, did, but I can apply compresses to bruises and sit by the bed and read aloud just as well as anyone! I can help with the bookkeeping, too. Mr. Stowe has given me a stack of ledgers and the responsibility of keeping track of the accounts. I hope my talent for mathematics makes me equal to the task. The pay is not much, but I keep reminding myself I am doing this for Hal after he has begged and begged me, though what good it will do me in the end I cannot say. At least V seems friendly and disposed to be agreeable, the neighborhood is pleasant, and I get my room and board for free. . . . "

Violet looked up at her sisters. "I was right. But I can hardly believe it."

"Believe what?" asked Rose.

"Right about what?" asked Jasmine.

Violet's voice held a note of awe. "See what it says here about falling down the cellar stairs? Remember I fell down into the cellar—because *there were no stairs*. And here's more about this person's heart problems—'her weak heart.' I think whoever wrote this diary entry was just starting a job looking after V. I've *got* to find out everything I can about V and Hal. It's not just for my earthquake project, you know. It's way more important than that." Violet turned the page. "Listen, there's more.

"January 20, ~~1905~~—no! 1906 now!

"Dear Diary,
    "I keep forgetting to write the correct year. It's the same every January when the old year has turned into the new. Perhaps it is my wish to turn back time, back to when life was simpler and I was happy. If I could turn back time two years, my parents would not yet have perished in the influenza epidemic. I would be a girl still, young and protected, looking forward to the future and to my eventual marriage. And, of course, I had already set my eyes on the very perfect man! It was two years ago that I met Hal. He was a young reporter working with my father on the newspaper. He seemed to like me, too. And he still does, that is clear—but my secret sadness is this: His regard for me is more brotherly than <u>loverly.</u> It is sheer torture for me to watch him showering his beloved V with affection while I, just the hired companion, stand at her side as their chaperone!
    "I have more or less settled into the routine of this job now and learned the ways of this family. Most of my hours are spent with V, who sometimes works in the shop, but more often is confined to bed upstairs. I sit in a big armchair near her bed and read to her, talk to her, and write down the letters she dictates to friends. Sometimes she will sit up and ask for her colored pencils, and we will

sketch together until she tires, which is very quickly indeed. I thought I would not like her, for she is in truth my rival, even though she knows nothing of my love for Hal, but I _do_ like her. This surprises me. In many ways she seems a gentle uncomplicated soul, eager not to be a burden and happy to talk to me as an equal rather than a servant. Yet she is more complicated underneath this sweet exterior. She can grow brooding, and she has odd dreams that tell her things.

"I had lost my watch and was frantic to find it—it had been my mother's—and V dreamt it had fallen into a crack beneath my bed. Sure enough, I found it there. Last week she urged her sister Rachel to stay home from school because she had dreamt the child would injure herself in some way. R was eager to comply, but Mrs. Stowe said such dreams were nonsense and sent the girl to school anyway. Surely enough, R was brought home midmorning by the principal. She had tripped on the playground and twisted her ankle. V was modest enough not to say anything. At least R was kept immobilized for a few days, so I had only the other twin to contend with!

"Yes, another aspect of my job is to keep the terrible twins out of V's room. They are riotous, undisciplined girls who blow into the house after school each day like twin tornadoes. They often upset poor V with their teasing. The Stowe parents are hard workers, both of them spending most of their time in the shop downstairs. When V drops off to sleep, they ask me to assist them at the sales counter. That is where I am now, writing in one of the old ledgers Mr. Stowe used for bookkeeping. There are empty pages in the back he says he has no use for. I keep the records in the current ledger and use the old books with their extra, empty pages for a diary. I have never kept one before. But this new experience warrants writing down. So much is new to me here.

"Mrs. Stowe designs the hats, sketching them in the evenings after our meal. Mr. Stowe builds the hats—many of them are amazing creations, fit to adorn the head of any lady in high society. Some are more modest, the sort I might purchase for myself, were there ever any time to go out on the town wearing it. Of course I _do_ get some time off; this was promised in the advertisement I answered. Each Sunday afternoon and one full Wednesday every other week. But Hal is working all day on Wednesdays and there is no possibility of seeing him, so the day is lost. On Sundays, at least, he occasionally calls on the family, and when he comes I stay around to bask in the warmth that emanates from him.

"I know myself to be pathetic, but I cannot see how to change things."

"Poor thing." Jasmine sighed as the train pulled in. "It sounds like a horrible job."

"That's cool about the dreams coming true," Rose said. "I wish mine would."

Violet held her finger in the ledger to mark the page as the girls filed onto the train and found seats together.

"What does the next entry say?" pressed Jasmine. "There are more, aren't there?"

"Just one more," said Violet, turning the page. She had to raise her voice a little as the train began moving. "The writing is a lot messier in this one. Harder to read.

"February 14, 1906

"Dear Diary,
"Valentine's Day, but no flowers for poor old me. Two dozen hothouse roses, though, for V from my own darling. It is nearly midnight now, and soon will be the 15th, just

another ordinary day, and so my pain will ebb. I watch V sleeping fitfully from my place here in the big armchair. She becomes more fragile daily, and the doctors come more often to visit. There's a problem with her heart, I am told, and it seems to be worsening. It's harder for me to keep her comfortable because she wants so much to be useful to her parents and lively with Hal when he comes to visit. Her father said today that he must not visit so often because it excites V and the excitement is not good for her heart. Still, they will write to each other. That is—I write the love notes she dictates. It is sometimes more than I can bear!

"She asked me to draw a picture of Hal, and so I did. A very good likeness, if I do say so myself. She then had me pencil in a grid across the sketch and transfer it to muslin so she could make a needlepoint pillow cover. 'So I can sleep with Hal's cheek pressed against my own,' she murmured. No doubt I will find it hard not to seize said pillow and press it instead right over her face as she sleeps!

"Jesting aside—and it is really most horrible of me to joke at all when V is truly so ill—the needlework seems to be all that engages V these days. I am glad to see her happily occupied, stitching Hal's hair or dark eyebrows onto cloth. While she is busy, she doesn't chatter so much. Really, her chattering is making me nervous. She says very strange things now and has nightmares nearly every night that disturb our sleep. She shouts about bridges and cries out that the children need help, and we must save the little girl . . . I ask her what bridge? What children? What girl? But she cannot tell me.

"My nights are broken, my days unbearably long."

Violet drew a shaky breath. *We must save the little girl*—

"That's it, then, isn't it?" asked Rose when Violet closed the ledger.

"That's what?" said Violet, shaking the vision of the shadow children out of her head.

"That's how V died, don't you think?" pressed Rose.

"What?" Jasmine looked confused. "What do you mean?"

"The needlepoint pillow," Rose said succinctly.

Violet's eyes grew round as she stared at her sister. "You could be right. This diary writer could have smothered her with it—just as she says she wants to!" Violet shivered as the train curved toward the bay. She shook her head. "I told you—I had a dream about needlepointing a man's face. And I've had—well, sort of a vision—about children crying for help. I've been feeling all along there's a tie to me, and now these entries prove it even more."

"What do you mean, you've had visions?" demanded Rose. "Have you turned psychic or something?" She glanced at Jasmine as if to say, *We don't believe this, do we?*

"I don't know," replied Violet. "The visions came to me during the earthquakes. Maybe they're not my visions. Maybe they're V's."

"You keep hinting about some big connection," Rose went on, sounding almost angry. "I think it's only fair that you tell us everything. After all, if it wasn't for us, you'd be locked up in jail by now, probably."

"You don't still think that Hal is writing letters to you, I hope," said Jasmine. "You don't think this diary writer is writing the diary to *you*, do you?"

"No," said Violet slowly. "Not *to* me—not exactly." She saw a man looking at her—no, looking at her *hair*—and she pulled her hood up and turned her back on him. "All right," she said softly, "I'll tell you," feeling strong, feeling powerful.

Rose and Jasmine leaned close in order to hear over the tumult of voices and the hum of the train as it rushed smoothly through the tunnel under the bay.

"Do you believe in magic?"

CHAPTER 11

"*I* believe in magic," said Jasmine. "At least, I want to believe."

It was after dinner that night, and the triplets sat curled up on the beds in Rose and Jasmine's pink-and-yellow bedroom.

Rose shook her head. "I'm not sure I do. The more I think about it, the more I'm sure the similarities between Vi's life and V's are just chance."

"But you have to admit there are an awful lot of parallels," said Jasmine.

"Well, yeah," conceded Rose.

Violet flashed her a smile. She couldn't blame Rose for not believing. She hardly believed it herself.

"I mean, okay," Rose was saying, "there *are* parallels. But I don't see why you jump to the conclusion that they *mean* anything." She snorted. "Am I supposed to believe that Prince Charming is going to come and elope with my baby sister?"

"I think—maybe it is a warning." Violet ignored Rose's sarcasm. "A warning to me. To beware."

"To beware of men coming through the window?" asked Rose incredulously.

"Whether it's magic or coincidence—there's still a pattern of similarities between my life and V's," reasoned Violet. "That means whatever happened to V could happen to me, too. Doesn't that make sense?"

Rose shrugged. Jasmine was looking worried.

Violet continued, her voice rising. "Maybe Hal didn't manage to elope with V because they were stopped by the earthquake. But maybe they were stopped in another way. Maybe he couldn't run off with her because she was murdered by the person who wrote the diary!"

"But you're just guessing that V was murdered," protested Rose. "Remember, the companion wrote that she was just joking about putting the pillow over V's face."

"Well, this part doesn't sound like much of a joke," said Jasmine, scanning the earlier diary entry Violet had found in the suitcase. She read aloud: *"I have done a terrible thing. She is dead and I am wracked with guilt."*

Rose frowned. "Well, we don't have proof that any of this is connected with Vi."

Violet felt cold. She belted her lavender robe more tightly. "How much proof am I supposed to wait for," she asked, "if my life's in danger?"

"What do you mean?" snapped Rose.

Jasmine put her hands to her mouth and peered at Violet with frightened blue eyes. "Oh, you don't really think—"

"I do think," Violet said slowly. Goose bumps prickled along the back of her neck. "I think someone may try to murder me."

Saying it aloud made it sound melodramatic. But wasn't a pattern from the past already there, written out before them?

"I think all of this is stupid," snapped Rose.

Lily poked her head into the room. "All three of you together?" she asked in glad surprise. "Still awake? Really, Baby, you look very pale. You need to get to bed now. It's late and there's school tomorrow."

"We were done anyway," said Violet softly.

"Homework, I suppose?"

"More or less," Rose fibbed quickly. "About Vi's science report on earthquakes."

"Mom, wait," called Jasmine as Lily turned away. "We wanted to ask you if we can go to San Francisco to the historical society. Vi needs to do research for her earthquake report, you know, and Rosy and I don't think she ought to go alone. We could take the BART after school—"

"Oh, my, I don't like the idea of you girls out alone in San Francisco."

"Mom! We did it before," complained Rose, and Violet kicked her. "Um—I mean when we went to clean on Saturday."

"That was different. It was daylight then, and early morning. I don't want you girls going to San Francisco after school. It gets dark too early now. I'd worry."

"How about on Saturday, then?" asked Jasmine. "You wanted us to go back and work on the shop again, right? Maybe we could go to the historical society first?"

"How about just calling?" suggested Lily. "It would be easier and more efficient." She kissed them all good night. "Now get to bed, girls. Especially you, Baby."

"Why didn't we think of that?" asked Jasmine when their mother had left the room.

"That's what mothers are for," replied Rose.

Violet slid off Rose's bed and headed for the door. "Good night."

"Wait a minute," said Jasmine. "Do you want to sleep in here with us?"

"Of course she doesn't," said Rose. "She *can't* be thinking someone is going to murder her. That is just too *creepy*."

Violet turned back in the doorway. "I'd feel safer if we had a plan," she told her sisters. "You guys help me watch out for—whomever. And we'll try really hard to find out more about V. The more we know, the more I'll know what to look out for, so that what happened to her doesn't happen to me."

"I'm still not sure about this," said Rose. "It's paranoid."

"Be sure not to mention anything to Mom and Dad," Violet added, thinking, *Maybe I am paranoid!* "They worry about me enough as it is."

"I'll help you," Jasmine vowed loyally. "Any way I can."

"Thanks," Violet whispered. She stepped into the hall, then looked back. "First thing in the morning we call the historical society place."

Rose saluted her. "Aye, aye, Captain!"

"And don't sleep too late," Violet instructed.

As Violet left the room, she heard Rose mutter to Jasmine, "Bossy, isn't she?"

And Jasmine answered, "Oh, I don't know. If it were me, I'd be *terrified*. I think Vi's being pretty brave about this. Maybe she's been brave all along, only we never noticed."

But Violet lay in bed unable to sleep. She was feeling anything but brave. She lay stiffly beneath her lavender quilt, fists clenched and aching. She was waiting, watching.

Whom did she need to watch out for?

What person posed a danger to her? V might have been

murdered by someone hired to be her companion, but Violet didn't have such a person in her own life. She lay rigid under her quilt, trying to think of anyone she knew who filled the role of V's companion in her own life. That she could think of no one should have been reassuring to her, but somehow was not. *I'm missing something*, she thought. She couldn't afford to miss anything, any warning, any sign at all.

In her dreams that night she was needlepointing again. Hal's face was coming along nicely, shaded in beige and brown thread. When she woke up she felt groggy but determined. The only way to save herself, if saving herself was possible, would be to push ahead and learn more about Hal and V and to discover the identity of the diary writer.

She tiptoed downstairs to the kitchen, brought the telephone directory to the counter, and sat leafing through it for several minutes before she realized the book was for the East Bay. The San Francisco directory must be up in her parents' room. Instead of going upstairs, she dialed 411—the information number. But when the operator asked her, "What city?" and she said, "San Francisco," he told her she had to dial a different number. Finally she linked up with an operator in San Francisco. She told him she wanted the historical society, and the operator asked which one. Violet sighed. *The one that has more letters from Hal*, she thought. But she said politely she didn't know which one, and if there were several historical societies, she'd take the numbers for all of them.

There were several. While Violet was writing down all the numbers, Jasmine and Rose tumbled into the kitchen.

"Hey," protested Rose. "I thought we were doing this together."

Violet finished writing down the numbers. Then she thanked the operator and hung up. "Keep your hair on," she told Rose. "I was only calling information."

"I think it's too early to call," objected Jasmine. "Most businesses don't open till nine."

Violet glanced at the kitchen clock. It was only just after seven. "But we'll be in school then," she moaned.

"Call from the cafeteria at lunchtime," suggested Rose practically, and Violet agreed that was what they'd do.

Waiting wasn't easy. Violet felt jumpy all morning. When Mrs. Lynch, the principal, roared at her for running in the hallway, Violet narrowed her eyes at her, wondering whether *she* could be the killer. When Casey Banks grabbed her arm on the stairs to ask her where Jasmine was, she shrieked so loudly that other kids stopped to see what was wrong. "Whoa!" howled Casey. "What did I do?"

"Sorry," muttered Violet. She hurried to her next class, embarrassed but still alive. *Do I really believe any of this?* she thought to herself. But the letters were real, and the pattern was real. The only question left to answer was what it all meant, and until she knew, it made sense to be careful.

Finally, the noon bell rang. Violet and her sisters avoided the crush in the cafeteria and hurried to the telephone in the hall. "What do I say?" asked Violet, fingering the coins in her pocket. "I mean, what should I tell them?"

"Do you want me to make the call for you?" asked Rose impatiently.

"No, she can do it," said Jasmine. "Don't panic. Just tell them the truth—that you're doing a project about the earthquake in 1906. And say that you saw the letter at the Academy of Sciences—and were told there might be more information at the historical society."

"Okay." Violet took a deep breath and dialed the first number she'd written down. The line was busy. So she hung up and tried the next. She was proud that her voice came out sounding so calm and grown-up as she explained her quest. The man who answered couldn't help them. Violet politely declined to send in an application for membership. Then she called the next number, and a woman said that yes, they did indeed accept donations of letters and documents from private homes. And yes, indeed, many of these were available to be read by the public. Did she have some to donate?

Violet gripped the phone tightly. "No, I'm sorry, I don't. But I'm trying to trace a letter that might have been donated to you." Then she told the woman about the letter she'd seen in the earthquake exhibit and how she wondered where it had come from.

"Just a moment. I'll check," said the woman.

"She's checking," Violet whispered to Jasmine and Rose. Her sisters crowded close, trying to hear.

The woman's voice was crisp. "That letter was sent in by a local woman. I remember telling her we wouldn't mind seeing any other letters she cared to donate—people sometimes have no idea that the old things they call junk are worth something to historians. But so far she hasn't sent us anything else."

Rose grabbed Violet's elbow. "Ask her the name of the person!"

"Can you tell me the name of the woman who brought you the letter?" asked Violet in her sweetest voice. "I'd like to—uh—write or call her or something. You know, to see if she can let me see the stuff. Maybe it'll help me out with my report."

There was a silence. Then an operator's voice—or was it a computerized voice?—interrupted. "Please insert sixty-five cents," it said. Violet dug into her pocket and came up with a quarter. She slipped it into the slot. "Give me some money!" she cried to her sisters, and both girls fished in their backpacks for change. "Please don't hang up," Violet called into the receiver.

Rose handed Violet two more quarters.

There were some clicks on the line. Then, "The name was Lauer," said the historical society woman. "*L-A-U-E-R.*"

"Get the phone number," hissed Jasmine, pressing close to Violet.

"Can you give me her number?" asked Violet, pushing Jasmine away. "Or address?"

"I'm sorry. I can't give you any further information."

Violet thought she probably *could,* but she thanked the woman and said good-bye. "The woman who donated the letter is named Lauer," Violet told her sisters excitedly. "We have to find her!"

"This is like being a detective," said Rose as Violet started turning the pages of the phone book attached to the phone booth by a thin chain. "One clue leading to another."

"Hurry up," pleaded Jasmine. "I have a math test next period and I still need to study." Then she grabbed the book out of Violet's hands. "This is the East Bay phone book!"

Violet dropped the book. It swung by its chain. "I'll have to call information again." She punched the buttons.

"Hurry, hurry!" said Jasmine. A bell rang, and the hallway grew loud with the crush of students passing by on their way outside. Violet had to raise her voice to speak to the San Francisco operator. She told the operator she wanted the phone number of someone named Lauer.

"First name?" asked the operator.

"I don't know."

"Address?" asked the operator.

"I don't know that, either."

The operator's voice sounded disapproving. "There are nine Lauers listed."

"Oh." Violet's head drooped in disappointment. "Could you—I know this is a lot to ask, but could you maybe give me all their phone numbers? And addresses? Please?"

"My dear," sighed the operator, "I don't have that kind of time, and we don't give out addresses, in any case. There are Lauers on Laguna, Maple, King, Twenty-ninth, Chance, Clementena—you'll have to go to a library and check the phone book for yourself."

"Wait a sec!" Violet pressed herself into the phone booth as a wave of rowdy boys, many of them leaping and shrieking, rushed down the hall. "Did you say Chance? Chance Street?"

Rose and Jasmine grabbed her shoulders in excitement.

"Well, I'd like that number," said Violet. "Just the Chance Street phone number, please." She wrote quickly. "And is that in the nine hundred block? . . . Oh—330? Right, that's what I meant. Thanks a lot!"

She hung up with a triumphant grin and her sisters threw their arms around her. "Hooray!" cried Jasmine. And Rose added, "330 Chance Street! That might just be a coincidence—but we don't believe in coincidences anymore, do we? I think we're on to something!"

The girls grinned at each other, and Violet basked in the warmth of her sisters' approval. She felt safer with them on her side. They were a team. And now she felt like a full player. "We have to go there," she said. "As soon as possible. Saturday."

She skipped along with her sisters, reaching the door of her classroom just as the late bell rang. She waved good-bye to them, then slipped into her seat, flipping another wave over at Beth, who sat in the next row. Beth was frowning.

"Hi," Violet whispered as Mr. Koch called the class to order.

"Why didn't you eat lunch?" demanded Beth. She wasn't even bothering to whisper.

"We had something to do," Violet hissed back. "Jazzy and Rosy and I."

"Oh, right. The famous Triplet Club," said Beth coldly.

What does that mean? wondered Violet. Beth sounded so angry.

Violet tried to explain. "We had something to do—about the letters. Wait till I tell you about the totally amazing adventure we had at the museum yesterday. You won't believe it!"

"I waited for you after school yesterday."

"Oh—sorry!" Violet's sudden guilt sounded in her voice. She should have told Beth about the change in plans. Or taken her along to the museum. "I'm really sorry, Beth."

"Did you mail the letter back?" Beth demanded.

"No, even better. We took it back in person!"

"We?" Beth's voice was harsh. *"We* who?"

"Jazzy, Rosy, and I," said Violet. "Who else?"

"Who else?" repeated Beth. She looked down at her book. "I should have known."

I said I was sorry, thought Violet. Beth looked so different when she was angry. Her normally sunny face turned hard, the eyes narrow and the mouth tight. Beth had been her best buddy for so long, her companion in everything, it was hard to understand why she should be . . .

Companion?

Violet's heart thudded. Was it possible—was *Beth* the one she needed to fear?

Mr. Koch began asking questions about sedimentary rock. Violet sat watching Beth out of the corner of her eye. Beth took notes. She raised her hand and answered a question about sedimentary rock. Correctly, of course.

I'm being crazy, thought Violet. This was Beth, her very best friend.

But maybe that's what V thought about her *companion, too. Before she died.*

Violet pushed the disturbing thought away. She opened her notebook and scribbled on a clean page: *Are you going to stay mad at me?* She cleared her throat and tipped the notebook so Beth could read the message.

Beth glanced over, then lowered her eyes, but not before Violet saw they were full of tears.

Understanding tinged with relief flooded Violet. She scribbled hastily in her notebook again: *Please come home with me after school. I promise I'll tell you <u>everything</u>!*

She tipped the notebook and cleared her throat again, but Beth kept her eyes firmly on the page in her textbook about sedimentary rock. Violet cleared her throat more loudly. Then she coughed, and coughed again. Finally Mr. Koch turned from the blackboard.

"Violet Jackstone, do you need to get a drink of water?"

Violet felt her face flush. "Uh—no. I'm okay."

When the teacher turned back to the board, Beth finally looked over. Her eyes skimmed Violet's message, and she shrugged.

It wasn't a very satisfactory answer, Violet thought. But it would have to do for now.

CHAPTER **12**

After school that day Violet kept her promise. She and her sisters brought Beth home and filled her in on the return of the stolen letter. They showed Beth the newly discovered diary entries and the needlepoint pattern, and invited her to come along on Saturday to check out the Lauer person on Chance Street.

Now it was Saturday and they were on their way. Violet sat next to Beth on the BART, chattering as if nothing had ever been wrong. She felt sorry that she'd hurt her friend's feelings by excluding her—she knew all too well how terrible it felt to be left out of things. She felt embarrassed that she'd considered Beth—even for a second—as the possible murderer. But she kept her eyes open, too, because if the person to beware of wasn't Beth, then she—or he—might still be lurking somewhere.

They gave Beth a tour of the Chance Street shop, pointing out all the changes. The triplets' father and mother had been busy during the past week. New track lighting had been installed in the front room. A telephone now hung on the wall by the sales counter. The cupboard doors had been re-fitted with strong new hinges and knobs and were closed tightly. Eight large cans of flat white paint waited by the windows with a large bag full of rollers and brushes. "Just leave the paint," their dad had cautioned before they set out today. "We'll have a family painting party once all the old wallpaper is off." He and Lily had decided they would do as much of the interior work as they could themselves, but would employ professionals to paint the exterior of the old building.

Beth and Violet stepped into the backyard, and Violet pointed out the cellar, its door now fitted with a new lock. "That's where I fell because the steps had rotted away. And over there"—she pointed to the back wall of the yard—"is where I imagined a stone bench and a flower garden with a birdbath. And then I read that V had fallen down the stairs, and then in the cellar we found an old stone bench *and* a carved stone birdbath stored against the back wall. Really bizarre." She didn't need to detail how frightened and exhilarated she had felt.

"Spooky," Beth agreed, glancing over her shoulder as if a ghost might be creeping up behind her. "It does seem you've got some connection to this place. The question is *why?*"

"That's what I'm hoping the Lauers can tell me." Violet led the way back into the shop, where Jasmine and Rose were just starting to pull strips of the old wallpaper off the front room walls. "Let's get going," she said, and her sisters jumped up.

The girls crossed the street to number 330. It was a Victorian row house similar to the Jackstones' shop, but this building was very clearly a family home. A skateboard lay at the foot of the steps, and a red tricycle was parked by the door. Rose tapped on the door, then pushed the buzzer. They waited. Violet reached into the back pocket of her jeans and fingered the folded pages of Hal's letters nervously.

"I'll do the talking," Rose murmured.

They had not telephoned ahead. It would be better, they decided, to approach the donor of the letter in person.

Then the door opened and a little girl with long brown braids hanging over her shoulders stood there. She was dressed in red overalls and stared out at them through the screen. "It's for you!" she screeched before the girls could say a word, and careened away. In another second there was a shuffling in the hallway and a boy peered out. "Yes?"

Violet recognized him immediately. Sam, the boy from the top of the mailbox. She felt her cheeks grow warm at the thought of how she must have looked to him then, and how she must look to him now that she had a purple sheen to her hair. He stood before them with his dark hair flopping over his forehead untidily and his eyes bright with interest. Rose and Jasmine broke into identical big smiles.

"Sam!" Jasmine exclaimed. "It's us—Jazzy and Rosy and Vi, remember?"

"How could I forget?" he asked in his gravelly voice. "It's the Maid-of-All-Work and Associates."

"This associate is Beth." Jasmine introduced her, since Violet remained silent. "Do you live here?"

"Huh?" he asked, still looking at Violet. "I mean, yeah." He opened the door. "I mean, hi. Come on in."

"I need you in here, Sam," called a woman's voice from the back of the house.

"It's my mom," he explained. "I'm helping her make pumpkin pies."

"Is your mom Mrs. Lauer?" asked Rose.

"Yup. How did you know that?"

"Could we talk to her?" asked Violet, finally finding her voice. She felt shy with him but had come on business and would not let herself be distracted. "We just want to ask her some questions."

"My mom?" He looked disappointed. Had he been hoping they'd all come to see *him?*

"Yes, please," Violet said in a firmer voice.

The girls followed Sam down the hall to the back of the house and into a large kitchen. The warm room smelled good—*cinnamon and nutmeg,* Violet thought. The smells reminded her of autumn, of fires crackling in the hearth, of Halloween and Thanksgiving. The little girl in red overalls was standing on a chair at the counter, using a wooden spoon to stir something in a big silver bowl. A baby in green overalls sat under the kitchen table, banging on a pot with another wooden spoon.

A television was chattering in the corner. It was another special report about the recent earthquakes, with a geologist using a pointer to indicate details on a big map. "These are the fault lines in California," she was saying, tapping the pointer on a frightening web of lines covering the state. "Many of them have only recently been discovered, and yet there are probably a hundred more we don't know about."

Violet looked away quickly and her glance fell on the newspaper spread over a kitchen chair. The headlines seemed to blare out as loudly as the TV geologist's words:

BAY AREA HOLDS ITS BREATH

WAITING FOR THE BIG ONE

DEALING WITH QUAKE-RELATED STRESS

There was no escape.

A large-boned woman wearing a loose flannel dress looked up from the piecrusts she was rolling out on the wooden cutting board. She had a smudge of flour across one cheek and a friendly smile. "Helpers!" she cried in a gravelly voice like Sam's. "And heaven-sent." Violet smiled at her, relieved to be distracted from the news.

"They're from across the street," said Sam. "Well, they don't really live there, but—"

"It's our new shop," explained Violet. "My parents' florist shop. My sisters and I have been cleaning it up to get ready."

"And we wanted to meet you," added Jasmine.

"We've already met Sam," said Rose politely. "I'm Rosy Jackstone. And this is Jazzy. And Vi. And Beth Madigan."

"We're triplets," said Violet. "Well, Beth isn't."

"Well I'm Ida Lauer, and I'm glad to meet you." Sam's mother tweaked one of the little girl's braids. "And this is our Annabel. That's Anthony under the table, playing the drums." Mrs. Lauer looked at each visitor in turn. "Now let's see. Triplets! Rosy must be short for Rose or Rosemary. And Vi is for Violet, right? But what about Jazzy?"

"It's really Jasmine," said Jasmine.

"Ah. Flower names for the florists' daughters, is that it?"

Jasmine nodded. "I think Mom and Dad got carried away."

"Mom's name is Lilian," said Rose. "But she goes by Lily."

"And your dad?" asked Sam. "Daffodil? Daffy for short?"

"Dad is just plain Greg," said Violet. She gave him a shy smile.

"It would be better if he were Basil or Sage or something."

"Oh, Sam." But his mother was laughing. "Well, I'm pleased to meet the whole bouquet. And Beth, too, of course." She tipped out more flour from the bag and spread it across the cutting board. "But I'm afraid I can't ask you to sit down for a neighborly chat just now. There's a bake sale at our church tomorrow, and I'm nowhere near ready with all the pies I promised to donate."

"They wanted to ask you something," Sam said.

"Well, ask away." Mrs. Lauer reached for her rolling pin and smoothed out a round of dough with deft strokes. "We can work and talk at the same time." She handed Violet a pie pan. "Here, honey. Can you flip this crust into the pan? I'll have another one ready in a sec. Oh, wait, better wash your hands."

Violet didn't mind being drafted into service. She washed her hands at the sink. Then she saw an apron hanging on the doorknob and tied it around her waist. She pulled out a chair at the kitchen table and sat down. Rose followed suit. Jasmine and Beth knelt on the floor and started clapping along in time to Anthony's banging. His round face was wreathed in smiles.

"Thank you, girls. You can help most by keeping the little ones out from underfoot," said Mrs. Lauer. "Here, Sam, open these last cans of pumpkin, would you?"

Violet started working on the second piecrust. She was pleased at the way the firm circles held together in her hands. Mrs. Lauer showed her how to crimp the dough around the edge. Annabel carried the big bowl of spiced pumpkin over to the table.

"My turn now?" she asked.

Mrs. Lauer helped Annabel spoon the creamy orange mixture into the crust Violet had prepared. From beneath the table, Jasmine poked Violet in the leg.

"We wanted to know about a letter you gave to the historical society," said Violet, returning Jasmine's poke with a little kick under the table.

Mrs. Lauer looked startled. "Now, how would you know a thing about that?"

"I saw it when I was on a field trip," explained Violet,

"and it really interested me because it seemed to be written by the same person who wrote other letters we found in our shop."

Mrs. Lauer raised her eyebrows. "How fascinating. And you cared enough to track me down? Now why would that be, I wonder."

Violet hesitated.

Rose took over. "Well, Vi is doing a science report on the 1906 earthquake. And so she was wondering if maybe you had any other stuff from that time."

"And she was wondering who Hal was," added Jasmine from under the table.

"Hal who?" asked Mrs. Lauer.

"The guy who wrote the letters," said Beth eagerly, standing up again. "You see, at first Vi thought the letters were written to her somehow, but now she doesn't, not exactly. But still, there is a link because the letters and diary entries keep coming true, and so the letters are sort of a warning—"

"Never mind about that!" interrupted Violet, and Beth broke off abruptly.

Violet bit her lip. It was hard work trying to be a detective and deal with a sensitive best friend at the same time.

Mrs. Lauer had stopped beating eggs and cream into a new batch of the pumpkin mixture. She raised her eyebrows. "A warning! This sounds more and more intriguing—"

Sam was staring across the table at Violet with unabashed curiosity. "You think the letters were written for *you*? But they're a million years old."

Before they could say anything more, Violet spoke quietly. "I just need to know where the letter came from in the first place."

Mrs. Lauer had resumed mixing the eggs and cream.

"Well, dear, all I know is that I found the letter inside one of the boxes I bought at our annual Chance Street sale a few years back. The boxes were full of old fabric scraps. Real pretty bits of lace, lots of ribbon, and pieces of felt. Even some feathers! Only a dollar a box. Seemed a bargain, because I'm always buying ribbon and suchlike for the wreaths I make to sell for the church."

Violet's mind was racing to process all this information. Rose spoke up first. "What *is* the Chance Street sale?" she asked Mrs. Lauer.

"It's like a block party and yard sale mixed together," explained Sam. "It's totally cool. Every year at the end of August, the street is roped off so there isn't any traffic. And then everybody on Chance Street can set up tables outside their houses. People sell all sorts of stuff real cheap. Last year I got a skateboard for five bucks—and it was hardly used."

Jasmine and Beth emerged from under the table to listen. Anthony crawled out of the room and Annabel followed him. "Go get them, Sam," said his mother. "They'll be up to mischief in there all alone." She turned her attention back to the girls.

"The merchants on the street have tables outside, too," Mrs. Lauer continued. "And the café sells sandwiches and drinks for half price. When the yard sale business slows down—usually around five o'clock—the people from other neighborhoods who came to shop go home, and then all the families have a big picnic. It's a wonderful tradition. Gone on for years now."

"And that's where you bought the box," murmured Jasmine. "But who was selling it? Do you remember?"

"Now that I *do* know," said Mrs. Lauer. She examined the pie shells Violet had made. "These are just fine. You have a nice touch."

"The box had to have come from our shop," pressed Violet, who had been silently listening. "But who lived there then?"

"It was old Miss Stowe," said Mrs. Lauer.

Stowe! The girls nudged each other.

"After I found the letter," explained Mrs. Lauer, "I called to ask if she wanted it. But she said she was leaving Chance Street to move into a nursing home. She didn't know anything about the letter and didn't want it back." Mrs. Lauer shook her head. "She's been gone about three years now— and her place has been empty all this time. The street doesn't seem the same without her."

Sam returned to the kitchen with Annabel on his shoulders and Anthony tucked under one arm like a sack of potatoes. "Nothing seems the same without the witch," Sam growled in a low, spooky voice, and then let out a piercing cackle. "And who's complaining?" Annabel laughed and pounded her hands on his head.

Violet looked at him sharply. "The witch?"

"Now, Sam, I don't like to hear such talk," chided his mother. "Old Miss Stowe was crotchety, I'll give you that. But she was having health problems. No one likes to hear skateboards whizzing up and down in front of their house when they're not feeling well."

"Stowe is the name of the family who used to live in our shop," said Jasmine.

"They made hats," added Rose.

"That's right," nodded Mrs. Lauer. "There were three sisters. Miss Stowe was the last of the family alive, if I recall rightly. The eldest sister died quite young, I remember hearing. Miss Stowe and her other sister were identical twins. The twins inherited the shop from their parents and kept it going until after World War Two, I believe. Then one sister died, and our Miss Stowe couldn't keep on by herself. None of the sisters ever married, and I guess there wasn't enough money to hire an assistant. The last Miss Stowe became something of a hermit—hardly ever came outside in later years. I hear she even had concrete poured over the back garden so she wouldn't have to go out and do the gardening."

It seemed criminal to Violet. "Those beautiful flowers and shrubs—all covered over by cement?" she protested.

Sam was looking at her intently. "Sounds as if you'd *seen* the garden."

"The old hat shop went out of business years ago," Mrs. Lauer said. "Long before we ever moved to Chance Street. People just don't wear hats the way they used to. I think Miss Stowe was living on her Social Security payments. We didn't know her well. She kept to herself, though I helped her from time to time with her shopping. As she grew older, she had one of those metal walkers and could only go a few feet before resting. It was hard for her to walk and pull her shopping cart along at the same time." Mrs. Lauer washed her hands and dried them on her apron. "Ah, well, we'll all grow old, God willing. It's still better than dying young, if you ask me!" She smiled over at Violet. "I'd like to see your letters, dear."

"Sure," said Jasmine brightly. "Vi?"

Violet shot Jasmine a look. She felt the folded pieces of paper in her back pocket. "Sure," she echoed slowly, feeling backed into a corner. *The letters are mine!* she wanted to cry. *It's up to me to decide whether to show them to people or not!* "Sometime. But, um, not today. Um, what we were hoping is that you would have more letters for us. Like the one you gave to the historical society. Maybe there are more in those boxes of lace and stuff you bought."

She noticed that Sam was looking at her intently, his brown eyes thoughtful. Did he suspect she had the letters in her pocket now, after all?

"Well, I'm fairly sure there aren't, but you girls are welcome to look. Sam, honey, go fetch the other box. It's up in the back of my closet with the craft supplies."

"This is really nice of you," said Beth politely as Mrs. Lauer led them from the kitchen into a living room littered with wooden blocks and plastic animals. They had to watch carefully to avoid stepping on them.

Violet and Beth sat with Mrs. Lauer on the couch, while Jasmine and Rose settled into the two armchairs by the fireplace. Annabel started building a tower with the blocks, and Anthony knocked the tower down. Violet braced herself for her screams of protest, but none came. Instead, she patiently started rebuilding the tower. Again Anthony knocked it down, laughing. Annabel laughed, too, and built a new tower.

Sam entered the room, lugging a large cardboard box. "Here it is. A zillion pounds of felt and lace and yarn. Mom's always making stuff—especially around Christmas."

Mrs. Lauer opened the flaps. The girls came forward to peer inside at the jumble of fabric. Violet's excitement died. She'd half expected to see bundles of letters from Hal tied up with ribbon. Carefully, Violet lifted the fabric and dug down to the bottom of the box. Then she turned to the girls.

"Nothing. There's nothing here." Their faces mirrored her disappointment.

"No, I didn't think there would be," said Mrs. Lauer. "Miss Stowe told me she was getting rid of all of her old things when she moved out. Her own personal stuff, she said, as well as old family things—even stuff left behind by the hired help."

"You can't take it with you," Sam intoned.

"But maybe she did!" Violet said. "Maybe she took some things to the nursing home with her. Maybe we could call and ask her."

The other girls grinned. "Good idea," Rose nodded. "Can you tell us where she lives?" she asked Mrs. Lauer.

"I think it was over in Oakland," the woman answered. "But—"

"Do you know the name of the place?" pressed Violet.

"I'm sorry. I have no idea. But I'm afraid it wouldn't do you any good even if I did. I heard from someone at church that Miss Stowe passed away last year. That's why your house—your new shop, I mean—came on the market."

Dead. The surviving Miss Stowe was now as dead as her two other sisters, and the trail of clues had reached a dead end as well. Violet stroked a swatch of blue velvet. She had been so certain that they were on Hal's trail. Now she felt lost again.

A spicy aroma wafted into the living room. "I'd better check on those pies," said Mrs. Lauer. She reached for Anthony as the little boy crawled past. "And this little one doesn't smell so good at all. Time for a diaper change, my sweet."

"I guess we'd better get going," said Rose regretfully, "if we're going to get any cleaning done at the shop."

"Yeah." Jasmine stood up, brushing off her jeans.

Beth nudged Violet, who remained sitting on the floor, stroking the cloth. Slowly Violet removed her apron and handed it to Mrs. Lauer. She made an effort to smile. "It was nice to meet you," she said. Annabel skipped along to the front hallway, leading the others.

"We're delighted that your parents bought old Miss Stowe's place," said Mrs. Lauer. "A pretty little florist shop ought to go a long way toward brightening up this old neighborhood."

They reached the front door when the floor dipped alarmingly and the glass panes rattled in the windows. "Uh-oh!"

cried Mrs. Lauer, snatching Annabel's hand and pulling the child to her.

"Not again!" squealed Beth.

"Hang on!" shouted Sam. "There—it's over already."

The others stood waiting, braced for whatever would come next, almost ready to laugh about it. Only Violet was holding her breath. Only Violet felt darkness lapping behind her closed eyes and saw the shadowy figures running in panic. *Flames!* The little girl fleeing from ruins of twisted metal, her mouth open in an anguished cry for help—

Sam laughed. Violet opened her eyes, dazed. She couldn't speak. The frightened pounding of her heart nearly drowned out the voices of the others.

"It was just that little old swarm of quakes," joked Rose. "Buzzing by again." And Jasmine giggled weakly.

"It's totally horrible the way you never know if a quake is just—you know, just a little one," complained Beth. "Or if it's the first of a whole lot of big ones."

"Well!" Mrs. Lauer hugged her little ones. "That seems to be all for this time. Everybody okay?"

"I guess so," said Jasmine.

"But I wish they'd stop," added Rose. "We've had enough."

Just as the girls started out the door, Sam brushed up against Violet and surreptitiously pressed something into her hand. Something smooth and square. Automatically, Violet closed her fingers around it. She raised her eyes to his questioningly. He winked.

Mrs. Lauer turned to her son. "Sam," she said, "why don't you go along and help these girls with some of the cleaning over there? Make yourself useful instead of risking your life on that skateboard all day."

"Sure," said Rose eagerly, turning back in the doorway.

"We could use another pair of hands to pull down the old wallpaper."

"Yeah," said Jasmine. "You know the old saying, don't you? 'Many hands make light work.' "

Sam shuffled his feet and looked embarrassed and pleased at the same time. "What about 'Too many cooks spoil the broth'?"

"Nonsense," said his mother. "You can smell how well the pies are turning out after all the help I had. Now run along."

Sam leaped down the front steps, followed by Jasmine and Rose. The three of them raced each other across the street while Beth and Violet followed more slowly.

"Are you okay?" Beth asked quietly. "You look really, I don't know, *freaked*."

Violet would never be okay on a planet that wouldn't keep still. But she took a deep breath and once again forced her fear back inside. "I'll get over it." She changed the subject. "I was so sure we'd find something at the Lauers. Oh well."

"We found Sam, though," said Beth cheerfully. "And his family. I like them. And know what? I think Sam likes *you*. In fact, maybe he's your Hal!"

Violet felt her cheeks grow warm. She went ahead of Beth into the shop, passed the others in the living room, and climbed upstairs on legs that shook. In the little bathroom, she sat on the edge of the tub and stared down at the thick square of paper Sam had given her. She could hear her heart beating. Was this a love note? Was he her Hal?

She unfolded the paper carefully. It was old, too old to be from Sam. It was a thin sheet of lined paper, the fold lines yellowed and brittle. The page was filled with the now-familiar, elegant brown script of the unknown diary writer. The date at the top was June 20, 1906. *That's after the big earthquake,* Violet remembered, *and after the other entry I found.* She began reading.

June 20, 1906

Dear Diary,

This will be fast because we shall be leaving shortly, but I have to tell someone. My heart is so full. It has happened at last, at long last! Hal is mine at last, truly and forever. We were married this afternoon before a judge, with two kindly people brought in off the street as witnesses. They had no idea they were witnessing not only a wedding ceremony but the fruition of all my hopes and plans. Everything is still in horrific disarray around us, but life goes on and we are making our plans to leave this ruined city. There are too many unhappy memories for me here, and for Hal, too, though I am positive with time I can change his sadness over poor Verity's death to gladness in the certainty that I am the right woman for him after all.

Her death is still very much on our minds—though in quite different ways, I imagine. He is remembering his dream girl, the beloved Sweet V he wanted to marry. I am remembering that same sweet V the day before the end.

I was helping her sit up in bed just a few days before she died when suddenly from outside in the street there came a loud clanging. She said softly, "Oh, listen, Laela— do you hear? Wedding bells! Wedding bells for me and Hal!" Her mind had seemed to be wandering in those last days, but I could hear the bells, too.

So I went to the window and looked out and saw the strangest sight. An old organ-grinder was walking by pushing a cart and banging with a stick on a pot dangling from a piece of rope. A very unusual sight on Chance Street. He had a little monkey riding high on his shoulder, wearing bells on his tiny fists. At least that's what I supposed they were, for as they passed, the little animal raised his arms over his fuzzy head and shook them, and little jingles mixed in with the loud clanging.

"Wedding bells," Verity said again from her nest of pillows.

"It's just an organ-grinder," I told Verity. "With a little monkey. Come, let me help you to the window so you can see them before they're gone."

But she had faded into sleep again. I shivered a little, though the room was warm. What she thought were wedding bells might have been her own death toll.

Verity, Violet thought, staring down at the page. V was Verity Stowe. And the diary writer's name was Laela. It looked like poor Verity had never married Hal after all. Instead Laela had—and very soon after the big earthquake . . . after Verity died. After Laela had killed her? But the way Laela wrote of Verity's death in this entry didn't sound like murder to Violet anymore.

But then how *had* Verity died? Violet bit her lip. It was vitally important that she know. The pattern was still there.

Slowly Violet folded the page and slipped it into her pocket. She opened the bathroom door and walked carefully down the stairs, gripping the banister extra tightly.

"Where's Sam?" she asked as Jasmine walked past the stairs, carrying a trash bag full of wallpaper scraps.

"Outside. We're taking the bags out as we fill them."

Violet joined Beth by the big bay windows and started helping to pull old wallpaper off in thin strips. Beth and Jasmine started singing along to the radio, but Violet worked silently, lost in thought.

It would be a relief not to have to look out for murderers anymore. But what if she got hit by a car? What if she tripped and cracked her head on the curb? A sudden heart attack?

There were so many ways to die. She looked out the window and watched a man across the street walk up toward the hardware store. What if he just pulled out a gun and turned and shot her—right through the window? Such things did happen sometimes. The newspapers were full of news like that.

If only she could find out exactly how Verity Stowe died, she'd know better what to look out for. She watched Sam and Rose walk around the house and up the front steps.

"What a job," complained Rose, entering the house. "Sam, how about if you hold the ladder for me, and I'll start on that corner?"

"Sam, how about if you help me rip the paper off here by the door?" asked Jasmine.

Sam just stood in the middle of the room and looked around. "It's weird thinking that this is where the witch lived. Was she a slob or what?"

"You should have seen it before we cleaned the first time," said Rose.

"Remember, the house was empty for years after she moved to the nursing home," said Beth. "That's a lot of time for the dust to pile up. Miss Stowe might have been neat as a pin."

Violet felt Sam's gaze on her and turned around. She liked his wide, happy grin. He would be a boy she'd like to get to know—but that probably wouldn't be possible now. She might not have much time left. Where had he found the diary entry? Why had he hidden it from the others? She would ask him—if she lived long enough to find time alone with him.

The thought brought tears to her eyes.

"Do you have something in your eye?" asked Sam, peering at Violet with concern.

"No!" Violet wiped her stinging eyes vigorously. "Nothing. I'm fine." She glanced past him up the stairs, imagined herself climbing them right up to the back bedroom. She had the strangest feeling that if she was to go to that window and look down at the backyard, she would see not a concrete alley, but a courtyard full of flowers—the same flowers poor V had looked out upon. Had they been the last thing she saw as she lay dying in her bed? Or had she died another way—by tripping down the stairs or choking on a fish bone?

Sam was looking at her strangely. "Are you sure? You don't look fine."

"No, I'm not. I mean, my eye is fine. But I'm not." He looked surprised, but she left the window and started for the stairs. "Come with me, Sam." When she saw her sisters looking over at them with identical smirks on their faces, she grabbed a spray bottle off the sales counter. "We're going to, um, clean windows."

CHAPTER 13

They faced each other in the bedroom that looked over the backyard. "So, what's with you?" asked Sam. "These windows shine like they've already been cleaned."

"Forget the windows. Tell me about the diary entry." Her voice was low and intense.

"Is that what it is? Could you read it?" Sam made an attempt to lower his foghorn voice to match hers. It came out a harsh whisper.

"Yes. Where did you get it?"

"It was at the bottom of the fabric box. I looked before I brought it down. It was right there, under everything in the bottom. I thought you should see it without having to share it with everybody else."

"Why did you think that?" asked Violet. "How could you know?"

"Well, it figures. If you're the one getting weird letters from the past, then you're the one who should at least see the thing first."

"You mean you didn't read it?"

"Well," he admitted, "I did sort of try. But it's hard to read all that curly writing. I couldn't make it out. Was it what you were looking for?"

"Sort of. But—" She looked helplessly out the window, down at the cement yard. There were no flowers there at all.

"What?"

"She died. She didn't marry Hal after all, and I don't know *how* she died!" Violet felt tears pricking behind her eyes again. She knew she wasn't making sense. Sam would think she was a total idiot.

There were sprinkles of dried wallpaper paste in Sam's dark hair. They blew loose as he shook his head. "I don't know who died or who Hal is. What is it you're afraid of?"

"Death." At his shocked expression, she sighed. "Sudden death, Sam. *My* death."

"I think you'd better spell everything out for me. I'm not getting this at all."

Would he believe any of it? She took a deep breath. "Okay, listen," she began slowly. "I know this is going to sound really weird, but there's a sort of *pattern*. From the past, I mean. The things that happened to a girl named Verity who lived here in this house almost a hundred years ago keep happening to me. Well, sort of." She gazed out the window as she spoke and told him all about it from the beginning, about the letters and the diary entries. Even about the stolen letter from the museum. Then she fingered the carefully folded letters and diary entries in her pocket. She drew them out and read them to him, pointing out the similarities between her life and Verity's.

"It's like we're connected somehow," she concluded. "And she died young, and so—well, you know."

"So you really think you'll die, too?" Sam's brown eyes were wide. "That's incredible."

She spritzed cleaning solution on the window and watched it dribble down the glass.

Sam squinted at the diary entry he had given her. "The name Verity is really nothing like your name—except for the first letter. And the other parallels—well, they're just coincidence. They've got to be. Lots of girls have two sisters. And sisters are always pains—I know that much myself, and I have only one of them."

"But Verity's sisters were twins—and their names were Jane and Rachel. My sisters look like twins—and their names start with *J* and *R*, too." Violet sighed. "Look, I know I can't convince you. It's just that—well, this is all so weird, I can't ignore what I'm finding."

"Hey, you're not the only one finding things, though. *I* found that last diary entry. Does that mean I'm going to die? Or my mom, since she bought the box from the old witch?"

She turned away from him. She put her hand on her heart and waited, trying to feel its beat. Was it erratic? She leaned her head against the window glass, feeling dizzy and helpless. "The letters are a warning to me. I just know it—even if it does make me sound crazy and paranoid to say so."

Beth's voice from the stairs made them both turn. "Hey, you two! Want something from the café?"

"Come on, let's go," said Sam, taking the spray bottle from Violet's hand and dropping it on the floor. "I'll hold your hand while we cross the street and keep you safe."

Violet let him take her hand and lead her downstairs. *I'm holding hands with a boy,* she thought, detached. She saw Rose, Jasmine, and Beth glance at each other in surprise when she and Sam came downstairs together.

Rose put her hands on her hips. "Well!" she said. "What have you two been up to?"

"We'll tell you about it at the café," murmured Sam.

"Really!" Beth wiggled her eyebrows. "Shouldn't some details be kept private?"

Jasmine and Rose giggled. "I hope," Jasmine said to Sam with mock severity, "that you haven't been putting the moves on our baby sister!"

Violet felt tears slipping down her cheeks. She felt stupid, but she couldn't help it, and she pulled her hand out of Sam's, pushed past them all, and walked toward the door. They could tease and joke all they wanted because they weren't the ones getting messages from the past. They could laugh! They didn't have to be watchful, as she did, searching out the dangers ahead. She just couldn't cope with every possible danger. She wouldn't know how to look out for them all. If it wasn't a murderer that killed her in the end, it would be a mugger, or a rabid dog, or her heart giving out, or a completely unpredictable slip in the bathtub sending her crashing down onto the hard tiles—

Or an earthquake.

"Hey, wait up," said Beth.

"Vi, we didn't mean anything!" Jasmine put her hand on Violet's arm.

"Don't be so sensitive," complained Rose. "You're no fun."

Violet shook the thought of earthquakes out of her head again. Sam led her out of the house. His booming voice was gentle. "I think you'd better show them the latest installment."

So over ice-cream sundaes served by the bubbly waitress, who flirted wildly with Sam when she brought their food, Violet showed her sisters and Beth the diary entry from Miss

Stowe's box. She read it all aloud—about the organ-grinder and the bells, about Verity Stowe's death and Laela's marriage to Hal. The other girls stopped eating while they listened, sitting wide-eyed as if it were a delightful mystery tale they were watching on TV. Violet wished she could share their excitement as she had before. But today she couldn't shake the feeling that something awful was going to happen.

"At least," said Rose, "we know V's name now."

"Verity means 'truth,' " said Beth, who often knew odd things like that.

"It's a pretty name," said Jasmine. "How can we find out more about her? I mean, if you're not famous, then there aren't books written about you or anything."

"Try the newspapers," said Sam.

"The papers?" asked Jasmine in surprise. "Why would she be in the newspapers?"

"If she had been murdered, then, of course, it would be in the papers," said Rose. "But in this last entry it doesn't sound like Laela murdered her after all. So there wouldn't be an article in the paper."

"I know," said Beth. "Sam means her death announcement." Violet wondered if it was because Beth's father had died in a car crash when she was little that she knew things like where to look for people's obituaries. Violet herself hadn't known that newspapers carried such information.

"Right," Sam was saying. "I can ask my dad to help us. He works at the *Chronicle*."

"We know the approximate date from the diary entry," said Jasmine. "Maybe the announcement will even tell us how she died."

"It would be good to know," Rose agreed. "So Vi can stop worrying."

"There's no news that will be good news," said Beth with

a sigh. "Unless we learn that Verity Stowe died of old age."

"Which we know didn't happen," said Jasmine, "since the letters always mention how young she is."

"Maybe we'd know more about Verity if we knew more about Laela," suggested Sam.

"But we don't know her last name," Beth pointed out. "So how could we look her up in the newspaper?"

"We know she married Hal," Jasmine pointed out. "If we could find out his last name, we could find out hers—at least her name once she married him. Women always took their husband's last name back in those days."

"The wedding announcement might have been in the paper, too," said Rose. "We can look at all the announcements for June of 1906 and see if anything turns up. Hey, Sam, let's ask your dad today."

"He's in Mendocino visiting my uncle. But I'll ask him as soon as he comes home, and then I'll call you." Sam gave her a rakish grin. "We'll crack this case if it's the last thing we do!"

His proclamation was followed by what sounded at first like bells ringing in the street. Then there came a loud clanging, jangling, and the scrape of metal against wood. They all looked at each other, then out the café windows. Other customers were craning their necks to see. Violet gasped and held her hands to her cheeks. She jumped up from their booth and ran to the door. She stepped out into the street, staring incredulously at the scene before her.

"No way," said Sam, right behind her. "No way." He put his hand on Violet's shoulder.

An organ-grinder, complete with old-fashioned wooden cart and a live monkey on his shoulder, was indeed a strange sight on Chance Street. People stepped out onto the sidewalks up and down the street to watch and wave. Down the street,

Mrs. Lauer stood on her front porch with little Annabel and baby Anthony, but Violet barely noticed them. All she could see was the organ-grinder, a grizzled old man with a thick gray beard and a big smile. His head was bare, but the little monkey wore a red felt cap, and this he tipped to the bystanders as the man stopped and removed an accordion from his cart. The organ-grinder started to play rollicking music that made the monkey leap down from his shoulder and dance on the top of the cart. The people of Chance Street laughed and clapped. Violet watched as if in a trance, remembering Laela's description of the organ-grinder she and Verity had seen.

When the music ended, the monkey held his little cap out and people crossed the street to drop coins into it. Then the organ-grinder, grinning his thanks, continued down the street and disappeared around the corner, bells jangling.

"Wow," breathed Sam. "I mean, *wow*."

"You call that a coincidence?" whispered Jasmine to Rose as they turned back to their table.

Beth was frowning.

Wedding bells? Violet wondered. *Or a death toll?*

CHAPTER 14

Violet lay on her bed in her alcove after dinner that evening, staring up at the ceiling. She put her hand on her heart and felt the beat. She thought there was a funny little flutter from time to time. She took deep regular breaths, willing her heart to keep on pumping.

How had Verity died?

It had been a long, hard day. Staying alive was difficult work, once you were concentrating on it. While her sisters and Beth and Sam had finished pulling down the old wallpaper, she had bundled the last of it into trash bags and hauled the bags to the back of the house. All the trash cans were full, so she dragged them one by one to the street. When she was heaving the last can into place at the curb, a motorcycle skidded around the corner onto Chance Street and roared past, narrowly missing her at the side of the road.

When the girls said good-bye to Sam and started walking down the street, Violet kept a keen eye out for people who might be muggers or thieves. The cable car was crowded and the four girls could not find seats together. Violet sat next to a woman who kept her hands in her pockets the entire time. When the cable car went around corners, the woman pressed against Violet, and Violet felt something hard poking her through the fabric of the woman's coat. *A gun? A knife?* She glanced at the woman, but the woman's eyes looked straight ahead. Violet edged away and was relieved when the cable car stopped. On the BART she worried that there would be an earthquake and the train would derail, or the tunnel under the bay would collapse, or there would be a terrible crash. Back at home she still didn't feel safe. Even if she could push aside the fear of earthquakes—which she could not—there were fires to worry about, and freak accidents. What if a plane crashed into their house? At dinner she thought the meat tasted off. There might be the danger of food poisoning, though when she'd mentioned this worry to her family, her father just roared at her to clean her plate. Jasmine was sympathetic, and for this Violet was grateful. But Rose maintained that Violet was letting her imagination run away with her and was becoming paranoid. After the meal both sisters had gone off to their bedroom to do their homework and now were downstairs watching TV as if they didn't have a care in the world.

Here in her alcove, Violet had only her heartbeat for company. And it seemed to her that heartbeat was growing more and more erratic every minute.

Violet sat up and looked around with dissatisfaction. You'd think that a girl marked for death at such a young age would at least get the chance to have a proper bedroom of her own. But she knew there was no use asking to room with Rosy and Jazzy. Their mother said two girls in a room was enough. And neither of her sisters would want to trade places and sleep in the alcove. They'd say there wasn't enough privacy.

Which there wasn't. *But I need privacy, too,* thought Violet. Once you feared for your life, you started thinking what you wanted to accomplish before the last breath was drawn. It was what those societies that grant dying kids their one last wish did, mused Violet. They knew that kids want something special—especially at a time when everything might be snatched away from them forever.

She thought about what she wanted. Kids in the newspapers always asked to go to Disneyland or to have dinner with their favorite sports hero. She had already been to Disneyland—and didn't think it was such a big deal, really, though that might have been because her parents were afraid to let her go on any of the really fast rides. And she didn't have any particular sports hero. She liked to watch the ice-skating during the Winter Olympics, but that was it.

What had Verity's last wish been?

"What I really want is my own room," she said aloud. "Is that so much to ask?"

But their house wasn't very big. Downstairs were the living room, dining room, kitchen, and a tiny bathroom. She'd read in a book about a family with a lot of kids who had turned their dining room into a bedroom—but she doubted her mom would go for the idea. Upstairs there were the two large bedrooms, one with the little alcove, and a second bathroom. There was one basement room they used for storage and for doing laundry. And there was the attic—

Violet hadn't been up there for ages.

She sat up and swung her legs off the bed. The attic was reached through the hallway linen closet. She went to the closet now and opened the door. Above her head a rope dangled. When she pulled on it, wooden steps mounted on a folding sort of ladder lowered down and clicked into place. Violet flicked the switch inside the linen closet that turned on the light in the attic, then climbed up.

The attic was a large narrow room that ran the length of the house. The sharp pitch of the roof made the walls slope to the floor, but two gable windows looked out on the street and would let in a lot of light, Violet suspected, in the daytime. Violet blessed her mother for being such an impeccable housekeeper that she included even the attic in her yearly spring cleaning. Although the attic was dusty, it could not be called dirty. In fact, the last time Violet had been up here was last April to help her dad, mom, and sisters wash the floor and windows. Greg had grumbled that there wasn't any point to cleaning a space they didn't even use, but Lily had replied firmly that the attic was part of the house and must not be overlooked. "We don't want mildew and mold, not to mention mice and spiders, getting into our boxes, now do we?" she'd asked. And, of course, everyone had to agree they wouldn't want any of that to happen.

Now Violet looked around at those same pest-free boxes. There were eight of them—large brown cardboard packing boxes filled with her parents' old yearbooks, the camping equipment, the cutest of the triplets' baby clothes Lily just hadn't been able to bring herself to give away, and assorted other household castoffs. There were also two lamps without shades, a ladder-back chair with a broken rung, and the scratched pine coffee table that hadn't sold at their garage sale last year, not even when Greg lowered the price to ten dollars. The attic looked wonderful to Violet. It was the answer to her last wish.

She heard a creak from the stairway and looked over to see a honey-colored head poking through the hole.

Jasmine frowned at her. "Didn't you hear Mom calling you?"

"Nope."

"She says to get ready for bed. What are you up here for?"

"Just checking it out. I'm going to move in."

"Hey, no kidding?" Jasmine looked around with interest. "It would make a cool bedroom if you painted the walls and hung up posters. But Mom and Dad will never let you. It's too far away from them at night, and too drafty in winter—and the stairs! You'd break your neck trying to get up and down them every day. Or what about in the middle of the night when you had to pee? You couldn't even turn on the light since the switch is down there in the closet."

"I don't care. I don't want to sleep in the alcove anymore. How would you like it? If I'm going to die young, I at least want my own bedroom."

"Oh, Vi." Jasmine's face was troubled. "How about if Rosy and I move up here and you take our room? It would be safer. Or if Rosy doesn't want to move, I will, and you can have my space."

Violet considered the offer. She'd always wanted to share the big bedroom with her sisters. But now that she'd decided on the attic, she was determined to have it for herself. "No. I want the attic."

"What?" came their mother's voice, and then the ladder stairs creaked as she climbed up. "Did I hear you say you want the attic, Baby? What does that mean?"

Lily's head appeared through the trapdoor. "It's bedtime. What are you two girls looking for up here?"

"Vi wants this to be her bedroom," Jasmine announced.

"What on earth!" cried Lily.

"Wait, Mom, wait," began Violet. "Don't say no yet. Please. Listen. I need a space of my own. Not the alcove, but all my own. I'll paint the walls myself, I'll dust and wash the windows and make curtains. I can do it all—and we can move my bed up here, and my rug and desk and dresser. I think the furniture will just fit through the hole—though we'll probably have to take the bed apart first. Please, Mom!"

Lily was shaking her head, but she stopped when Violet's eyes welled with tears. "Baby, I don't think it's a good idea. But come down and discuss it with Dad. Let's see what he thinks."

Violet took a deep breath and wiped her eyes. She didn't want to break down and cry. That would only reinforce their sense that she was the weak little runt of the family. She must be strong and speak clearly and explain why she needed the attic.

Lily climbed back down the steps, Jasmine and Violet following. "Don't mention that you're afraid you're going to— you know," Jasmine whispered back at Violet. "That will only freak them out."

Violet went to her alcove and changed into her night-gown. Then she washed her face and brushed her teeth, studying her pale face in the mirror. Her hair wasn't quite so purple anymore, she decided. But it would need another dozen washings before it looked truly back to normal. She resolved to take a lot of showers in the next week. It would be horrible if she died and then looked stupid at her funeral.

But she was going to try very hard not to die. She held tightly to the handrail as she went downstairs to confront her dad with the news that she planned to move into the attic.

He and Rose were sitting in the living room working a jig-saw puzzle. Lily bustled in from the kitchen carrying a large vase of fresh flowers. She set the vase on top of the bookcase by the windows, then came to sit down. "All right," she said. "Ex-plain to your dad and me again why you don't like the alcove."

At least they were going to pretend to listen to her. Violet took a deep breath and began telling them how she was as old as Jazzy and Rosy, and how she didn't like feeling like a baby. She told them that sleeping in the little alcove where her baby crib used to be made her feel they thought she still needed to be hooked up to a heart monitor at night. She told them how nice the attic would be once the walls were painted and her furniture had been moved up.

Greg listened, nodding. "You have some good points," he said.

Lily shot him an incredulous look. "But the problems

outweigh the good points, don't you think, Greg? I mean, think about the stairs, for one thing. I don't want Vi having to climb up and down that rickety ladder all the time. And the light switch is downstairs. That's very awkward. And you know what it's like up there in winter. She'd freeze."

Jasmine had come into the room while Violet was talking and now spoke up hurriedly. "I offered to sleep in the attic, Dad. I wouldn't mind. It's neat up there."

"I don't really want you going up that ladder, either, Jazzy," said Lily with a frown. "And in winter—"

"If Vi really doesn't want the alcove anymore," began Rose in a noble tone, "I guess we could probably squeeze her in with us. Maybe if Jazzy and I had bunk beds..."

"No! You guys don't get it!" wailed Violet, though inwardly she was impressed that Rose had actually offered to make room for her. "I want to be able to have a room of my own—just once, okay? Just once before I die!"

Jasmine and Rose glared at her. Lily gasped. Greg looked stunned. After a moment, Greg said mildly, "No one is expecting you to die, sweetheart."

"Oh yeah? That's not how it seems to me," stormed Violet. "The way you all worry and fuss at me all the time. You act like I can't do anything for myself! Like maybe my heart really isn't fixed right and I'll have heart failure on the way to school! And you never know, I could catch a new deadly virus, or I could be in a car crash. It doesn't have to be my heart at all—it could be a murderer!" She heard herself and knew she sounded hysterical. So she forced herself to stop. It would be awful to die angry at your family. They'd always remember you that way. She took a deep breath. "Anyway," she continued in as calm a voice as she could muster, "I would really like to try the attic. I'll be very careful on the ladder. I'll take extra quilts up there. I'll be fine. And if I'm not—then I'll move downstairs again. Okay? Just let me try it."

Lily was shaking her head, but to Violet's relief, she saw her dad nodding. "Let's get clear on one matter first, before we discuss this any further," Greg said gently. "Baby, you were born with a bad heart murmur and there was a problem with one of the valves. You had a rough start. But the operation you had when you were six was completely successful. Mom and I are not afraid you are going to drop dead of heart failure or anything else, and I don't want you worrying about it, either. Maybe we do worry about your health more than we should—I guess it's because we nearly lost you. Worrying about you became a habit." He reached out and ruffled her dark hair, so like his own. "I think maybe Mom and I have been overreacting, and your sisters have caught it from us. I'm sorry about that, honey. You're just *fine*. Got it?"

"Yes," she whispered gratefully, her eyes filling with tears.

Lily reached over and hugged her tightly. "You're a strong, healthy girl," she whispered.

"Good," Greg said. "Okay then. When I was looking through renovators' catalogs to get ideas for fixing up the new shop, I saw some ads for staircases. They weren't really very expensive at all, and I bet we could find one that would fit right inside the linen closet. Maybe a spiral staircase. Something that would give easy and safe access to the attic—and we could do away with the ladder entirely."

"Oh, Dad! That would be perfect!" cried Violet.

He smiled at her. "I'll look into it on Monday."

"But the cold, Greg," objected Lily, tightening her arms around Violet. "And the light switch. And there's no bathroom!"

"Lily, dear," Greg chided her, "we've just promised not to fuss so much."

"I'll just come down the stairs," Violet said quickly. "Or—or use a chamber pot like—" She'd been about to say "like Verity must have," but she swallowed the words. "Like in the old days," she finished. "People had to go outside to outhouses," she told her mom. "And they didn't have central heating. And *they* did all right. I'll manage."

Lily released her with a little laugh. "You're certainly determined, I'll give you that."

"We'll have to see what can be done," Greg said. "It might be worth insulating the attic anyway—help keep the heating costs down. And it would be a small job to put some outlets up there. The wiring is already there, after all." He was getting interested, Violet was pleased to see. Renovation projects always held an appeal for him.

Jasmine and Rose grinned at her. She smiled back at them for a moment, feeling strong and proud and healthy. It wasn't Disneyland or a dinner with a sports hero, but it looked like she might get this last wish after all. She felt that, despite her dad's reassurances about her health, whatever happened to Verity Stowe was quite likely just around the corner for her. But until it made itself known to her, Violet resolved, she would keep on trying for a few more last wishes. Who knew? She might live longer now that she was aware of the danger. She might be lucky.

One other last wish, she realized after she'd kissed her parents good night and climbed the stairs, carefully holding the rail, was to go to the middle school dance. Why should Jazzy and Rosy be old enough to ask boys to the Halloween Ball but not Vi?

And Violet knew just the boy she'd like to invite.

She'd call Sam tomorrow and see if her luck held.

CHAPTER 15

That night Violet dreamed of Mr. Koch. He was taking the science class on a field trip to San Francisco, and they were all walking across the Golden Gate Bridge to get there. The hot sun directly overhead blazed down and cars rushed past. As Violet walked, she looked down over the side of the bridge and saw sailboats floating languidly on the bay. There seemed to be no breeze to fill their sails. And yet, mysteriously, the bridge under her feet began trembling, then swinging back and forth as if propelled by mighty winds. It felt as if the whole contraption were a new ride at an amusement park—the kind of ride Violet hated. Cars slid into each other and burst into flames. From the smoking, twisted metal of a car just in front of Violet, three figures emerged. It was hard to see through the black smoke now swirling everywhere, but Violet knew they were children. Their cries rose above the crackle of flame—and she clutched Mr. Koch, calling for him to help them, but he kept trying to thrust a pile of books into her arms. "Have you started on your report?" he boomed, his voice louder even than the screams all around them.

Violet cried out as she awoke. "Save them! The bridge—!" Then she sat up, her limbs feeling heavy, her head groggy, and groaned aloud. *Why is this happening to me? What does it mean?* She leaned forward till her head rested on her knees and the dream receded. She lifted her head and saw that the morning was gray, covered by mist.

She was *just* like Verity now, talking in her sleep and having visions of doom.

On the other hand, Beth would say the dream was just a sign of a guilty conscience. Violet still had not started on her science project and the deadline was approaching fast.

Whatever it was, vision of doom or reflection of guilty conscience, the dream kept Violet lying in bed for a long time. She lay with her hand over her heart, counting the beats. She listened to her breath. In, out; in, out. She thought about breathing. How could it be that her lungs drew breath and expelled it, on and on and on throughout the day and throughout the night, then more days and nights—for years, for her whole life long? How could it be that her heart—she pictured it looking like a fist-sized piece of uncooked roast beef—could beat steadily on and on without her even having to think about it? That seemed nothing short of magic.

Magic—like the organ-grinder. Like the letters, the diary entries, the other strange connections between now and then. *Magic?* she thought. *Or a miracle?* The miracle of life, as much as the steady beating of her heart was a miracle. *Or part of a plan?*

She stretched in her bed, feeling stronger. No longer heavy and groggy, her body now felt energetic; she was ready to face the day. She glanced over at the alarm clock. Only

6:30. Plan One—she could go over to her desk and start reading some of Mr. Koch's books. Or Plan Two—she could go down and surprise everyone by making breakfast.

Then there was Plan Three—she could take a long shower before her sisters were awake and phone Sam before making breakfast and working on her paper. Plan Three won.

She washed her hair half a dozen times in the pounding shower. Close inspection in the mirror revealed that the purple traces in her hair had faded even more. Already she couldn't recapture the urgency that she'd felt only days ago to look like her sisters. The last few days had provided more troubling matters to ponder than whether the three of them matched.

Shivering, she raced back to her alcove wrapped in a towel, murmuring hello to her parents, who were just beginning to stir. She dressed warmly in jeans and a white sweater and socks, then found the piece of paper on which Sam had written his phone number. She went downstairs to the kitchen. It was pretty early to call anyone, especially on a weekend, but she told herself that most families with little kids were up early anyway. She sat at the counter near the phone. She pushed Sam's number. Mrs. Lauer answered on the second ring.

"Hold on just a minute and I'll see if I can pull him out of bed," Mrs. Lauer said with a laugh after Violet identified herself and asked to speak to Sam. "He's usually a terrible beast in the mornings, but a call from you might just be enough to lure him out of his lair."

It took quite a while before Sam's groggy voice came through the receiver. During the wait, Violet stretched the phone cord across to the counter and grabbed an apple from the big blue pottery bowl. She stared out the kitchen window above the sink and admired the crisp red leaves on the bushes outside. When your life was in jeopardy, the world became a more beautiful place.

"Hello? Maid-of-All-Work? What's up at this ungodly hour of the morning?"

She swallowed her bite of apple quickly. "Hi, Sam. I know it's early, but I'm calling to see if you—well, I mean, to invite you—" She stopped and swallowed again, feeling shy.

"To your birthday party? Do triplets have one big party or three little ones?" His gravelly voice was teasing.

She cleared her throat. "It's not a birthday party. Our birthday isn't until the spring. But there's this dance at school this coming Friday. A Halloween Ball. It's probably going to be stupid, but I thought it would be more fun if maybe you could come, too. With me."

There. She'd said it.

"Well, I'd kind of like to," Sam said slowly, and his voice grew softer. "But, I mean, I don't know how to dance."

"No problem," replied Violet. "I don't know how to, either. I don't think anybody does."

"Oh."

She wasn't sure whether that meant he'd come or not. "If you want to, you could come over to Berkeley by BART after school on Friday and have supper with us before the dance. Then maybe you could sleep over here and go home in the morning when we all go back to work on the Chance Street shop. We have a sleeping bag you could use—" She was making these plans up as she went along and just hoped they would be all right with her parents.

"Okay, cool," said Sam. "Let me ask."

She ate more apple while he was gone, remembering the way his dark hair dipped into his eyes. Nice dark hair, just the color of hers, or the color hers used to be—would soon be again.

In a few minutes he was back with the news that he could come. "But my mom wants to clear it with yours," he said.

"That's great," said Violet. "But my mom's not up yet. I'll have her call your mom later." Then she fell silent. She wasn't sure what else to say. Fortunately Sam had something to say instead.

"I asked my dad about looking up old newspaper articles and stuff," he said. "And he told me, no problem. He can do it for us and print out whatever he finds. He just needs to know what names to look for."

"Well, we don't know Hal's last name—or Laela's, either," said Violet. "But if it's not too much trouble for him to look at all the wedding announcements for June of 1906, we might find something. And he could look up Verity Stowe. Or any of the Stowes, really."

"I'll see what he can do," promised Sam. "And I'll bring whatever I get when I come on Friday. And—uh—about this ball. Is it, you know, something fancy?"

"Just wear a costume," said Violet. "My sisters and I were planning to be aliens and dress all in black, with antennae. But I don't know, I might decide on something else."

He laughed. "How about an organ-grinder?"

Magic? Miracle? Or a plan?

That hadn't been so hard after all, Violet thought after they'd said good-bye and hung up. She didn't know why she'd said she might not be an alien. Maybe it had something to do with how she didn't want to be part of a threesome around him. She wanted to stand out.

But now there was the long week to get through—going to school, writing her paper...and watching for death traps—until she would see him on Friday.

Later that day the whole family helped Violet wash down the walls in the attic and wipe up the dust, and on Monday

Greg bought two gallons of cream-colored paint. "Not lavender?" asked Lily wistfully. "It's always been your color, Baby."

"No," said Violet decisively. "If I want color on the walls, I'll hang up some posters."

On Tuesday Lily gave Violet the old dining-room rug for her new bedroom. It was an oriental pattern in deep reds. Unrolled and vacuumed, it made the attic room seem larger and cozier. Violet hugged herself with anticipation. On Wednesday she brought Beth home after school and they made cream puffs filled with vanilla yogurt and carried the after-school snacks up to Violet's attic. In a last-ditch effort to remove all the purple traces from her hair, Violet and Beth washed her hair for a half hour, using up most of the shampoo. Beth scrubbed so hard that Violet screeched that her scalp would come off—and afterward Jasmine and Rose agreed there was no more than a sort of sheen left. Going to a dance with purple hair—even dressed as an alien—would be bad enough, but *dying* with purple hair would be even worse.

Violet had to smile at herself. She had never felt farther from death.

On Thursday at school, Mr. Koch stood by the window and glowered at the class. He said he was looking forward to reading everyone's report, due in class on Monday, and Halloween was no excuse. No late papers accepted. Thursday night Violet *meant* to get busy writing about the 1906 earthquake, but Greg and Lily started moving Violet's furniture up to the attic and, of course, she wanted to help. She still didn't really know what to write, anyway. All the bits of information she'd learned about 1906 didn't seem the sort of things that belonged in a paper for Mr. Koch.

Violet's bed had to be taken apart and reassembled in the attic, but everything else fit up through the hole. Her sisters came in to sit on the bed, and both proclaimed the room better than theirs and said they were jealous.

On Friday morning, Halloween, a series of small, sharp jolts sent the Jackstones bolting from their beds and into the doorways and under tables and desks. Violet huddled under her desk in the attic, fighting back the swirling smoke and cries of children in her head by concentrating on breathing. In, out; in, out. She heard a crash and cautiously edged across the attic to the hole in the floor. "Dad!" she wailed. "Help!" The ladder's bolts had shaken loose, and the ladder had fallen to the floor of the hallway below.

Lily and Greg emerged from their bedroom, and Lily gasped when she saw the ladder. "This is just too much, Greg," she quavered. "These quakes have got to stop."

Greg stood the ladder back up and held it while Violet climbed down. "I agree with you completely," he said, hugging Violet. "I'll tell them to stop immediately."

Jasmine and Rose pelted into the hallway. "It's not funny, Dad!" Jasmine cried.

But Rose was laughing. "What a way to wake up!"

"Give me an alarm clock any day," said Violet. Her heart was still racing.

"Poor Baby," her father said. "We'll have to see about that new staircase right away."

Over breakfast the family listened to the news. "An unwelcome Halloween trick was experienced by much of the Bay Area this morning as a chain of thumps jolted people from their beds," said the newscaster. Her voice was cheerful, as if the quakes were part of a pleasant weather forecast she was relating. "The largest of those jolts measured 2.9 on the Richter scale and seemed to be centered about three miles offshore along what geologists say may be a previously uncharted branch of the San Andreas fault."

Violet reached over and pushed the "off" button.

"Hey!" objected Rose.

"Leave it off," directed Lily. "I've heard much more than I wanted to hear."

At school everyone was talking about the quakes. The principal, Ms. Lynch, called an assembly to review earthquake preparedness. Violet diligently took notes about how much bottled water to have on hand, which supplies to put by, and how to stock the first-aid kit in anticipation of a really large quake. But the information didn't reassure her. The swaying bridge and crying children were shadows hovering nearby.

School ended with Mr. Koch's admonitions not to let the Halloween Ball interfere with their science papers. He would be chaperoning the dance with his wife and so would be on hand, he informed them with a smirk, to remind them. Most of the class groaned good-naturedly, but Violet's groan held real dismay.

Finally, she was hurrying home again. She went straight up to her attic room—the ladder now bolted firmly in place by Greg—determined to stop procrastinating. But first she laid out the clothes she would wear to the dance. The girls had decided on black tights and black sweatshirts. Their mom had fashioned black head scarves with antennae made from green florist's wire and orange pom-poms.

Violet's scarf lay on her bed, ready to be tried on. She stood in front of her mirror and pulled the band off her ponytail. She fluffed her hair with her fingers till it stood out around her face in a dark cloud. The purple highlights, at least in this light, were nearly invisible. The gymnasium, where the dance was to be held, would also be fairly dark. The scarf would hide most of her hair anyway. *What I really need,* she thought, *is one of those gigantic hats the Stowes used to make!*

She remembered that Lily had a big straw hat wrapped

with a green velvet bow. Her mom and dad had dressed in Victorian costumes for a party last Halloween. The long dress was still at the back of Lily's closet, Violet knew—a confection of green and black satin. For a second, as she pictured the dress, Violet could almost feel the long skirt swirl around her legs. Verity would have worn long skirts. Laela, too.

I wonder if Jazzy and Rosy would mind? she wondered, and started for her ladder. Would her mom be annoyed that the third alien head scarf wouldn't be worn?

She climbed down and ran downstairs to ask her mom about the Victorian costume. Lily had taken the afternoon off from work to help the girls get ready for the ball. She was happy to let Violet wear the dress, and they went back upstairs to find the hat that went with it.

"I don't have time to hem it for you," said Lily when Violet pirouetted in front of the long mirror on the back of the bathroom door. "But we can shorten the skirt with safety pins. No one will see them."

"That'll be great, Mom!" Violet twirled around again, the wide skirt billowing. She held her arms out as if she were dancing, as if she knew how to dance. She felt happy and foolish at once, lighthearted for the first time since being jolted from her bed that morning. In less than an hour Sam would arrive.

Less than an hour! And she still hadn't opened a single book about earthquakes.

She slipped out of the dress, left it on her parents' bed for her mom to pin, and hurried back up to her attic. She sat at her desk and reached for the pile of Mr. Koch's books. She had not gone to the library to look for others. These alone would have to do.

There were four books. The first was a geology text called, intimidatingly, *Plate Tectonics*. Violet blinked uncertainly. The next book, *Shining City,* looked more promising. It contained photographs of San Francisco before the quake, one hundred years ago and more. Violet studied the pictures.

In some, the hilly streets were crowded with horses and trains. In others, people walked the streets. Violet looked closely at the narrow streets of Chinatown and the wider streets off Russian Hill with large, ornate Victorian houses. She looked especially at the people. It was odd to think that any one of these people could have known Verity or Hal or Laela—could even *be* Verity or Hal or Laela.

In all the photos the men wore hats and the boys wore caps. The women, in dresses with skirts so long they swept the sidewalks, also wore hats as they walked along carrying shopping baskets or pushing huge wicker baby buggies. Little girls wearing white pinafores sported straw hats or wore huge floppy bows in their hair. It was a good time, Violet could see, for the Stowes' millinery shop to be in business.

The next book, *The Earth Shook, the Sky Burned,* described the 1906 quake in horrifying detail. Violet turned the pages quickly past the scenes of fire, of piles of rubble, a dead horse in the street, long lines of suddenly homeless people waiting for free bowls of soup. She had seen pictures like these before—but in color—on the evening news after earthquakes had hit the Bay Area or Los Angeles, or devastated cities in Mexico or Japan.

What had it been like for Hal, she wondered, when the big quake hit? He must have been an early bird to be awake so early in the morning. But he had been writing to V of his plan to take her away when the room began to shake and the bricks began to fall from the fireplace. He had jumped up, no doubt, spilling his ink but never noticing. He had run out of the house—but where did he live? Had he run to Chance Street to save Verity?

She sighed, picking up the last book and flipping through

it. *Our New San Francisco* was an old book. It seemed to be a compilation of newspaper articles and editorials about the rebuilding of the city after the destruction by the quake. She froze when she saw the name penned in flowing ink on the flyleaf—a name written in the distinctive handwriting she knew so well: *Hal Emerson, 1910.*

Could that be *her* Hal? Hal's own book? Her finger trembled as she traced the name. Had Hal's own book been lying here on her desk even before she'd found the first of the letters from him? But how could Mr. Koch have come to have Hal's book in the first place?

Just one more strange coincidence? Or one more odd piece that would fit—somehow—into this puzzle from the past?

Violet dropped the book, and it landed with a thud on her desk. A folded paper flew out of the back cover. Stooping to pick it up, she caught her breath. She held it in both hands, a part of her wanting to feel shocked, another part acknowledging that this was fate at work, once again.

It was a diary entry—in Laela's tightly curled handwriting.

November 1, 1906

Dear Diary,
  It is early morning now and I hold my pen with trembling hand. I awoke a short time ago, crying from a fearful dream, and though Hal held me close and comforted me, I could not stop shaking. He asked me to tell him what I'd dreamt, and I've tried—but my words did not convey my sense that this isn't just any old dream, that it means something more than the nighttime workings of an overactive imagination. Now he has gone back to sleep, but I must write this down.
  Because, you see, it isn't just my dream. It was V's

dream, too! It was the same old nightmare that jolted her awake so often in the last weeks of her life—the one about the bridge. "Something bad is going to happen, Laela," she kept saying. And then she would struggle to sit up, imploring me to help. "The people! The earth will take care of itself, but who will help the people?" I would try to soothe her back to sleep.

After the earthquake, I wondered if she had somehow foreseen that terrible event. She always had something mystical about her, with her great dark eyes and gentle languor. If the bridge dream foretells earthquakes, then what am I to do now that I've had it? V told me, and I didn't listen. I've told Hal, but he says I'm just remembering the dream because V had told me about it. And yet that cannot be, because I can picture everything so very clearly and V never described such details to me. The bridge was a fabulous golden bridge that spanned the entire bay. It was so huge it seemed to soar high in the sky before coming through the clouds again to touch land on the other side. It must have been high noon. I stood on this bridge looking down at the sailboats, with the sun directly overhead, warming me. And slowly I became aware that there was a dark-haired girl at my side. She did not speak. Then suddenly the bridge was shaking, and I grabbed the golden girder for support. But unlike real gold it was not solid, and seemed to melt away under my hand. Fire shot up around me, and through the smoke I saw three shadows reaching out their hands to me. Then we were falling, and falling around us, too, were strange vehicles, like horseless carriages or automobiles, but sleek and smooth and all shiny colors. There were people trapped inside, men, women, children—all screaming as we plummeted toward the churning water.

I awoke then, sick and miserable.

Poor sleepy Hal tried to reason it out. He said it is only natural, since we have lost Verity, that I should dream of a dark-haired girl at my side. He said it is only natural, since we survived the great destruction of San Francisco, that I should dream of other earthquakes. "You're not the only one who will forever link Verity and the quake in your memory," he said, reminding me of the letter he gave me soon after Verity's death, when I was still living at the Stowes'. He had been writing it to Verity at the exact moment the earthquake struck. An inkblot covered half the page. I kept that letter—hid it away in the back of my dresser and meant to take it with me when I left. There are no doubt other letters from Hal still stashed in secret cracks and crannies at that house on Chance Street—letters that I missed when I packed my bags to leave the Stowes' employ. No matter—the letters were only a poor substitute for the real Hal, <u>my</u> real Hal, who sat up comforting me tonight. "It was all a dream," he promised me, and I long to find solace in his words.

But I find I cannot. The dream felt more than a dream, though I don't know myself what I can mean by that. I don't believe the girl at my side was Verity at all; she did not have Verity's tremulous air but one of firmer resolve. And the quake that dissolved the golden bridge, I feel quite certain, was not the quake we suffered. It was a different quake, a different girl, a different time.

By dreaming of it all I feel I have been inexplicably altered. I feel Verity's urgency now in wishing I could help those poor people.

But how? Who are they? Where—and when?

Violet slipped the page from Laela's diary back into Hal's book and gently placed the book in the center of the desk. She realized she was holding her breath and expelled it in a soft puff. She sensed that she, too, had in the last moment been altered.

She stood up, picked up the book, and moved slowly toward the attic ladder. She walked, trying to hold in her urge to run, to pelt headlong down the ladder in panic, to race to the safety and warmth of her parents' and sisters' presence. She stood in the upstairs hallway and called out for them. "Jazzy? Rosy?" Her voice sounded odd to her ears, flat, warped as if she were speaking from inside a tunnel.

"In here," came Jasmine's voice.

Violet walked to her sisters' room, and there they were, trying on their black head scarves with the bobbing antennae. They looked up and saw her in the doorway, and Jasmine waggled her head to make the pom-poms dance.

"It's just us, Vi," Rose teased. "You don't have to look as if you've seen a ghost!"

Violet's laugh was shaky. "Almost." She closed the door behind her and came into their room. "I'm not sure what's going on, but—something's changed. We have to talk. Right now."

"Okay." Rose tossed back her long hair. "What about?"

"Bridges," said Violet.

Jasmine raised a delicate brow. "The girl with purple hair suddenly spoke about bridges," she stated. She glanced at Rose. "Go ahead, Rosy. Yes and no questions only."

"Is the purple hair a wig?" asked Rose.

"Nope."

"Is the girl with purple hair an alien?"

"Yes!" Jasmine giggled.

"Is it a *real* bridge she wants to talk about? Or the card game?"

"Who knows?" said Jasmine. "Anyway, it's yes and no questions only."

"Come on, you guys. I'm serious," interrupted Violet.

Rose sighed dramatically. "You mean it's not another lateral thinking riddle? No? Well, that's okay. Bridges. It's an interesting enough topic, but *I* would rather talk about highways or train stations. Wouldn't you, Jazz?"

"Quit joking," Violet said harshly. "*Listen* to me, you two."

"We are your captive audience," declared Rose magnanimously, and flopped down on her bed. Jasmine collapsed next to her, antennae bobbing.

Violet stood staring down at her sisters. In this silly mood they were unlikely to be receptive to her new theory. And yet she had to try. "All these letters and diary entries," she began firmly. "There's a reason that we're finding them. That *I'm* finding them."

"We know," said Rose. "You think they're like a prophecy—whatever happened to Verity Stowe happens to you. We've already gone through that, Baby."

"I know, I know. And I still do think it's true, but there's more. I think I've figured something out. The letters aren't just a warning to *me*—it's not just that *I* might die. It's bigger than that. We *all* might die."

"I feel perfectly healthy," said Jasmine. "And you're healthy, too, Vi."

"Physically healthy maybe, but I told you, she's getting paranoid," said Rose glumly.

"It's been too easy," Violet continued, ignoring their comments. How could she explain the vague theory that had come to her as she read Laela's dream?

"All these papers and letters and things have practically been planted in my path! Think of it—the first letter fell out of the old sales cupboard. The second from the wall after that little quake. The first diary entry in the old suitcase. The letter in the museum! Another diary entry in the box of cast-off things at the Academy. Another in the box at Sam's house— and he'd even pulled it out and saved it for me. It's as if I just walk along collecting these things, don't you see?"

"You're giving me the creeps, Vi," murmured Jasmine, sitting up and looking distinctly nervous. She untied her scarf and tossed it on the bed. "It's like a—a trail."

"It gives me the creeps, too," said Violet. "And it gets worse. Because just now I was sitting in my room working on my history project, and what should fall out of one of the books? *Another* diary entry! And not only that," she went on, ignoring her sisters' excited exclamations, "the book I found it in belonged to someone named Hal Emerson. He wrote his name inside."

"Hal?" squeaked Jasmine. "Was Hal's last name Emerson?"

"I think it was. At least, the handwriting is exactly the same as in the letters."

"I don't believe it," snorted Rose. "That is just too much coincidence!"

Violet looked at her sisters and couldn't help the note of triumph that crept into her voice. "Exactly! It *is* too much coincidence. That must mean—it *isn't* coincidence."

The three of them stared at each other for a long moment. Then Rose jumped up. "Well, come on, let's see the book and the entry!"

"In a minute. First I have to tell the dream I had—"

"A dream?" yelled Rose. "Who cares about a dream?"

"We want to see the diary entry first," insisted Jasmine.

"No, just *listen*. The dream matters. It's another—connection. I dreamed that I was on the Golden Gate Bridge with my science class. It was noon, I could tell because the sun was right overhead. And suddenly there was an earthquake and the bridge was shaking like crazy—and ghostly children were screaming and crying, and there were flames— and then Mr. Koch was pushing books at me and yelling that I needed to get busy on my work. Then I woke up. It wasn't even really a scary dream—I mean, I've had dreams of those children before. But then I read Laela's diary entry." She unfolded it. "Listen to this."

She read them Laela's dream, then handed them the page to inspect for themselves. She also showed them Hal's signature in the book. "Do you see what I mean?"

"You think that there's going to be another earthquake," Rose stated flatly.

"Yes," said Violet.

"Well, of *course* there is. This is California. We've already had zillions of quakes."

"No, I mean a *big* one. Like the one in 1906. Big enough to destroy the bridge."

Jasmine shook her head. "The Golden Gate Bridge? Oh, Vi, I don't think so. The bridges were all retrofitted after the earthquake in 1989, remember? We saw that on the news."

Rose spoke up. "And you're forgetting that the bridges weren't even built across the bay when Laela wrote this entry. So she couldn't be talking about the Golden Gate Bridge."

"But that's just what I mean," Violet said fiercely. "Verity and Laela didn't even know what they were dreaming. It's as if their dreams are a prophecy. Look, Laela mentions strange, shiny vehicles. Those are modern cars, of course—but she didn't know that. She didn't know there would be a golden bridge, either, but there is one. And I had the very same sort of dream—with an important difference. In my dream, Mr. Koch was pushing books on me. I thought it meant I'd better get started on my science project, but now I think it was a message that I should open the books he gave me and find Laela's diary entry."

"I wonder how Mr. Koch got hold of Hal's book in the first place," mused Jasmine.

"I'm going to call him now and ask," said Violet, jumping up.

"What!" Rose looked shocked. "Call a teacher at home?"

"Why not? This is important."

"Brave Baby," said Jasmine. "But why not just wait a couple hours and you can ask him at the dance. He and his wife agreed to be some of our chaperones, so I know he'll be there."

"Girls!" interrupted the voice of their mother calling up the stairs. "Your dad and Sam are here!"

"Send Sam up!" called Violet, and she went to the top of the stairs to meet him, her sisters close behind.

"Hi, Vi!" he said cheerfully. "Good evening, Ladies of Mars. Or is it Venus?"

"Jupiter," said Rose. "Where's *your* costume?"

He was wearing blue jeans and a red sweatshirt, his dark mop of hair windblown. He looked wonderful, but Vi's earlier excitement about the dance was overshadowed by this new development.

"Don't worry about that now," said Violet, taking his arm and propelling him into the pink-and-yellow bedroom. "We have something really important to talk about."

"I brought a mask," he told her. "Not an organ-grinder, though. Not even a monkey." He reached into his back pocket and pulled out a rubber Frankenstein mask.

"That'll be great, Sam," she said, hardly looking at it. "But listen. Something's happened." She thrust the book and diary page into his hands.

He looked around the room and grinned at Rose and

Jasmine. "I guess it's got to be business before pleasure." But he sat down obediently next to Violet on Jasmine's bed and struggled to read Laela's handwriting.

"Violet thinks there's going to be a big earthquake that destroys the Golden Gate Bridge," Rose told him as he finished reading Laela's dream. "She says she had the same sort of dream herself."

"Hmm," Sam said, looking intrigued now. "And why do you think this is all happening? I mean, who or what is making it happen? Is it magic?"

"Whooooo," wailed Rose. "It's a ghost!"

But Violet didn't laugh with the others. "Rosy, I think you're right."

"Oh, come on," said Jasmine. "Not ghosts now! You don't believe in ghosts."

"Laela's ghost," Violet said, her mind whirling to fit this new puzzle piece. "Trying to do a good deed to make up for getting rid of Verity so *she* could marry Hal."

"I thought we had decided that she *didn't* kill Verity," said Rose.

"Well, she did *something*." Violet chewed her lip. "Something she felt was wrong."

"Look, I've got something to show you," Sam said before Rose could respond. "My dad looked in the newspaper archives for me and printed out copies of what he found." He reached for his backpack and unzipped it, pulling out a manila envelope. "It's not much, but it does answer some of the big questions."

He handed it to Violet. She lifted the flap and pulled out the folded papers. Her sisters pressed close to see.

First there was a short article with the headline: FASHIONABLE HATS FILCHED. "Look at the byline," Sam said, pointing. "Look who wrote it."

"By Hal Emerson," shrieked Rose.

"He worked for the paper!" Violet said, and felt as if another piece of a puzzle had dropped into place. "He was a reporter. That explains why he was awake when the earthquake hit. Reporters must keep all sorts of weird hours in order to cover stories for the newspaper." She read the article aloud.

"FASHIONABLE HATS FILCHED
—by Hal Emerson

"Police were called to the Stowe Millinery shop on Chance Street on Friday after the owner, Mr. Albert Stowe, raised the alarm that a thief had entered sometime during the afternoon and stolen a dozen made-to-order ladies' hats. The shop room was untended for a short time because the Stowe family members, who all work in the business, were helping one of the daughters, Miss Verity Stowe, who had fallen down the stairs in the back of the building, sustaining both a strained back and a twisted ankle. By the time the family had settled Miss Stowe in her bedchamber and returned to the shop room, the hats were gone.

"Police speculate that the thief was a passerby— or even a potential customer—who, upon entering the shop and finding it empty, took the chance to make off with the beautiful creations meant to adorn the heads of San Francisco's finest matrons. Mr. Stowe has promised to make new hats for the customers whose hats were stolen, but for some, the replacements will come too late. Mrs. Gilbert Morrison, of Haight Street, had planned to wear her new hat to an engagement that same evening. 'Nonetheless,' she is reported as saying, 'I will continue to patronize Stowe's Millinery. Mr. Stowe and his wife are simply the finest milliners in all of California.'

"Any information leading to the return of the stolen hats and the apprehension of the thief should be directed to the Chief of Police.

"It's weird, isn't it," said Violet, laying down the paper, "reading about the Stowes—and knowing that Hal wrote this himself."

"Yeah," agreed Rose. "It makes them all seem more real. I bet this is how Hal met the Stowes in the first place. Remember Laela's diary entry that mentions how her 'poor charge' had fallen down the stairs, and that's why they needed to hire a companion? Probably Hal met the family when he came to cover this burglary for the newspaper, and he met Verity then, too."

"And fell in love with her," added Jasmine. "But for some reason the parents wouldn't let him date her—"

"They didn't call it dating in those days," said Sam. "He probably asked to court her, and the parents said no—because she was too sickly. We keep reading about how weak she was."

"But he didn't want to take no for an answer," said Violet dreamily, taking up the story. "So he had the idea of asking his friend Laela to apply for the companion job. He probably wanted to use Laela as a way to get to know Verity. He didn't know that Laela was in love with him."

"Look at the next article," Sam directed her. "It tells you more."

Violet looked down at the page in her hand and drew a ragged breath. It was an obituary. She sat staring at it until Sam gently removed it from her hand and read aloud:

"STOWE, VERITY ELIZABETH—

"Miss Verity Stowe, age 18 years, passed away on April 17, at her home on Chance Street in San Francisco after a long decline. The eldest daughter of Albert and Eleanor Stowe, owners and proprietors of Stowe Millinery, Miss Verity Stowe was at first thought to have perished in the earthquake which struck early the next morning.

But her companion, Miss Laela Baublitz, hired to assist with her care in these past months, reported that Miss Stowe drew her last breath shortly after retiring for the night. Doctors concur that death occurred due to heart failure, not an uncommon occurrence in wasting diseases of the sort from which Miss Stowe long had suffered. Miss Stowe is survived by her parents and two sisters, Jane and Rachel Stowe, age 12, also of Chance Street. A memorial service will be held on Saturday at St. Paul's Church."

Heart failure, Violet thought uncomfortably.

"She was only eighteen," whispered Jasmine.

"But," said Rose, "she died of an illness. So that lets Laela off the hook."

Sam looked puzzled. "But why should she feel guilty if she didn't have anything to do with Verity's death?"

Violet tried to ignore her heart. Was it really fluttering madly—or was she just imagining it? "Baublitz," she read aloud from the clipping. "So now we know Laela's last name, too. Is there anything else, Sam?" She reached for the papers he held. "Oh, listen to this one. It's you-know-who's wedding announcement!

"BAUBLITZ-EMERSON

"Miss Laela Baublitz and Mr. Hal Emerson, both of San Francisco, were married on June 20, 1906, at the Courthouse in this city. Miss Baublitz, now Mrs. Emerson, worked until her marriage as a nurse/companion, employed by the Albert Stowe family of Chance Street. Mr. Emerson, a well-respected reporter with this newspaper, was born in San Francisco. The couple plan to make their home in New Jersey, where Mr. Emerson will work for the *Trenton Times.*"

"Laela got her man," said Jasmine with satisfaction.

"I still want to know what Laela did to feel so guilty about," muttered Sam.

"And I," said Violet, "want to know why I had the same dream that she and Verity did. That's the key, I'll bet you anything, and—"

She broke off when Greg called up the stairs for them all to come down for supper. Lily had ordered two large pizzas, which were set out in the dining room along with a big bowl of fresh salad and tall glasses of juice. "Now don't stuff yourselves too much or you won't be able to dance!" Lily told them with a smile as they trooped into the room.

They settled themselves at the table and heaped their plates with salad and hot pizza. "Don't mention Hal and Laela," Violet warned Sam in a whisper. "My mom and dad don't know anything."

She was silent, only picking at her pizza while the others talked about normal everyday things like school and Halloween and earthquakes. She kept feeling that despite all the incredible connections between the past and the present, between Verity's life and her own, there was still some connection they were meant to make but hadn't. And time was passing.

The first trick-or-treaters were arriving as they finished eating. Lily went to the door with a basket of chocolate bars.

Sam waited in the living room, talking to Greg while the girls rushed upstairs. Violet dressed in the green-and-black Victorian-style dress. She fluffed out her hair the way she'd done earlier, then tied the large hat with the green velvet ribbon under her chin. She even dabbed on some lip gloss.

Her sisters looked up in surprise when she joined them in the living room. They appeared identical in their alien costumes, golden hair streaming over their shoulders from under the black scarves.

"I changed my mind," Violet said simply. "Hope you don't mind."

"No," said Rose, with a little frown. "But—"

"You look gorgeous!" cried Jasmine.

"Are you Verity or Laela?" Sam asked in a low voice. He pulled the rubber Frankenstein mask out of his jacket pocket. "Wish I had a Hal mask instead!"

The needlepoint portrait flashed in Violet's head. *"Ssh,"* she cautioned him as her parents came in from the kitchen with a camera. "I like Frankenstein just fine."

They posed for photographs, first all together, then just the aliens, then Frankenstein and the Victorian Lady, then the triplets with Violet in the middle. She knew she stood apart from her sisters more than ever tonight—but now she didn't care.

She *was* different. She was special. She was the one who was part of a plan, the one to whom past and future were revealed.

16

Greg drove them to the Halloween Ball, where they met Beth, who was standing with Casey Banks and Brett Hudson in the school gym. Beth wore a black witch's hat and a long cape. She was fending off the boys, both wearing vampire costumes, with her broomstick.

The gym had been transformed with dim lights, pulsing music, a multitude of leering jack-o'-lanterns, and scarecrows strategically placed in corners to hide the storage lockers. Long tables covered by cheerful pumpkin-sprigged tablecloths were stocked with snacks and cold drinks. There was no place to talk quietly to tell Beth about the latest diary entry, the book with Hal's inscription, and the news clippings Sam had brought. The music was too loud, the gym too crowded with costumed creatures. But it had been arranged that Beth would sleep over at the Jackstones, so there would be time to catch up later.

Sam grabbed Violet's hand and swung her into the crowd,

and there were Beth and Rose and Jasmine all bobbing around amid ghosts, ghouls, and a dragon, all holding soft drinks sloshing in their hands and wearing wild smiles on their painted faces. The music pounded with Violet's heartbeat.

She had been so excited about coming to the dance with Sam. And yet she felt an urgency connected with Laela's dream. There was something she had missed, something vitally important *not* to miss. She felt dizzy and frightened.

She saw Mr. Koch with some of the other teachers and parents near the door, holding drinks and swaying to the music. None were in costume. Some of them looked bored, some amused. Mr. Koch looked as if he'd like to dance. A pretty, dark woman in a tight red dress stood next to him.

After the song ended, Violet stepped away from the circle of her friends. "I'll be back in a minute," she shouted to Sam over the music, and pushed through the mass of dancers.

"Hello, Violet," Mr. Koch shouted when she reached him. "You look stunning in that hat." He nodded at the woman in the red dress. "My wife wore one like that at our wedding!"

"It wasn't nearly that big!" laughed the woman.

"I need to talk to you," Violet said urgently.

Mr. Koch looked surprised. "Are you all right?"

"I feel dizzy—"

"Let me get you a Coke." His wife turned to the table.

"I need to ask you something," Violet said quickly. The teacher leaned closer in order to hear her over the din. "Those books you loaned me for my paper. Where did you get them?"

"They were some things I got after my mother died and we had to clear out her house."

"Your mother—?" Violet repeated faintly. She looked up at his face. "Did your mother know someone named Hal Emerson?"

"Why, yes," Mr. Koch replied in surprise. "I should think she did! He was her father."

"You mean Hal Emerson was your *grandfather*?" Violet was incredulous. "Was Laela Baublitz your grandmother?"

"That's right—but how could you know?" He looked amazed. "Tell me about it."

Violet accepted the cold drink from Mrs. Koch and sipped it. She wasn't sure what to say. She didn't know how to tell him about Hal's letters to Verity, about Laela's diary pages, written nearly a century ago, having landed by something far stranger than coincidence in Violet's possession. How could she explain to Mr. Koch that there was something going on, some pattern she now believed she was meant to follow, set in motion by these papers from the past and centering, somehow, around an earthquake?

"Did you ever hear of anyone named Verity?" she asked.

He couldn't hear her, so she had to shout it. "Did you ever know someone named Verity?"

He set his glass down and shouted back at her. "Verity was my mother's name!"

Violet was staring at him. "How could your mother be Verity? I know she died before she even got married—"

"Whoa, slow down." The teacher took hold of Violet's arm and steered her toward the door of the gym. "Mind if we just talk in the hall a minute? It's so loud I can't hear a thing." He pushed open the door and led her through. In the hallway the air was cool and the beat of the music receded.

Violet clasped her hands in front of her. She had so many questions and didn't know where to begin. She had completely forgotten about Sam. Mr. Koch folded his arms across his chest and leaned back against the wall. "Now, if you don't mind, tell me what's going on."

She nodded. "I'd love to tell you—but I just don't know what's going on! I really don't! Oh, it's hard to explain, but weird things have been happening. I've been finding out all sorts of things. I know that an eighteen-year-old girl named Verity Stowe died in 1906—just hours before the big earthquake. But she couldn't have been your mother, could she?"

"No," he said. "My mother's maiden name was Verity Emerson. So it's a different Verity. But I wonder—*hmm*." He looked at the ceiling thoughtfully, trying to remember something. "I know that my mother was named for a dear friend of her parents. Maybe that was your Verity Stowe." He frowned at her. "Now tell me more about these 'weird things' that are happening, as you say. Are you saying they're somehow connected to your science paper? Is this a novel excuse for telling me you won't have the paper done on time?"

Violet didn't answer. Her thoughts were racing along as she shuffled a few new pieces of the puzzle and worked them into place. Laela and Hal had married after Verity was dead, she knew that much already. Then later they must have had a daughter—and named her Verity after Verity Stowe.

"Are your grandparents still alive?" she asked abruptly. It would be amazing if she could actually meet Hal and Laela and talk to them, ask Laela what she'd felt so guilty about. Ask what she was supposed to do about the dreams. But her hopes were dashed when Mr. Koch shook his head.

"Oh, no, they've been dead a good thirty years. And my mother died last year—that's when I cleaned out the house she'd lived in and came into possession of my grandparents' books and papers. I suppose my mother must have inherited them from her parents years ago. But I'd never seen them until I had to clear out my mother's house." He looked at her thoughtfully. "There was a letter among my grandfather's papers you might be interested in seeing. It's very personal— a sort of family treasure. But since you already know something about my grandparents, you might like to see it."

"A letter?" Violet's voice was sharp. "From Hal?"

"No—from a woman named Verity, who apparently loved him very much. Possibly it's the Verity Stowe you know about. It's a very melodramatic letter, but rather sweet at the same time. I'll let you read it if you like."

"Oh yes, please, Mr. Koch! Do you have it with you now?" Violet felt like jumping up and down. "Oh, please, Mr. Koch—it could be so important!"

"I don't have it with me, no," the teacher replied dryly. "I can't say I usually bring old family letters with me to a school dance. I'll bring it to school on Monday." Her face fell, and he continued. "Or—I live only around the corner from school—you can walk over with me and get it right after the dance."

"Oh, thank you, Mr. Koch! Oh, that would be wonderful!" exclaimed Violet. She glanced at the closed gym door, worrying that Sam or one of her sisters would come barging out looking for her. "Can we go now?"

He raised a bushy eyebrow. "How about you first tell me why you want to know? This seems to me to have very little to do with your assignment."

She studied the tiled floor for a moment, then shook her head. "I'm—I'm sorry," she stuttered. "It's pretty complicated." She looked up into his face, saw the puzzled expression. "I think it's sort of to do with what you said in class the other week—about how the past is all around us, if we could only see it? Well, I've—I think I've been seeing bits of it."

"Go on," he said.

"Well, I meant to write about fault lines and geology, you know, and the 1906 quake. But I sort of got sidetracked away from the *earth*—and on to the *people* who lived then."

"They're connected," he reminded her.

"Anyway, I've been looking at lots of, um, original sources."

"And you're writing all this up for your project?"

"Oh, could I? I mean, yes! That's what I'm trying to do."

"Scientists need proof." Mr. Koch frowned. "And this all sounds very mysterious. I'm not sure I see how anything you've found out about my family can be connected to your earthquake paper."

"But you've just said people are connected with the earth," Violet explained hesitantly. She wasn't used to challenging Mr. Koch on anything. "I think I do have proof—"

The door to the gym opened and the thud of the music swelled. Frankenstein poked his head out. "Vi?" he called to her, sounding surprised. "I've been looking everywhere for you. Aren't you coming?"

She nodded. "Sorry, Sam! Just a second." She turned back to Mr. Koch and spoke hurriedly. "I think the people I've been researching are connected to the earthquakes just like fissures in the earth connect the fault lines. I have proof—but I need more. And so, um, anything you can tell me about your grandparents will help me understand—things—better, I think."

Sam stepped out into the hallway with them and closed the door.

"Info about my grandparents!" Mr. Koch grinned at Sam. "In this getup she looks like she could *be* one of my grandparents." He looked back at Violet curiously. "That's one of the more unusual requests I've had from a student. But if you think it will help your paper, I'm happy to oblige. My grandfather was a journalist, I know that much. He married my grandmother just a few months after the 1906 quake. She had been a nurse."

Violet was nodding. "A companion—to a sick girl," she said softly. Next to her, Sam gave a start of surprise.

"Was she?" Mr. Koch said. "Well, women usually didn't work once they married, you know, and my grandmother didn't either, after she married my grandfather. They moved to the East Coast—to New Jersey. My mother was born there—quite a few years later. She was their only child. She grew up and married my dad, who was from California. So my brothers and I were born here—and here I still am today, with two kids already in college, and I live, as I told you, just around the corner."

Mr. Koch opened the door to the gym so they could return to the dance. A wave of music rolled over them.

"Mr. Koch?" Violet had to shout again. "Did your grandmother—um—I mean, was she a *nice* person? Did you like her?" Maybe Mr. Koch knew what guilty secret Laela had carried with her to the grave.

"I was just a kid when she died," he replied. "But she was a very sweet old lady."

"And did your grandfather love her?" *Why did Hal ever marry her in the first place?* she wanted to ask. He was passionately in love with Verity, and yet just months after her death he'd gone and married Laela. What had made him do such a thing?

"They were devoted to each other," Mr. Koch shouted over the din. "My mother often spoke about her happy childhood." He smiled at Violet as he held the door for her to pass through. "But just wait till you see the letter. It gives the word *romance* a new meaning."

"I can't wait!" she yelled back at him.

"But you have to!" Then he walked back over to his wife. Violet reached for Sam's hand.

"Weirder and weirder," he said. "What was all that about?"

She led him across the dance floor, looking for her sisters and Beth. The identical aliens were thick in the throng of dancers, antennae jiggling wildly, but Beth was standing by herself near the food tables, munching cookies disconsolately. At the sight of Violet, she brightened.

"Hey!" Sam yelled, his foghorn voice easily rising over the noise. "She ditched me, too!" His words were light, but Violet sensed that his mask hid an unhappy expression.

"I'm really sorry," she said to both Beth and Sam. "But I had to talk to Mr. Koch."

"What?" Beth couldn't hear her through the music.

"I'll tell you both about it later," she shouted. "Let's dance."

Sam took her hand gladly and then reached out for Beth's as well. He pulled both girls back into the middle of the surging crowd of kids. As they danced, other kids joined them till there was a circle of dancers. Beth's face lost her tense expression and Sam started laughing. By the time the song ended, everyone was singing along. They all danced as a group for the next song, and the next. When a slow song started, the group broke into pairs. Beth slipped away with several other witches.

Sam drew Violet close. He wrapped his arms around her waist. No one knew how to dance, she reflected, but it was nice to hang on to each other, to feel the beat of Sam's heart through his sweatshirt. *Eat, drink, and be merry,* she thought, twining her arms around him tightly and pushing back her hat to rest her head against his shoulder. *For tomorrow we may die.*

It was an old saying her father sometimes quoted, and it seemed particularly appropriate now. The puzzle from the past was connected to the present, with a strange dream at its center. No one could ever be sure what tomorrow would bring—but the dream held a clue to the future. There would be another earthquake; Violet knew that now as a certainty. But when?

CHAPTER 17

After the Halloween Ball was over, most of the students vanished into cars lined up at the curb, but Violet waited for Mr. Koch and his wife. Sam, Beth, Jasmine, and Rose were sitting outside on the stone steps of the school waiting for Mr. Jackstone, who was coming to pick them all up. "I just have to get something from Mr. Koch's house," she told them as the teacher and his wife emerged from the big front doors. "I'll run right back."

"There you are, Violet," said Mr. Koch genially. "Ready?"

"Oh yes!"

"I'm coming with you," said Sam, stuffing his mask into his jacket pocket and hurrying after her through the crisp October dark. A few late-lingering trick-or-treaters straggled past them with bulging sacks of goodies. Sam tucked his arm through Violet's as they walked behind the Koches. "What is he going to give you that can't wait till Monday?"

"Something for my project," she murmured, unsure why she wanted to keep this newest letter to herself until she'd read it. *Maybe,* she thought uneasily, *I'm afraid of what it will say.*

The teacher's house was just around the corner. Violet and Sam waited in the front hallway while Mr. Koch rummaged around in the drawers of a desk in the living room and his wife hung up their jackets. It seemed funny to see Mr. Koch inside a regular house, very much like Violet's own, rather than at the front of a classroom.

In seconds he had found what he was searching for, and he handed Violet the long white envelope with a flourish. "Take good care of it, and return it to me on Monday."

"Oh yes. I will." She held the letter securely with two hands in front of her.

"She'll guard it with her life," Sam promised. Then, as they left the house, he whispered to Violet, "And I'll guard yours with mine."

Before Sam could ask again about the letter, Violet took his hand and started running back to the others, the motion of her long skirt sending dry leaves flying. Just as they turned the corner, they saw Violet's dad driving up to the curb in front of the school, tooting the horn.

"What were you getting?" asked Beth as everyone was climbing in.

"Tell you later," replied Violet in a whisper, removing her large hat. *After I've read it myself.* She slipped the envelope into the pocket of her skirt.

But she didn't have a chance until much later. First, before they went up to bed, Lily and Greg had to hear all about the dance over a late-night snack of leftover pizza and slices of apple pie. Rose suggested popcorn. Violet, seeing her chance, volunteered to make it.

She read the letter in the kitchen while corn popped in the microwave. She read it straight through, then read it again. *This is bizarre,* she thought. She knew she had to share the letter now, try to have the others make sense of it for her.

When she carried the big bowl of fragrant popcorn back to the living room, her parents were gone. Sam was rolling out his borrowed sleeping bag on the living-room floor, and Jasmine, Rose, and Beth were all lazing around on the couches chatting with him.

She set the bowl down in front of Sam, then walked to the fireplace and stood in front of it. She cleared her throat, swishing her long skirt dramatically. She pulled the white envelope out of her pocket and waved it in the air.

"Look at Vi," yawned Rose. "Waving the white flag. Are you surrendering?"

"Was there a war? Did I miss something?" murmured Jasmine.

Beth's voice was as sharp as the point on her witch's hat. "Come on, come on, already. Let's see it!"

"Wait a second—is that *another* letter?" shrieked Rose, antennae bobbing madly. "Where on earth did you get it?"

"Don't tell me it's from Hal or I'll faint," moaned Jasmine. "I swear I will."

Sam sat down on top of his sleeping bag. He just looked at her, waiting.

"It's not a letter from Hal this time," Violet told them. "It's *to* Hal. It's been in Mr. Koch's family for years."

"Why would it be in Mr. Koch's family?" demanded Beth.

"Just another one of those coincidences," Violet said slowly, "which can't be coincidences at all. It turns out Hal and Laela were his grandparents."

She braced herself for the shrieks and screeches that would surely follow this announcement, but the others were silent. After a long moment, Sam summed up their reaction with a single word: *"Wow."*

"The letter's really hard to read," Violet continued. "The writing is faint and all sort of cramped up together and blotchy, with ink stains and smudges. It's not handwriting I've seen before." Their silence filled the room with expectancy, and then Violet began to read aloud:

"April 17, 1906, 8:00 in the evening—

"My dear Hal,
"I hope you will be able to read this. Always before I have dictated to Laela the letters I've sent you. But this time I must write to you privately.
"This is a very difficult letter to write to one I hold in such high esteem, but write I must. You have been a stalwart friend to me since we first spoke at length last winter when you came to report the burglary. I have regarded you since then as someone special. I know it may not be seemly for me to write to you in such a frank manner, but I have little time left to waste in mannered conventions. I must tell you what is in my heart.
"I know you say you love me and want to save me from my family; I know you have planned a wonderful, dashing escape. But I would not be fair to myself or to you—nor, indeed, to our mutual friend, Laela—if I did not tell you right now that I cannot marry you. No, Hal. I shall never marry you.
"I am very ill indeed, though I know you have not wanted to believe this. The unvarnished truth is that I do not have long to live. The doctors have said this—I overheard them telling my father—and I feel it inside. My heart and my blood are so weak, I can barely lift my hand. But I must.
"You have told me many times you will marry no

one if you cannot have me because to do so would spoil the memory of our 'amazing love'—to quote your own words. Oh, Hal, I need to tell you you have built up a fantasy world. There can be no happily-ever-after for us.

"I will not live long, but you will. And I want you to marry and be happy in that life. Your vow to marry no one saddens me, and my love and affection for you compel me to beg you to reconsider. I do not require that sort of sacrifice from you. Indeed, I will be unable to rest in my grave. You have been so good to me. You have brought me much joy. Your letters have been a wonderful diversion for me in my illness. They, coupled with Laela's company, have helped me to cope with being bedridden and weak for so long now.

"It is Laela I wish now to discuss. <u>She</u> is the woman I want you to marry instead of me. Yes, Hal. Laela loves you as much as or even more than I do. You have had a paragon as your friend for a long time now, but have been blind to her charms. It is time to open your eyes now, Hal, that you may see what perfect happiness you might have together.

"She knows nothing of this note. I am writing it under great strain. I am so weak that my fingers are as water.

"I will die very soon, Hal, and it saddens me that I cannot ever become your wife.

"But Laela can—and it is my most pressing desire that you and she should make each other happy. I beg you, Hal, as my dying wish, to have her as your wife. And I give you both my blessing, and shall watch you from above.

Your V"

Violet laid the letter on the coffee table.

"Wow," Sam said again, very softly. "That's heavy stuff." He reached for the letter as if to assure himself that the words Violet had read them really were there on the paper. He passed the letter to Beth, who read it and passed it on to Rose and Jasmine. Their twin heads bumped as they bent over it. Violet sat on the floor near the couch and waited.

"What does it mean?" asked Beth finally.

"It explains why Hal married Laela," replied Violet. "It's amazing."

"What's even more amazing," said Sam, "is the way pieces of the story keep falling into your hands. I agree with you now, it *is* too amazing to be chance."

"It's what I keep saying." Violet reached over and smoothed the old letter. "One thing just keeps leading to the next."

"A real paper trail," Beth said.

"And an earthquake trail," said Violet pointedly. "Because all along there have been little quakes or tremors—almost every time I've found something. It's all got to be connected."

"But how can it be?" demanded Rose. She had been sitting silently through all their discussion, her expression tight and worried. "It can't be!"

"There were those jolts this morning, right?" Violet leaned toward Rose, her voice hushed. "And now more information has appeared. Laela's dream entry. Hal's name in the book. And Mr. Koch's letter from Verity."

"I don't like this," mumbled Rose. "Things like this can't really happen."

"How do you know?" asked Sam mildly.

"That's right." Jasmine nodded. "Whether they *can* happen or not, they *are* happening."

Violet nodded, too. "And there's going to be another quake. A big one." She shuddered, wrapping her arms tightly around her knees. "It's part of—whatever all this is about. I *know* it."

"I think this is stupid!" cried Rose, slapping her hand down on Verity's letter. The others jumped. "What's the point of learning all this stuff about Verity and Hal and everything if all it does is warn us that there's going to be a big earthquake sometime? I mean, there's nothing anyone can do about that, is there? It would have made more sense if it was what Vi was worried about in the first place, that somehow the letters were a warning personally for *her*—to keep her from being murdered. At least then we'd have a chance of *doing* something. You know, guarding her with our lives, looking out for killers in the bushes. *Something!*" Two bright red spots stained Rose's cheeks, signs, Violet knew, that her sister was very upset. "This is all a waste of time. Instead of sitting down here getting scared about something we can't do anything about, we should just go to bed." Rose stood up. "Which is where I'm going. Good night."

The others watched in silence as she stalked out of the room.

"She's scared," observed Beth. "You can't blame her, really."

"And she's probably right." Jasmine sighed, also getting up. "It seems like we're in the thick of some really cool mystery, and the story of Laela and Hal is part of it, but in the end, we don't know why we're getting this story, and the story doesn't really have anything to do with the earthquakes, either. So I'm confused, and I'm exhausted, and I'm on the cleanup committee that has to be at the gym tomorrow at nine o'clock." She yawned. "So I'm going to bed, too. See you guys in the morning."

After her sisters left, Violet turned to Sam and Beth. "What are we supposed to do?"

"That's just it," Sam said gently. "I don't think we can do anything about anything. There's no way to pinpoint when a quake will hit. If Laela's dream were really any use, it would have told us *when*."

"I think we should just keep researching the story of Laela and Hal," Beth murmured. "We can at least do that. I want to know what happened after Hal got this letter from Verity."

"We *know* what happened," said Violet with a sigh. "Verity was dying and she wrote this totally generous letter to Hal, so even though Hal loved *her,* he went along with her wishes that he should marry *Laela*. And that was nice for Laela, because she'd loved him all along anyway. But we still don't know what Laela felt so guilty about."

"The point is," Beth said wearily, "that there are all these tantalizing bits of information floating around, and they seem to lead to something—but then they don't."

"Is it magic?" mused Sam. "Or is it the ghost of Laela feeling guilty about something and trying to tell her story? Is it some mysterious force of nature that just sort of points out weird parallels between the life of a girl called Verity who lived ninety years ago and the life of a girl called Violet who lives now? Maybe. We don't know."

"Rosy and Jazzy are right," Beth said. "The best thing to do is just go to bed!"

She and Violet said good night to Sam and left him on the living-room floor, stretched out in his sleeping bag. They went upstairs and brushed their teeth in the bathroom, then climbed up the ladder into Violet's attic bedroom.

"I like your new room," murmured Beth, wiggling into her sleeping bag on the floor next to Violet's bed. "It's cozy. I wonder why you didn't think of moving up here ages ago?"

Violet hung the Victorian dress up on a hook in the rafters. She set the big hat on her desk. Then she climbed into bed and lay very still under her lavender quilt. Pieces of the day turned like a kaleidoscope in her mind: Hal's name in the book. Laela's diary entry. The dance. Mr. Koch's grandparents. The letter from Verity.

She thought about her new room. *Why did I move up here?*

She'd made her decision to claim the attic for her own when she thought she might not have long to live. She'd invited Sam to the dance then, too. She was making braver decisions—all on her own—since she'd found Hal's letters.

If she hadn't decided to go to the Chance Street shop that first day, would one of her sisters have found the letter from Hal? Or had it been meant only for her? Mr. Koch's books with Laela's diary entry and Hal's name inside were on her desk even before she'd found the first letter. Her topic—the 1906 earthquake—had already been assigned by Mr. Koch, the grandson of Laela and Hal.

Violet sighed and turned over in bed. The pieces of this mystery were as baffling as one of Jasmine's lateral thinking puzzles.

Then Violet sat up suddenly. *Maybe that is what this is!* she thought wildly. Maybe the pieces of the puzzle didn't fit together in the way she'd been trying to fit them. Maybe the meaning of all that had been happening would become clear if she could shift the pieces into a different perspective.

The story of Hal and Verity and Laela had shown her how the past had parallels in the present. Not just parallels between Violet's own life and Verity's, but other parallels, too. The letters from Hal and the diary entries had taught Violet to believe in parallels and to see past her own situation to *other* parallel situations. Like the earthquakes that happened then and now. Like the dreams of bridges.

Violet pushed back her quilt and swung her legs over the side of the bed. "Beth!"

There was no answer. Violet peered into the darkness. She saw the peak of Beth's witch's hat on the floor. She heard Beth's deep, even breathing. Beth was fast asleep.

Cautiously Violet edged out of bed, stepping around her sleeping friend. She went to her desk and opened the drawer, withdrew the packet of letters and diary entries, then switched on her desk lamp. She read them through, trying hard to forget all the previous connections she'd made.

A man lies dead in a cabin on the side of a mountain, she thought. But the man wasn't the sort of stalwart backpacker you imagined, and the cabin wasn't a house. Nothing was what it seemed to be. You had to let your preconceptions drop away; you had to look at the facts in a new light before the puzzle pieces dropped into place.

She read Laela's description of her dream about the golden bridge. She reread it. She read the date: *November 1, 1906.*

She glanced up at her own calendar hanging from a nail above her desk.

The light shifted. A puzzle piece dropped into place.

CHAPTER 18

Violet climbed back into bed and pulled the quilt up to her chin. She was trembling with excitement and apprehension.

Laela's dream entry was dated November 1. Violet's calendar showed that the next day's date was November 1. In Laela's dream the golden bridge had begun to sway and fall when the sun was directly overhead at high noon. In Violet's dream she had also known it was exactly noon.

Was something going to happen at noon the next day on the Golden Gate Bridge?

Maybe the parallels meant nothing. Maybe she was misinterpreting them. But maybe she wasn't, and so much was at stake, she couldn't just ignore her fears. Something had to be done. Worse than that—*she* was the one who had to do something.

Violet lay in bed trying to think what to do. No one could stop an earthquake from coming. She couldn't just tell her parents and hope they would take over and fix things. She could hardly ride through the entire Bay Area on her bike, a modern-day Paul Revere, warning people to evacuate their homes.

What *could* she do? How could she make sure that no one was on the Golden Gate Bridge at noon the next day?

She stared up at the ceiling for a long, long time. Finally, just as sleep overtook her, she hit upon a plan. It was daring, it was outrageous; it was also illegal. And yet, she told herself, she'd already embarked on a life of crime, hadn't she? Was this plan really so much worse than stealing a letter from a museum exhibit?

Yes, whispered her conscience, but she quieted it by falling asleep. And in the morning when she awoke, she knew there was no time to lose.

At breakfast Greg and Lily were making plans for the day. "It's such a lovely autumn day," said Lily, "I thought we could pack a picnic and drive over the Golden Gate Bridge to the scenic overlook before we take Sam home. It's a touristy thing to do, but fun, and on such a clear day we'll be able to see for miles. How does that sound, kids?"

Violet, entering the kitchen with Beth right behind her, stopped in the doorway and stared at her mother in horror.

Sam grinned. "Sounds cool to me."

"Remember, Mom, Rosy and I have to be at school from nine till ten to clean up the gym," Jasmine said. "But we can go after that."

"And, Beth, of course you are welcome to come with us," Lily said with a smile. "That is, if you won't mind helping out again at the shop. The new sign is being hung outside today, and I want to make sure it's done right. 'Jackstone Florists.' It should look great."

"There's also more cleaning to do before the new refrigerators and display cases are delivered on Monday," Greg added.

"I'd love to help," said Beth. "Let me just call my mom and see if it's okay with her."

Violet felt as if her tongue were stuck to the roof of her mouth. "N–no!" she burst out. "We have to stay home today."

"Are you sick, Baby?" asked Greg. "Or just tired? Come let me feel your forehead. I hope you kids didn't stay up all night partying."

"Oh, dear," said Lily worriedly. "Maybe it's not such a good idea, Greg, her sleeping up in the attic like this. I'm sure it's colder up there than in the alcove. She's already caught a chill."

"No, I haven't," said Violet desperately. "It's just that—well, listen, everybody. I think there's going to be a big earthquake today. I *know* there's going to be! We have to stay home."

"Vi!" shrieked Rose. "You can't know that!"

"Yes, I can. I do know it. You'd know it, too, if you'd just—"

She broke off as her father cleared his throat. "Now, Baby," Greg said reprovingly. "Do you really want us to cancel our plans just because you're afraid of earthquakes?"

"Yes!" she cried. Then she pressed her lips together and looked beseechingly at her sisters and Beth and Sam. *Help me out*, she thought. *You read the letters, too.* She would have to get them alone so she could tell them how she'd figured out the date and time. Then they'd believe her. She glanced at the clock by the stove. Already 8:30. There wasn't much time left.

"It's natural to be worried about earthquakes," Lily was

saying soothingly as she brought a basket of bagels to the table. "With all the little ones we've had lately and all the talk about them, it's no wonder you're frightened, honey." She brought a plate of lox and a tub of cream cheese to the table and sat down. "Help yourselves everybody."

"Even Vi's science project is about earthquakes," Jasmine added.

"Just remember—little quakes let off steam," Sam offered, spearing a piece of lox with his fork. "We don't have to worry about big quakes as long as we have little ones. That's what my dad says, anyway."

"Sounds like a good theory to me," Greg said.

"Me, too," said Rose.

"*Please* let's stay home," begged Violet.

"No, dear." Lily shook her head. "But how about this? If you're really worried, you may stay home by yourself. You can work on your paper for school. In fact, maybe you should. Have you finished it yet?"

"Nearly." Violet spread cream cheese on half a bagel and bit into it. It was no use trying to convince her parents. But after breakfast she would tell the others. *They* would believe her.

But they didn't. Up in Jasmine and Rose's bedroom while the two girls hurriedly braided each other's hair, Violet showed the others Laela's diary entry and told them about her realizations of the night before. "The date is the same," she finished. "I think it's a sign."

Jasmine shook her head. "I think you're taking things too far."

Rose sighed. "*Really,* Baby. Get a grip." She fastened an elastic band around Jasmine's thick braid with an audible snap.

Even Sam just sat looking faintly embarrassed, as if he

thought Violet were making a fool of herself. And maybe she was. Only Beth looked worried.

Violet appealed to her friend.

"Look at the date on this entry, Beth!" she insisted. "It's November first, same as today. And the time—with the sun directly overhead, that would be noon! You know how at first I thought all the parallels between Verity's time and mine were there to warn me about murderers or heart failure, but—"

"You've got a huge ego, Baby," reproved Rose. "Always thinking things are about you!"

"But that's what I'm trying to tell you," cried Violet. "It's bigger than that!" She put her hand on Beth's arm. "Don't you get it? We might be driving across that bridge at noon on our way to have a picnic, and there will be other people, too. On a beautiful day like this, loads of people will be out on the bridge. There are always kids skating or walking across, and joggers—not to mention all the cars crashing and burning and falling. Do you want people falling to their deaths? Do you want *us* to be on that bridge, too?"

"I just don't know what to think," Beth murmured.

Flumes, remembered Violet. *Children running from the ruins.* Could the wreckage be a car? Could the shadow children be not ghosts but specters of a disaster yet to come? *"Help us!"* cried the little girl. Was Violet the one who could help?

Sam cleared his throat. "Even if we do believe you, Vi," he said, "the problem of what you can do about it is the same. Like, even if you stay home today, what about all those other people? Are you going to stand at the entrance of the bridge and hold up a sign saying 'Go Back or Else!'?"

"People will think you're cracked," said Jasmine. "Come on Rose. We're already late." She and Rose left the room.

"I don't care what people think," declared Violet, and realized that in this case it was true. "Of course there's a chance I've got it all wrong. But what if I don't? I'm not willing to take that risk." There were the children to save, and all the other people. There was her own family to save—and her friends.

"Oh, Vi." Beth looked torn. "The picnic will be fun. It's so unlikely that anything will happen . . . You know I want to be on your side, but—"

"I am not driving over that bridge. No way."

Violet and Beth looked at each other. Violet felt near tears. "Well, how about if we take BART?" suggested Beth. "Will you come with us then, Vi?"

"No." Violet shivered at the idea of being on the train under the bay when the quake hit.

"How about the ferry?" asked Sam. "Then if there's a quake, we'll just bob around."

"Yeah, good idea," said Beth. "Let's go ask your parents. The ferry will be more fun, anyway! I haven't been on one for years, and we can even eat our picnic while we're out on the water." She jumped up and ran down the stairs.

Violet hadn't said she would go on the ferry, but she followed her friends downstairs. When Lily agreed they would go to San Francisco by ferry as long as Violet came, too, Violet felt she had to say she would. But that still didn't help the people who would be on the Golden Gate Bridge at noon.

Beth and Sam watched morning cartoons, laughing uproariously, while they waited for Jasmine and Rose to return from cleaning up at the school. Lily and Greg drank coffee at the kitchen counter and talked about their new shop. Violet sat on the front steps, squinting up at the sun. Every minute it moved higher in the sky. At noon it would be directly overhead. What would happen then to all the people on the bridge? What would happen to the children?

Only one thing might help those people, and Violet was going to try it. But she wouldn't tell her sisters or Beth or Sam. No sense getting them in trouble if things went wrong.

She waited until her sisters returned and everyone was downstairs, almost ready to leave for Jack London Square, where they'd get the ferry across to San Francisco. She didn't want to put her plan into action too early. Then she said, "I've got to go to the bathroom. I'll be down in a minute."

Jasmine and Rose looked exasperated. "We'll wait in the van," said Greg. Beth hesitated at the foot of the stairs, almost as if she sensed that Violet was not going to the bathroom at all. Violet longed to have Beth at her side now, as they had been together in so many games before.

But this was not a game. And Violet knew she must act alone.

She gave Beth a little smile. "I'll be right back," she said, and ran upstairs to her parents' bedroom. She sat on the bed. She reached for the telephone, then drew back. What if her call could be traced to this phone? She didn't dare—her parents would be in terrible trouble.

It was already 10:25 now. There was very little time. She sidled down the stairs, pressing against the wall. Her sisters and Beth and Sam were laughing as they followed Lily and Greg out of the house. Violet edged down the hallway, raced through the dining room to the kitchen, opened the back door, and slipped out. Then, bending nearly double to avoid being seen, she skittered past the bushes and around the next-door neighbors' house. Breaking into a run, she tore through several backyards to the next corner, where there was a pay phone outside a little Chinese grocery.

Did she have enough money? She felt in her pockets and

came up with only a dime. But wait—you didn't need money to call 911.

She pressed the buttons, holding her breath.

The dispatcher answered immediately. "Hello, what is your emergency?"

For a second Violet couldn't speak. She felt as if her voice were frozen in her throat. "Hello?" repeated the voice urgently. "What is your emergency? Can you hear me?"

"There's a bomb," Violet whispered into the receiver.

"Excuse me? Can you speak louder?"

"A bomb! On the Golden Gate Bridge." There. She'd done it.

"May I have your name, please?" the dispatcher asked quickly.

"You don't need my name. But it's true, I know it! There's a bomb set to go off on the Golden Gate Bridge— at noon. At noon today! You need to close the bridge, get everyone off!"

"How do you know this?" asked the voice on the other end of the line.

Violet thought quickly. "Um—my brother! Yes, I overheard something about a bomb—my brother and his friends set it. They're going to try to blow up the whole bridge. At noon today, that's the important thing. You need to get the police to close the bridge before noon. Get everyone off before it starts—I mean, before it blows up!" Abruptly, before the voice could ask anything else, she slammed down the receiver. She was shaking, and her heart was pounding so loud she was sure the people coming out of the little grocery store could hear it.

Quickly she turned away from the phone booth and pelted back through the yards to North Street. She collapsed on the back steps of her house, panting.

The door opened and Lily peered down at her. "Violet! We were looking everywhere for you! You said you were going up to the bathroom. What in the world are you doing outside?"

"I—um—I thought, um, I thought I'd left some of my schoolbooks out here." The lie brought a flush to her cheeks.

"Maybe you do have a fever. Come inside and let me check. I'm sure it wasn't good for you to stay up so late last night."

"That's right," Violet agreed readily. "Probably I'm too sick to go anywhere today—and you should all stay home to take care of me."

Lily looked at her searchingly. "I'm getting very worried about you." But when they went in to the kitchen and Lily pressed the plastic temperature strip to Violet's forehead, there was no fever.

Rose and Jasmine appeared in the doorway. "Oh, *there* she is," said Rose.

"Are you okay?" asked Jasmine.

"She's fine," replied Lily.

"Good, so can we go now?" Rose asked impatiently. "Everybody's waiting."

Greg, Sam, and Beth were sitting in the van. Sam had made himself comfortable during the long wait with his feet propped on his backpack. "The ferry leaves in twenty minutes," Greg said with a frown. "We'll have to hurry if we're going to make it now."

Violet looked at her watch. 10:35. By the time they caught the ferry and got to San Francisco, it would be nearly 11:30. Then they needed to take the cable car—they would arrive just before noon. At least she hoped they'd be there by noon. She didn't want to be on a cable car going up a steep hill at noon.

"Wait a sec," she said as they all piled into the Jackstones' van. "I need to go back inside." Her father sighed dramatically but handed her the key, and she ran back into the house. She emerged a moment later carrying the family's first-aid kit from the bathroom cupboard. "We may need this," she said, climbing into the van.

Rose rolled her eyes. But Violet settled herself on the seat next to her, buckling the seat belt resolutely. She had done what she could. There was nothing else to do.

Whatever happened next, at least she would know she had tried.

The ferry ride seemed to last forever. Violet stood at the bow and stared down at the choppy waves. Planes flew overhead, slivers of silver among the clouds, heading east. The brisk, salt-scented wind whipped Violet's hair into a tangle. Her sisters were wearing neat braids—but she had been so caught up in her worries that matching her sisters was the last thing on her mind. Her parents, sisters, and Beth stood nearby, munching sandwiches and grapes.

Sam came up behind her. "Are you okay, Vi?" he asked. "Aren't you hungry?"

"No, I'm nervous," she said stiffly. "But at least we're not driving over the Golden Gate Bridge."

"I guess I feel nervous, too," he confided, "whenever I let myself think about earthquakes. But I try not to—"

"That's not good enough," she said curtly. "Not today, anyway. If Laela's dream and my dream are right, then there's going to be another earthquake at noon, and the Golden Gate Bridge is going to fall." She checked her watch. "In about half an hour."

"You're pretty sure about this, aren't you?" he asked.

"It makes about as much sense as everything else that's

been happening," Violet replied. "But I hope I'm wrong. I hope nothing happens at all."

"I wish I believed it would help to go to the bridge and report the quake to the people at the toll plaza so they could stop the cars from going across," Sam said. "But they'd never believe me in a million years."

"I know," said Violet. She had to bite the insides of her mouth to keep from blurting out that she'd already reported something more compelling. No one must know what she had done. She peered across the water to the bridge, hazy in the distance. Were the police evacuating the bridge now because of the anonymous bomb threat? She couldn't tell.

The ferry ride ended and Violet's family and friends started walking for the cable car. She saw a policeman driving by in a patrol car and felt her cheeks grow warm. What was he doing up here when he should be over at the Golden Gate Bridge, shutting it off to travelers? Was he out looking for mad bombers? Or for crazy girls who called in fake bomb threats? Violet checked her watch again.

They hopped on a cable car at the terminus. As they traveled along, Violet stared out at the streets, trying to picture how they had looked back in 1906 after the earthquake and fire. Picturing the past was hard, but it was all too easy to picture how the city would look if an earthquake hit now. She tried to push out of her mind the images of houses jolted off their foundations, piles of rubble in the streets, and homeless, injured people everywhere.

Finally they arrived. Chance Street shimmered in the autumn sunshine. Dry brown leaves skittered along in the gutter, driven by the brisk wind. To Violet, the street seemed unusually noisy. Birds were everywhere, chirping from the trees and telephone wires. There were a lot of dogs barking from behind fences and inside houses. *Funny.* She'd never noticed all this noise on Chance Street before. Could it be true what she'd heard on the news about animals becoming agitated just before a quake?

"I'll just drop my stuff off at home," Sam was saying. "Then I'll come over."

"Thank you, dear," said Lily, smiling at him approvingly. Jasmine and Rose nudged Violet behind their mother's back, grinning.

Inside the shop, Lily and Greg started assigning chores. "Jazzy and Rosy, you two girls can lay shelf paper on the shelves over here. Beth, dear, would you please sweep once more—making sure to get in those corners? Baby—"

"I'll sweep the courtyard," Violet said hastily. She didn't want to stay in the old shop. It had survived the 1906 quake, true, but its old walls seemed none too safe to her now.

"Fine. I'll send Sam to help you when he comes back." Lily switched on the portable radio they'd brought from home. Rock music blared as Violet escaped out the back door.

She swept dead leaves off the pavement slabs and imagined how the garden might have looked before old Miss Stowe had covered it over with concrete, back in the days when Laela worked here, when Verity lay in bed in the room overlooking the garden, when Hal planned to elope with her. There would have been beds of flowers and bushes along the back, probably, and the stone birdbath over there—and the bench there by the wall. She could practically smell how fresh and lovely it once was, how small and cozy and inviting, the perfect place to sit with tea and needlework. She was standing there leaning on her broom and musing that here was another place where layers of time cracked, letting bits of the past filter through, when the screen door burst open and Rose stood in the doorway.

"Vi!" she said, and her voice sounded strange.

"What?"

"You'll never believe what we just heard on the radio! The Golden Gate Bridge has been closed. There was a bomb threat, and the police have stopped all traffic!"

Violet glanced at her watch. It was 11:53. Seven minutes till noon.

"That's good," she said calmly. "Did the report say how long they'll keep it closed?"

Sam and Jasmine appeared at the door behind Rose. "Apparently the bomb is supposed to go off at noon," Sam said. "So the bridge will be closed at least till then. The bomb squad has been called out."

"Oh no." Violet hadn't expected that. "They shouldn't let *anyone* on the bridge—"

"Baby," said Rose, narrowing her eyes. "What do you know about this?"

"How many times do I have to tell you not to call me Baby?"

"Don't change the subject, *Violet Emily Jackstone*! What do you know about this?"

"Me?" Violet widened her eyes. "How could I know anything about *bombs*? I just hope that no one is on the bridge when it goes off, that's all."

"Hmm," said Jasmine, pushing past the others to come outside to the yard. "If I didn't know you so well, Vi, I'd wonder if you had done something..."

"Done what? Planted a bomb on the bridge?" Violet tried to make her voice sound outraged, but it came out as a little squeak. "Where would I get a bomb?" She looked at her watch again. 11:55. Five minutes till noon.

"Come on out here, you guys. *Fast!*"

"What for?" asked Rose, not moving.

"It's almost noon!" She wasn't sure the courtyard would

be any safer than the house, but at least the walls wouldn't be able to collapse on them outside.

"Even if there is a bomb on the bridge," said Rose scornfully, "it won't reach us here."

"But you're not really worried about the bomb," Sam said slowly. "Are you?"

"You still think there's going to be an earthquake, don't you?" Jasmine jumped off the stoop. "Okay, come on, Rosy. It can't hurt to humor her about this."

"No, I suppose not," Rose agreed. "But what about Mom and Dad? And Beth?"

"We have to get them, too," said Violet urgently now, glancing at the time. "The house is too rickety to be safe. Out here we have a chance. Tell them—"

"Want to do another faint?" asked Rose. "Like in the museum?

"No—just say I need to show them something. *All* of them!"

Rose vanished back inside. Violet reached out and grabbed Jasmine and Sam by the hands. "Come over here," she said, pulling them to the far corner of the yard. "Away from the buildings. Most people in quakes are killed by falling roof tile and stuff, right?"

Rose and Beth came outside, but there was no sign of Lily or Greg.

"Oh, Vi, the things I do for my friends." But Beth's giggle sounded nervous.

"I couldn't get them to come," Rose said. She didn't seem worried. "Mom is upstairs screwing new lighting fixtures into the ceilings. And Dad is holding the ladder. They said whatever it is you want to show them can wait."

"But it can't!" cried Violet. Her watch read 11:57. She watched the second hand sweep around, and then it was

11:58. Two minutes longer! She sank to the ground. "Hurry, Rose, tell them I've fainted." She felt strange and dizzy—so frightened now at what might indeed be coming, she thought she might *really* faint.

Rose sauntered back inside while Sam, Beth, and Jasmine crouched over Violet. "Calm down," Sam said soothingly. "Nothing is going to happen."

11:59 . . . 12:00. Violet held her breath. Rose appeared again, with Lily and Greg behind her. They came outside, down the steps into the concrete yard.

"What is it, Baby?" cried Greg, hurrying over. "Rosy said you felt faint!"

"Oh, I *knew* she was up too late last night," moaned Lily. "All this activity can't be good for her heart!"

Violet sat motionless, her head drooping low between her raised knees. She flicked a glance at her watch. 12:01 . . . 12:02. The autumn sun hung directly overhead. She could feel the touch of warmth on her head despite the brisk breeze. Had she been wrong, then? Was it all a mistake?

But then there was a hush, as if all the city held its breath. And next, far down within the earth, beneath layers of soil and bedrock, miles deeper than anything could live, there came a rumble. It was an ominous rumble, a sudden slow shifting as if a giant animal under the earth had awoken from a long sleep and stretched—*Yyyaaawwwnnn.* That rumble was a portent of more rumbles to come, and as the Jackstone family and Beth and Sam huddled in the concrete courtyard, the rumbling changed to a groan. Then the shaking began.

Violet closed her eyes and grabbed the nearest hand—she didn't know whose.

"Stay where you are, everybody," she heard her father shout. "Hold on tight!"

The ground bucked and rolled. The concrete rippled. The

trees creaked and groaned. Somewhere nearby there were crashes and a scream, the grate of metal, the thud of heavy objects falling to the ground. Cars squealed out in the street, horns blared, and the rolling and heaving of the ground continued.

There was nowhere to run to that could be safer than where they were, Violet knew that, yet some part of her wanted to dart into the house for safety. "*Safe as houses*," she thought wildly. *Isn't that how the old saying goes?* Yet houses were not safe when the walls dipped and cracked, when the plaster was raining down and tiles spilled off the roof. Where could you go when nowhere was safe?

"Help!" cried Rose as the bricks from the chimney smashed to the ground only a few feet from where they huddled. Greg drew her into his arms.

Jasmine and Beth were sobbing in terror. Lily leaned over the girls protectively, her arms outstretched as a mother hen might shield her chicks with her wings. Sam was looking wildly around him, starting at each crash or bang from the street. It was his hand Violet was clutching, and he held on tightly as if she were the anchor that would keep him from being flung out to sea. Violet sat frozen while all around her the cries and sobs and thumps and crashes merged together into one great cacophony.

She squeezed her eyes closed and immediately there were flames—*flames!*—and the acrid smell of burning rubber. She could not breathe. The shadow children were there, reaching out to her, crying for help—no, not crying after all. They were shouting something. Not reaching out to her—they were waving. The smoke cleared and the three children stood hand in hand, two boys and the little girl. Behind them stood their car, unburnt, and the dark figures of their parents, waiting for them. The shadow children turned and walked toward them, the little girl turning back once more to wave. Violet felt their gratitude wash over her, like water extinguishing flame, as the dark shape of their car drove away into nothingness.

And then there was silence and in the silence she opened her eyes and looked up to see a girl a few years older, a girl with russet hair pulled back into a neat bun at the nape of her neck, standing right in front of her. The girl was wearing a long dark skirt and a white blouse with a high collar, and she was holding out her hand to Violet. Although the girl appeared to be part of the little group out in the backyard, Violet knew with a shiver that she was not really part of anything anymore.

"Laela?" whispered Violet. "Or are you Verity?"

But even as she spoke, the girl faded away and all that was left was the silence in the backyard and the huddle of her family and friends around her.

"It's over," came Rose's tremulous voice.

"Careful, everybody," warned Greg, "there may be aftershocks."

No one moved. They waited, frozen, but nothing happened. After another moment, Lily gave a little laugh and hugged whichever girls she could get her hands on. "Everybody okay? Are you girls okay? And you, Sam?"

"I'm okay," said Sam weakly.

"Did you see her?" asked Violet, but her voice came out a whisper. "Did you see Laela?"

"That must have been the 'big one,'" murmured Jasmine. "It *must* have been. There couldn't be anything bigger than that."

"I thought it was the end of the world," said Beth, pushing her hair from her eyes. She looked around at everyone and managed a smile. "I really thought it was the end."

"What about you, Baby?" Greg knelt next to Violet. "We came out because Rosy told us you'd fainted. What happened? Are you okay now?"

Then suddenly everyone was looking down at Violet where she sat on the hard concrete. She was staring up at the sky, where the glint of an airplane shone silver through the clouds. *The people up there missed it,* she thought aimlessly. *They don't even know*...Then she blinked and saw her family and the wonder in their eyes.

"Did you see Laela?" she asked. "I did."

They weren't listening to her. They were just marveling over her.

"It was just as you said, Vi!" exclaimed Jasmine. "An earthquake at noon."

"We have a prophet amongst us!" Rose exclaimed dramatically.

"But really," marveled Greg, "it's the most amazing coincidence."

In the distance, sirens started wailing. Violet wondered if the Golden Gate Bridge was still standing.

CHAPTER 19

"But of course you couldn't really have known," Lily said anxiously, helping Violet to her feet. Lily's eyes were wide with fear. "Right, sweetheart? It was just a guess, wasn't it?"

Obediently, Violet nodded.

They brushed themselves off and walked tentatively up the back steps into the Chance Street shop. "Oh no," moaned Jasmine as she stepped inside.

"All that cleaning!" wailed Rose. "All for nothing!"

The house was a shambles. Plaster dust had sifted down over everything. The clean floors and windows now looked as dusty as if they had been untended for a decade.

"But at least the walls are standing," Greg said with satisfaction. "This is a well-made building."

"And fortunately we don't have much in the way of furnishings in here," said Lily. "You're right, dear. It could be a lot worse. But what about our things at home?"

"I'd better get home and see if everything's all right at

my house," said Sam. He picked his way through the fallen plaster and turned back by the front door. "Um, thanks for everything. The Halloween Ball and the sleep-over and everything. I'll come back to help you clean up here once I see what's happening at home."

"Let us know if there's anything we can do for your family," Lily said. And when Sam had left she added, "What a nice, polite boy you've found, Vi."

Violet stood at the window. She could see Sam's house still standing across the street. In fact, all the houses on Chance Street seemed to be unharmed except for the scattered bricks from fallen chimneys and some broken window glass. People were rushing out into the streets now, checking on neighbors, calling dogs and cats home.

Greg walked to the wall in the front room and pressed the light switch. Nothing. "Electricity is out," he said. He picked up the telephone. "There's a dial tone. Beth, you'd better try to reach your mom. She'll be worried about you. I'll go turn off the gas before we all explode." He strode away.

"I'd better cancel the sign for the shop," said Lily slowly. "No sense hanging it today, when we won't be opening on time."

"The radio still works," called Rose from the back room. "It's on batteries. Let's listen for the news." She came into the room carrying the portable radio.

"*Whoa*, folks!" the disc jockey was exclaiming. "That one sure shook things up, didn't it? Just hang on to your hats for another minute and we'll be bringing you a news update. We're lucky we still have power!" His voice was lighthearted, carefree, but Violet detected a giddy tone. She felt near to hysteria herself but forced herself to listen to the newscaster who came on next. Her sisters and Beth crowded close to listen.

"Today's quake hit at 12:02 P.M.," began the newscaster in an appropriately grave voice. "The epicenter has been determined to be on a recently discovered branch of the San Andreas fault, three to four miles out in the ocean off the coast of San Francisco. Seismologists are still trying to calculate an exact reading on the Richter scale, but early reports say it was at least a 7.3. The water turbulence generated by the quake is severe, and there is currently some concern about tidal waves. Communities along the coast as far north as Mendocino and as far south as Carmel are being evacuated. We're getting updates right now—" He broke off, then continued excitedly.

"There is a fire at Fisherman's Wharf, and the area is currently being evacuated. Word has just come in that several blocks in downtown Oakland will also have to be evacuated due to the danger of explosions. And wait—what's this? A report just now that police and firefighters are on the scene at the Golden Gate Bridge, where a cable has fallen across the deck, causing a collapse to part of the road! Let's see if we can transfer over to Jenna Fisher, reporting live from our helicopter."

Crackling, then a woman's voice came scratchily over the airwaves. "Yes, Dave, there's a lot going on on the Golden Gate Bridge just now. But despite the usually high volume of traffic over the bridge, there are no reports of injuries at this time owing to the bridge's having been closed shortly before the quake. In what police are terming an 'amazing stroke of good fortune,' a bomb threat was called in this morning, forcing immediate closure of the bridge."

"Thank you, Jenna," the newscaster said. "And now let's link up with Police Chief Darren Parker at the Golden Gate Bridge. Chief Parker? Can you tell us about this bomb threat?"

Violet, her eyes downcast, fists shoved deep into the

pockets of her jeans, listened as the deep, harassed-sounding voice of the police chief came on the air. "We received a 911 call this morning from what sounded like a young girl. The call was made from a pay phone in Berkeley, but we have found no traces of the caller. She stated that she'd overheard her brother talking about planting a bomb to go off on the bridge today at noon, and begged us to close the bridge. She sounded quite upset, and in any case we must treat all such threats as potentially genuine. There was something about her tone . . . So the bridge was closed immediately and traffic re-routed. It's just amazing that the bridge cable should break in the earthquake and come crashing down like this with the bridge totally empty of cars. If there had been traffic crossing as usual, we might be looking at hundreds of fatalities!"

"And what about the bomb?" asked the newscaster. "Did it go off?"

"No sign of any bomb," replied the chief. "We have our bomb crew still checking, but there's nothing so far."

"Thank you, Chief Parker," said the newscaster. "And now, to recap: The earthquake measured 7.3 on the Richter scale and hit at 12:02. Reports are still coming in about the massive damage to the coastal town of Bolinas . . ."

"Vi was right all along," Jasmine said in a voice tinged with awe. "I can't believe it. She was right about the earthquake *and* about the bridge!"

"We might have been driving on the bridge when the cable fell, who knows?" said Beth. "If Vi hadn't made us take the ferry instead—"

Rose remained silent, her arms wrapped tightly around herself as if for warmth or comfort.

"Wasn't it lucky about that bomb threat?" trilled Lily, her voice unnaturally high. "So no one was on the bridge at all—amazing! I just don't know what to think!"

"Things like this make me *sure* there's a God," said Greg solemnly. "Perfect timing."

Violet walked to the front door and let herself out onto the front steps. Her heart was racing. The bridge had not fallen just as it had in the dreams, but when had anything come true *exactly* as it was foretold in the letters? It was enough that the quake had occurred almost exactly when the dreams predicted. It was enough that the bridge cable had fallen. *Not* my *death at all.* Hundreds of people might have been killed, but were not. She sank down on the step, hugging her knees. *That's what all this was about,* she thought triumphantly.

Sam came running across the street. "Hey, did you hear the news—about the bridge?"

She nodded, grinning, her heart too full to speak.

"Vi—?" He sat down next to her and put his hand on her knee. "Did you do it?"

She couldn't look at him. "Do what?"

"You know. They said on TV it was a girl's voice, calling from Berkeley. Was it you?"

"*Was* it?" echoed Jasmine's voice. She was at the door with Rose and Beth behind her.

"She wouldn't dare," sniffed Rose, coming out onto the steps. "Not in a million years."

"Oh yes, she would," Beth defended her friend. "She's braver than you think!"

"No shrinking violet, not *our* Baby," said Rose. "I still don't believe she had anything to do with it."

"But you'll never know for sure, will you?" said Violet coolly. She stood up and brushed her hands together in a businesslike gesture. "Well, I guess we've got some more cleaning up to do." She left the others still sitting on the steps and went to find her parents. But despite her offhand tone, she was smiling inside. She had done it! She and Laela and Verity.

Violet followed the sound of the radio newscaster's voice and found Lily and Greg upstairs in the front bedroom. "It's not too bad in here," Lily was saying as she swept mounds of fallen plaster into a black garbage bag. "If I could get the vacuum cleaner up here—"

"Don't worry," Greg said. "The electricity will be back on eventually. But I think we ought to leave this mess now and get home. There could be a gas leak—or broken water pipes. Some of the roads are blocked, and the BART is closed for a safety check. So are all the bridges. The radio says the ferries are still running so far, but they're going to be crowded." He saw Violet at the bedroom door. "Please go down and tell the other girls that we're leaving in five minutes."

"Sure." Violet started back for the stairs, then stopped as the floor shook under her feet and she heard a crash from the back bedroom. She braced herself for the vision, the terror—but they didn't come.

Then she ran down the hall with her parents close behind. "Watch out!" she called out, stopping abruptly in the doorway.

The earthquake had weakened the already loose plaster and it had rained down during the quake to cover the room, like snow. But the aftershock had cracked the exposed wooden beam and it now dipped dangerously. The crash they'd heard was the light fixture falling off the wall at the crack. It lay shattered on the floor amidst the plaster dust.

"I guess we can't open this place until I have a structural engineer out to check it for safety," Greg said with a weary sigh. "We can't very well have the roof coming down on the heads of our customers."

Lily's shoulders drooped dejectedly. "So much trouble," she said.

"Well, this is what's known as one of those Acts of God on insurance forms," said Greg. "But at least we're all safe. That's the main thing. Nothing we can do but clean up and keep going." He put his hand on Violet's shoulder. "Come on, sweetheart. There may be more aftershocks."

But Violet walked into the room despite the protests of both parents. She had seen something and couldn't leave without investigating. It was over by the window, by the cracked wooden beam. Something dark green beneath the white dust. Something familiar. She reached out and tugged—and out of the wall slid another of Albert Stowe's ledgers.

"Now why should that be tucked inside the wall?" asked Lily in surprise. She reached for it, but Violet held it close against her chest.

"I found it," she said softly. "I get to look first."

"Well, look by all means," said Greg. "But bring it with you. We've got to get home." He started down the hall. "*If* we can get home at all."

Violet rifled through the book. "It's just another ledger," she told her mother. But her heart was pounding.

"How odd!" cried Lily, reaching for it again. This time Violet handed it over. "How boring!" she cried, opening the first page and seeing a list of expenditures made by Albert Stowe, Milliner, in 1903. "As a girl I always dreamed of finding someone's old diary or some romantic love letters or something hidden away. But this looks just like the other ledgers you found in that suitcase. Too bad."

"Yeah," agreed Violet, taking it back. Although the label declared the book belonged to Albert Stowe in 1903, she had recognized the writing on the pages in the back.

"Oh, well, bring it along home," said Lily. "It might be interesting anyway. After all, someone took the trouble to hide it, didn't they? I wonder why?" She headed down the stairs. "I bet there's a story there, somewhere."

Violet wondered, as she followed her mother down the stairs, whether she might hold the end to the story right here, right now, in her hands.

She felt weak and shaky on the long trip home. The cable cars were not running and so they had to walk all the way down the hill to the ferry building. It took ages. Lily suggested staying overnight at the Chance Street shop—or at Sam's house—but Greg was determined to get his family and Beth home to Berkeley. The ferries were running, but not on their usual schedule, and they were crowded. Violet stood in a crowd of people, all chattering wildly about where they'd been during the quake and speculating about damages to property. She pressed herself against the railing on the upper deck and stared across the choppy water at the Golden Gate Bridge, letting the din of the crowd wash over her. She remembered the shadow children, how they'd waved and smiled and then driven off in a car with their parents.

Were they the children Verity had seen in her visions? Would they have been among those killed on the bridge during the quake had Violet and Laela and Verity not tried to save them? No way to know, but with the wind on her face and the thrum of the ferry's engines sending a comforting throb through her body, Violet felt sure she would not see them again. The shadow children, part of the earth as much as everything else, had gone. Whoever they were, they were safe now.

All the passengers cheered when the ferry finally docked at Jack London Square. The Jackstones and Beth cheered when they saw the Jackstones' van parked where they'd left it, undamaged.

Even the normally short drive from Oakland to Berkeley took much longer than usual because the roads were clogged with cars and many streets were filled with broken branches and roof tiles. Some cars had pulled over to the side and seemed to be abandoned. Violet wondered whether they had broken down in the quake, or whether their occupants had simply been unable to drive on the blocked roads. People were in the streets, pulling debris out of the way so cars could pass. At one large intersection, a traffic light had crashed down onto a fire hydrant and traffic was being routed around the mess. Their van crawled along, taking detour after detour around fallen brick chimneys, signs, and trees.

They dropped Beth off at her apartment by the freeway and stayed to talk to Beth's mother and brother, Tom. An outside staircase on the side of their building had crumbled during the quake. "I saw it!" Tom yelled excitedly. "I was just coming home from a walk with the dog, and I saw it happen!" Beth's old schnauzer, Romps, panted at his side.

Finally they were home. Many of their neighbors stood outside in the street as they drove up, checking that all the street's residents were accounted for and that no one had been hurt.

"Glad to see you," said Mr. Green as they climbed out of the van. "Wasn't sure you'd be able to make it home. Hear some of the roads are blocked." He was bent over, collecting trash that had tumbled out of his garbage cans during the quake.

"We took the ferry," Lily told the old man. "Lucky for us it was running. Otherwise we'd have had to spend the night in our San Francisco shop—and that's a mess. I'm afraid to look at the house."

Jasmine started helping to gather litter from the bushes and sidewalk. She stuffed it into Mr. Green's garbage can.

"All my dishes!" moaned Mrs. Carruthers from next door. "They flew right out of the cupboards. Our wedding china!"

"I never thought I'd be glad to have those childproof locks on my cupboards," Mrs. Rabinski said with a satisfied nod. "But my daughter-in-law is a stickler for safety where her kiddies are concerned and wouldn't let them stay overnight at my house unless I locked the cupboards. Glad I did now. All *my* china stayed put!"

"Lucky for you," sniffed Mrs. Carruthers. "Of course, when I'm old enough to have grandchildren, maybe I'll have locks on my cupboards, too—"

"I was down at the grocery store," old Dr. Edmunds from across the street said quickly. "We had to duck and cover our heads. I was in the cereal aisle, thank goodness. At least those boxes aren't heavy. My wife was by the soup. One of the cans landed right on her foot."

"Yes, and others were flying right past my eyes!" Frail Mrs. Edmunds took up the tale in her quavery voice. "Then we came home—to this." She pointed at the white picket fence that had bordered her yard but now lay bent and splintered across the sidewalk. "What about you girls? Were you frightened?"

" 'Course they were frightened, who wouldn't be?" said Mrs. Carruthers.

"We were *terrified*," agreed Rose. "The shaking seemed to go on for the *longest* time."

"We were outside when it happened—in the backyard," said Jasmine, "because Vi had warned us—"

"Let's go inside," Violet interrupted hastily.

"*Warned* you?" echoed Mr. Green.

"Now how could she know—," began Dr. Edmunds.

"And speaking of warnings, did you hear on the news

about the bomb threat?" Mrs. Rabinski interrupted. "I heard it on the TV. The Golden Gate Bridge was shut down just an hour before the quake hit. No one was on it at the time—and lucky thing, too, since a massive cable came plonking down. Destroyed a whole stretch of the road."

"Similar to what happened with the Bay Bridge back in 1989," said Greg.

"Think how bad it would have been if cars had been on the bridge today as usual," said Dr. Edmunds, and he shook his head. "We don't usually have anything to thank bombers for, but in this case, I bet a lot of people are grateful."

"It wasn't even really a bomb, I don't think," said Lily. "Just a bomb threat."

"Well, whoever called it in is a hero," maintained the old doctor. "That's what I say."

Violet climbed the steps to the porch without another word. She walked quietly through the rooms of her house, noting the damage. At first glance it looked as if vandals had trashed the place. But on closer inspection it was clear that there was no major damage. Several plants had tipped off shelves and lay in piles of black dirt on the carpets. Three of the stools at the kitchen counter lay on the floor. Books had been flung from the shelves and skittered across the rooms. In the living room there was a large wet patch on the floor. Violet walked over to it, perplexed, then realized water must have sloshed out of the fish tank. There were no fish on the carpet, though, and Violet was glad to see the tiny, brightly hued tropical fish swimming rapidly in circles in the several inches of water that were left.

"Poor little things," she murmured. "We'll fill your tank up again soon."

She went upstairs, clutching the ledger. A flick of the wall switch in the hallway linen closet revealed the electricity was out, but Violet climbed the ladder to her attic bedroom. The late afternoon light coming through the windows was dim, but she could see her room had been untouched by the quake, except for the contents of her desktop, which now lay scattered on the floor. Nothing else had been disturbed. She picked up Mr. Koch's books, then threw herself across the bed, quite overcome by the events of the day. *Death warmed over,* she thought grimly, closing her eyes.

But she had not died in the quake. Nor had the people who would have been on the Golden Gate Bridge. Eyes closed, she heaved a great sigh of relief and exhaustion.

She might have slept for a few minutes because she didn't hear her sisters ascend the ladder. But her eyes flew open with a start when Rose's voice rasped at her ear.

"Okay, Baby, let's see it."

"Don't call me Baby." Violet propped herself up on one elbow. "See what?"

"The ledger. Mom said you'd found one."

"Yes, I did." Her voice sounded smug.

"Weren't you going to tell us?" asked Jasmine. "I thought we were all in this together!"

"We are. I just didn't have a chance." Violet glanced over at the desk where she had laid the ledger. "I haven't even read it yet."

"Let's do it now," demanded Rose.

And so Violet fetched the book off the desk and opened it, turning past the pages of carefully recorded columns to the now-familiar elegant handwriting. She read it to them aloud:

"February 26, 1906

"Dear Diary,
"I write at night when Verity is asleep. It is the only time I can snatch for my own. During the days I am kept busy from dawn till dark, coping with Verity and also with

the terrible twins, Rachel and Jane. As if that weren't enough to do, I am pressed to help out in the shop in Verity's place. I never supposed when I applied for this position at Hal's behest that I should become a workhorse. And yet I do it for my dear Hal. At least I get to savor his letters when he writes to Verity, and to imagine they are written to me. And I have the pleasure of answering them as well, though of course only as Verity dictates.

"I admit, dear Diary, that it grows increasingly difficult not to show my envy as we huddle like two schoolgirls over the letters, giggling over what she would like to write and what is <u>seemly.</u> It is indeed hard to hear her whisper of longing to cover his face with kisses—the very same longing I have myself.

"Hal writes to her once a week and slips me the letters on my Sunday afternoons off. I meet him for tea and try to soak up enough of the happiness his presence brings me to last me until I next see him. Then I take his letter back to Chance Street, to his own beloved Verity. I bide my time until the Stowe family is at the dinner table and I am taking my meal with Verity alone. I sleep in her room now, on a pallet on the floor near her bed. Although she tries to be strong during the day, at night she often awakens with sweats and pains and needs my attentions. She is so weak I must help her to turn over in bed. Really, I should not begrudge her the happiness her love for Hal gives her. She is very ill, I fear.

"Hal's letters must now be kept secret as indeed must the whole romance between them because Mr. Stowe has expressly forbidden any contact between his ailing eldest daughter and 'that upstart reporter.' He says he fears the excitement Hal engenders in her will harm her health.

"But in the evenings after Verity has read Hal's letter and dictated her reply, she entrusts both letters to me. My instructions are clear: Her letters to him must be hidden in my pocket and slipped to Hal when I next meet him. And his letters to her must be burned to ashes.

"I have a confession to make, dear Diary. And it pains me that I cannot do the honorable thing and follow Verity's orders. But because the letters are written by my own Hal—because his long fingers held the pen and his warm hand smoothed the page—I can never destroy them. I hide them instead deep in the crack in the wall by the window or under the shelf lining in the sales counter. They are perfect hiding places. No one will ever find them there. I hide my own writing there as well—and in several other spots around the house when I am writing while I should be at work and am caught short by someone's approach.

"I will close now as morning comes all too swiftly."

Violet looked up from the page. "I wouldn't like having Laela's job."

"Me, neither," said Rose. "It's horrible having to take care of sick people. You're always worrying they're going to die, and the whole household revolves around them, and—"

"Rosy," said Jasmine in a chiding tone, and Rose shut her mouth.

Violet regarded them both for a long moment, then read the next entry in a firm voice:

"March 2, 1906

"Dear Diary,
"I am so tired. I had no idea the job would be this demanding. After such a long day of work, there's hardly any time to write. But I find these pages to be the only

242

place anymore where I can tell the truth about how I feel. Good thing Mr. Stowe has left so many ledgers in the shop with empty pages at the back. I have been using these pages for my diary, and tearing them out when I remember to, to hide away with Hal's letters.

"My back aches from carrying bolts of new fabric—who would think that several loads of woolen cloth could be so heavy?—from the shop up to the attic for storage. No more Winter Hats, now we shall make only Spring Hats. I am hoping the lightweight fabric will be easier for me to lug around. You'd never know from how I spend my days that I am the hired companion for Verity. I pictured myself sitting by her bedside reading to her or chatting; I even thought we might become friends. After all, we have one very important someone in common, though she does not suspect my deepest feelings of love. I have been very discreet, as Hal wishes me to be. Verity thinks only that we are casual acquaintances. But I didn't bargain on having to work in the shop as well as playing nursemaid, and, really, the sisters, Jane and Rachel, are hopeless. At twelve years old they could help in the shop themselves, I feel. But they come home from school and run around and get in everyone's way, making noise and disturbing Verity's rest. They never go near Poor Baby, for they're afraid of contagion, though the doctor feels quite certain that the wasting disease is in her blood and compounded by her weak heart—and not anything at all in the air we breathe around her. She is really much sicker than I thought at first, and I have tried to tell Hal, but he doesn't want to believe me. I fear he thinks I am falling for the family's version of things, and who knows, maybe I am. Maybe it's just my wishful thinking that would keep him and Verity apart if I could!"

"Isn't that too bad," said Violet. "Verity died so young. Hal must have been miserable."

"But not for too long, with Laela to help him get on with his life." Jasmine drew up her knees and wrapped her arms around them. "It's a good thing Verity wrote to Hal telling him to marry Laela, otherwise he might never have married anyone and would have *stayed* miserable."

Violet turned the page and read the next diary entry aloud:

"April 5, 1906

"Dear Diary,
"Verity is so weak and listless most of the time now that it came as a great shock when she perked up today and said she wanted to see Hal and that I must help her. Most of the time she sleeps or tries to work her needlepoint portrait. But her fingers aren't so nimble anymore, and only last night she asked me to pick out nearly all the stitches she'd put in this week.

"We had to let the twins in on the plan because I needed to get a message to Hal. Jane and Rachel promised to deliver it to him at the newspaper office if we would let them come along to Kauffman's—the restaurant down the street. It wasn't the best way to arrange a secret rendezvous, I know, but it was the easiest and quickest.

"We set the time for four o'clock because I knew Mr. Stowe would be out of the shop on deliveries, and Mrs. Stowe would be busy with a fitting.

"The twins and I sat near the door, leaving Verity to slip away alone to a table in the back. I plied the younger girls with cakes and hot chocolate, and, of course, Jane spilled hers and Rachel had a coughing fit over some crumbs. At last, from the window I saw my darling Hal's approach. He

cut a handsome figure, indeed, in his jacket and bowler, and looked every inch a gentleman. Yet I felt a heavy sadness despite my pleasure—for though his face lights with joy, his smile dazzles, and his eyes crinkle at the corners, none of this is for me. It is all for Verity.

"He acted as if he did not see me and went quickly to sit with his beloved. They had their heads close together for so long, I considered taking the twins home. But Verity had made me promise to remain—for propriety's sake as much as for safety's. She needs my assistance throughout the day and depends on me to be at her side.

"I tried to keep the twins occupied by playing guessing games about the other customers. We decided the man with the walrus mustache, sitting alone and reading the newspaper, was a spy; the two fine ladies drinking tea were his contacts from the other side. We also thought the ladies would do well to order their next hats from Stowe's, as the ones they wore were clearly inferior and unfashionable.

"Soon the girls tired of this game and left their seats, giggling. Before I could stop them, they were in the back of the restaurant, confronting their sister and Hal. 'Buy us some ice cream or I'll tell Papa you're here,' cried Jane. 'I think I shall tell him whether you get us ice cream or not!' added Rachel. Two more obnoxious girls I've never seen.

"Verity's face grew alarmingly pale. I endeavored to reach her, but Hal was faster and gripped her shoulders. He turned to scold the twins, but Verity, to all our surprise, spoke first. And a rare scene was witnessed by the patrons of Kauffman's restaurant as Verity shouted for the girls to leave her in peace, pronounced them horrible brats, and vowed that if they even once mentioned Hal to their father or mother, she would personally cut off all their hair while they slept and throw it in the fire!

"It was a thrilling scene. Walrus Mustache called out 'Hear, hear!' and The Unfashionable Hats tittered behind their hands. Some men would have been put off by such unseemly behavior, but I could see the admiration in Hal's eyes as he took V's arm and spoke soothingly. I dragged the girls home; they seemed mortified by all the commotion. But it was no less than they deserved!

"From my window I could see the restaurant, and I watched as Hal kissed V good-bye.

"Diary, I confess, I wept."

"Poor Laela," murmured Jasmine.

"That must be what Hal meant in the first letter I found," Violet pointed out matter-of-factly, "when he said Verity was 'wonderfully vibrant' after a quarrel with her sisters in a restaurant." She wasn't sure whether she felt sorrier for Laela or Verity.

"Good for Verity!" Rose approved.

"Yeah, but poor Laela," repeated Jasmine. "What's the next one say?"

"April 7, 1906

"Dear Diary,

"The strange dreams have begun again and keep me awake at night. V tosses and twitches and cries out about disaster. She moans about bridges—Bridges! of all things!— and makes me promise to help the children . . .

"Help? It seems all I do these days is try to help, but nothing makes V any better or affords her any peace of mind. She has not seen Hal again since the scene in the restaurant nor has she spoken of him.

"Mr. and Mrs. Stowe sat with her a long time this

afternoon, and then after supper they had the doctor here once again. They do not tell me what is going on.

"Even the twins are subdued now. I wonder if they, too, feel the coldness of the shadow of death? We all know, I think, it hovers very near.

"Bridges again," murmured Violet, quickly turning to the next entry.

"April 11, 1906

"Dear Diary,

"Today on my afternoon off I went to the newspaper office and waited till Hal had his break, just long enough for us to take a walk, and I could deliver to him another of the letters from Verity. She dictated this most recent one to me in a voice so weak it was no more than a whisper. But she says she adores Hal, and I know if she were stronger, she would climb out of bed and go to him. But she cannot, so I continue to be her messenger. When she reads a letter from Hal her eyes shine with joy—much as I suppose my own eyes shine when I read the letter later and hide it away. I can't help it, Diary; I still pretend his notes are for me!

"I know it is childish to do so, but I cannot help myself. And who will ever know?

"Today when Hal read the note I'd brought, he began talking of his plans for their married life together, and oh, I could bear it no longer. I felt he must be made to understand how sick she is, how she won't recover, how their married life is nothing but a sad fancy. I wanted him to acknowledge that she is dying so that he can loosen the ties between his heart and hers. A little voice inside me wonders whether I might not also want to hurt him—to punish him for loving her.

"I hope not, dear Diary. I want my love for him to be purer than that.

"Hal swears that if Death prevents him from marrying V, he will never marry at all.

"We walked along, and he reminisced about how he and Verity had met last summer. Of course I've heard the story a million times from both of them, but I had no choice except to listen.

"The first time he saw her was at an Exhibition of Art that he himself was covering for the newspaper. Verity had become separated from her family and Hal found her, nearly weeping, behind some potted palms. He was able to restore her to her family—not that they were particularly gracious at seeing her in a strange man's company! They hardly exchanged two words, but that was when he fell in love with her, head over heels, as they say.

"The next time he saw her he was covering a burglary at the shop for the newspaper, and Verity had just fallen down the stairs and injured her ankle. She may have been desperately ill already but didn't look poorly yet, and I guess it was easy, when he interviewed her about the burglary, for his love to increase to desperate passion.

"I interrupted to tell him how she looks like a skeleton now, all wasted and bony with her long black hair spread on the pillow like an ink stain. I told him that she is now so weak she barely lifts her head for the broth I give her on a spoon.

"He grew angry, Diary! He grabbed my arm and swore to me he will convince her father to let them marry even though her father maintains she is far too ill for suitors. Hal is convinced that her weak heart is only an excuse contrived by her parents to keep him away because he is a lowly *reporter instead of an editor at the paper. Yet I see with my own eyes that Mr. and Mrs. Stowe are dreadfully worried about their oldest daughter and would give anything to have her healthy enough to be courted.*

"Hal's big plan now is to take her away with him somehow, and he begs my help in arranging her escape. If I care for him at all, he says, I will help them. My own heart boils with love for him, but oh, what good does my love do? I nearly weep when I watch his eyes and listen as he talks about <u>her,</u> his Poor Baby, his beautiful darling V held prisoner by her evil parents. She's no prisoner, I tell him, except of her own ill health. And she's no beauty, I told him today as we walked, and she's desperately sick, and you'll probably kill her if you take her away. Her parents are right about this—she's too ill to see him and too weak to climb from her bed, much less out the window..."

Violet looked up from the page. Her sisters waited for more. "That's it," Violet told them. "That's the end." She leafed through the last few blank pages at the back of the ledger, then stopped. "No, wait a minute, there's one more entry. It's a letter to Hal! But it's really hard to read because it's got all these crossed-out words and scribbles in the margins."

"Let me see," said Rose, and Violet handed her the journal. "It looks like a draft, like something Laela was trying to get just perfect."

"Like what we do with our essays for school," Jasmine added. "You know how Ms. Martuscelli goes on about *revision* all the time."

"Let me read it," demanded Violet, and she took the ledger back from Rose. "I'll just try to work in all the corrections."

The handwriting was definitely Laela's, but the many

crossed-out words made reading aloud hard. Violet motioned for her sisters to read silently along with her.

"April 17, 1906, 8:00 in the evening—

"My dear Hal,
"I hope you will be able to read this. ~~It is hard to write.~~ Always before I have dictated to Laela the letters I've sent you. But this time I must write to you ~~alone~~ privately.

"Hey, wait a minute." Violet lowered the ledger, frowning. She checked the signature at the end of the letter. "This is the same letter that Verity wrote to Hal. The one that Mr. Koch gave me!"

"How can it be?" asked Rose. "It's in *Laela's* handwriting!"

"Maybe—maybe Verity was dictating it to Laela?" Jasmine suggested.

"No, it says right here that Verity is writing this herself." Violet pointed to the page. "But we know Verity *isn't* writing it—because this is definitely Laela's handwriting!" Violet stared at her sisters. "It's a rough draft."

"Read out some more," ordered Rose. "Let's see if it's exactly the same."

"I've got Mr. Koch's version right here," said Violet, opening the drawer to her desk. She removed the packet of letters and diary entries and sifted through the pages until she found Verity's letter to Hal. She spread it out on the bed next to the open ledger. "Okay. This is from Laela's diary:

"This is a very difficult letter to write to one I ~~love so much~~ hold in such high esteem, but write I must. You

have been a stalwart friend to me since we first spoke at length last winter when you came to report the burglary. I have regarded you since then as someone ~~more precious than life itself~~ *special. I know it may not be seemly for me to write to you in such a frank manner, but I have little time left to waste in mannered conventions.* ~~Before I die~~ *I must tell you what is in my heart.*

"It's exactly the same," said Violet, wonderingly. "Except for the crossed-out words."

"Go on," said Jasmine. "Keep reading!"

"I know you say you love me and want to save me from my family; I know you have planned a wonderful, dashing escape. But I would not be fair to myself or to you—nor, indeed, to our mutual friend, Laela—if I did not tell you right now that I cannot marry you. No, Hal. I shall <u>never</u> marry you ~~despite all we have planned together, our elopement, our home together, even our children.~~

~~*"I am very ill indeed, though I know you have not*~~ *wanted to believe this. The* ^{unvarnished} *truth is that I do not have long to live."*

Violet tried to puzzle it out as she read. "Here it comes," she said after another two paragraphs. "This is where the part about Laela comes in:

"It is Laela I wish now to discuss. <u>She</u> is the woman I want you to marry instead of me. Yes, Hal. Laela loves you ~~much more than I do~~ *as much as or even more than I do. You have had a paragon as your*

friend for a long time now, but have been blind to her
~~beauty grace~~ charms. ~~If you would only~~ It is time to
open your eyes now, Hal, that you may see what
perfect happiness you might have together.

"She knows nothing of this note. I am writing it
~~in terrible pain~~ under great strain. I am so weak that
my fingers are as water."

"But this means Laela was writing it herself—and pretending to be Verity." Jasmine looked puzzled. "Why would she do that?"

"*Shh*, wait a sec. Listen to the end," ordered Rose.

"I will die very soon, Hal, ~~but even if I were to
recover miraculously and live to be ninety, Laela is
really the true love for you~~ and it saddens me that I
cannot ever become your wife.

"But Laela can—and it is my most pressing desire
that you and she should make each other happy. I beg
you, Hal, as my dying wish, to have her as your wife.
And I give you both my blessing, and shall watch you
from ~~heaven~~ above.

Your V"

Violet closed the ledger. She looked at her sisters. Rose was frowning. Jasmine looked bewildered.

"The draft is in Laela's diary," said Violet. "In her own handwriting—the same handwriting that wrote all the other diary entries. So she must have written it."

The identical sisters stared at each other, reminding Violet of how they looked when struggling to solve other puzzles. *The man in the mask,* thought Violet. This puzzle was no less confusing.

"But what about the letter Mr. Koch gave Vi?" Jasmine asked after a long moment. "That's in *Verity's* handwriting."

"Is it?" Rose reached for the letter Mr. Koch had given Violet. "Look how funny and cramped the writing is."

Violet leaned over and studied it, too. "I thought at first it was messy because Verity was so ill and weak she couldn't hold the pen. But now I think—" She hesitated a moment, then went doggedly on. "I bet Laela faked it. She wrote the draft herself, then copied it over, trying to disguise her handwriting so Hal would think the letter was from Verity."

"But *why?*" demanded Rose, and at the same time Jasmine asked, "But wouldn't Hal notice that the handwriting wasn't Verity's?"

Violet just sat there, her thoughts tumbling around in her brain like acrobats. She tried to hold them still, tried to fix them in place so she could understand what seemed so close. . . .

"Why?" she repeated, echoing Rose. "Why? Because she loved him and didn't want him to marry Verity. She knew Verity was dying anyway, but Hal had said he wouldn't marry anyone else if he couldn't have Verity. So Laela must have decided that if Hal believed Verity hadn't loved him, and that Verity wanted him to marry Laela—well, then, maybe he would."

"But the handwriting—," began Jasmine.

"Faked," said Violet firmly. "And Hal would never know because, remember, Verity had always dictated her letters to him through Laela. So every letter he had from Verity was actually in Laela's handwriting. When he got this one—all messy and hard to read—he would have thought it was Verity's own writing. Just as Laela meant him to."

"Pretty crafty," said Rose admiringly.

"I don't know," objected Jasmine. "I think it's creepy. I

don't like Laela very much. And how could she just send on this letter? Wouldn't Verity find out what she'd done?"

"Not necessarily," said Violet slowly. "Not if she was dead by then."

The strange story from the past, learned in slivers through the bits of paper that had fallen into Violet's path, was coming clear now. Violet sat quietly, trying to sort it all out in her head. Hal had loved Verity, and Verity had loved Hal. But Laela had loved Hal, too. And she'd taken the job as companion to Verity as a favor to Hal. How it must have hurt her to have to take dictation from Verity and write love letters to Hal—all the things she probably longed to write to him herself but couldn't. How relieved she must have been at the fact that despite Verity's love for Hal, she was too ill ever to marry him. That left the way clear for Laela—that is, except for Hal's vow never to marry.

So Laela would have thought of a plan. She would have written a letter, making it seem as if it were a letter from Verity. Laela would have given that letter to Hal while Verity lay dying—or perhaps *after* she had died—saying it was Verity's deathbed letter to him, and an expression of her truest wishes.

Violet could almost *see* it. Laela writing this letter by lamplight, sitting in her big armchair by the side of Verity's bed, then sealing it, and later giving it to Hal, trying to hide her feelings as she told him it was a last letter from his beloved, sealed with a kiss, for his eyes alone.

And then, since Hal loved Verity so much, he would want to honor the wishes expressed in her last letter, and grant her dying wish that he marry someone else. And that someone else was Laela.

Violet told her sisters what she thought had happened, finishing up, "And so Hal did marry Laela, and she got what she'd always wanted."

"And they lived happily ever after." Rose smirked.

"Unless she felt guilty," said Jasmine. "I think *I* would. Wouldn't you, Vi?"

"Yes, I would," said Violet. And then she realized what Laela's guilty secret had been. It was this faked letter. Laela's conscience would always have plagued her, even after long years of marriage to Hal.

Violet scrabbled through the pile of pages on her bed until she found the diary entry she had discovered in the old suitcase from the cellar. It was dated May 10, 1906—*after* the earthquake, and after Verity Stowe's death. She read from the entry aloud.

"For so long I have been wounded by the irony of it all. Small wonder, then, that I have been driven to desperate measures.

"The 'desperate measures' being a faked letter to make Hal turn to her." Everything was coming clear to Violet now.

"The facts remain unalterable. I have done a terrible thing. She is dead and I am wracked with guilt."

"Laela must have written her letter right after Verity died—or even while she was dying," said Jasmine. "That's pretty horrible."

"She was desperate," Violet said.

"I don't know," said Rose. "It still sounds like murder to me."

"No, listen to this—it fits with what we know happened later," cried Violet eagerly, and read the next lines.

"She is dead, but I am not. And Hal must never know how we have come together. Indeed, I shall endeavor all my life to ensure he never discovers the truth.

"She and Hal came together—just as she says—because she tricked him into believing Verity's dying wish was that they should get married!" Violet continued. "Remember, he had said he'd never marry anyone if he couldn't have Verity. But then Laela always felt guilty because she had tricked him—*not* because she had killed Verity. I guess Verity died of what it said in the newspaper. A wasting disease."

"Maybe leukemia," Jasmine said softly. "Like Nana had. She got so weak she couldn't lift her spoon, either. Just like Verity."

"You might be right, Vi," Rose conceded. "If Verity was too weak to hold a spoon, she was bound to be too weak to hold a pen. So she died—and then Laela sat there at her side and wrote the fake letter. It still doesn't make Laela look very good, does it? Sort of cold and unfeeling."

"Yeah, maybe," agreed Violet. "But she got him, and I'm glad. And Mr. Koch said they had a happy marriage as far as he could tell. And if Laela and Hal never married, they wouldn't have had a daughter, who had a son who turned out to be my science teacher. And if he hadn't given me the earthquake assignment, maybe..." Violet's voice trailed off as the chain of events overwhelmed her.

"Are you going to show Mr. Koch the draft of this letter?" asked Jasmine practically.

"Yeah," said Rose. "Don't you think he should know what his grandmother did?"

Violet smiled at her sisters as she gathered all the letters and diary pages together in a single pile. There they were, the three of them, sitting together as equals, talking just as she'd always longed for them to do. And she felt her heart beating steadily in her chest, felt her lungs expand healthily as she sucked in the crisp breeze from the open attic window, and she knew her body was strong and young, with a full life ahead. The other two girls were wearing matching blue sweat-shirts and she, Violet, was wearing a purple one. But being part of a matching set was no longer one of her goals. She marveled that it ever had been, and such a short time ago, too. So much had changed since that first earthquake only two weeks ago.

She felt a tickle at the back of her neck, the sort you might feel when someone is staring at you from behind. She turned, half expecting to see again the figure of the russet-haired young woman in the long skirt. But no one was there.

Violet shook her head. "I won't be telling Mr. Koch a thing," she said, as much in answer to her sisters' questions as to reassure the ghostly presence.

Laela's guilty revelation wasn't the only secret Violet was determined to keep.

CHAPTER **20**

That evening the Jackstones ate a simple cold supper of tuna salad, bread, and fruit, then set to work tidying up the house. The electricity was still off, but Lily set candles on all the tables and handed out flashlights. She used a broom to sweep up the worst of the dirt from the fallen plants, and Greg walked around checking the walls for cracks or other damage. While upstairs, he measured the space where the new staircase would be installed. Violet and Jasmine cleaned and refilled the fish tank while Rose replaced the scattered books and papers. When everything was again in order, the family sat together by candlelight and listened to the news coverage of the earthquake on their battery-operated radio.

The situation was not as bad as people might have thought, the newscasters reported optimistically. Though electricity had been interrupted throughout most of the Bay Area, very few gas mains had broken. The fires were all under control at this time. The main damage was to property—

tumbled chimneys, cracked walls, broken furnishings—and to roads. And, of course, there was the broken cable on the Golden Gate Bridge and the damaged roadbed. That would take several weeks to repair, but in the meantime commuters could take the Bay Bridge, the BART, or the ferry across the bay. Slower traffic seemed a small price to pay for such a large earthquake. There had been a few oversize waves sighted, but no tidal waves, and now people who had left their homes along the coast were returning.

But the best news of all, the newscasters continued, was that more people had not been hurt or killed. The hospitals were caring for the several dozen unfortunate people injured by crashing brick, falls, or car collisions during the quake. But hundreds more people were thankful that the Golden Gate Bridge had been closed just as they'd hoped to drive across it. "Sure we were annoyed," said one man cheerfully. "Most bomb threats are crank calls, anyway. This one was, too, wasn't it? There was no bomb in the end—but thanks to that girl who called in the threat, my car wasn't on that bridge when the cable snapped. That's what I call a piece of good luck!"

Violet went up to bed early. She felt exhausted and fell asleep almost as soon as she pulled up her quilt. In the morning she was awakened by her sisters, who climbed onto the bed, shaking a newspaper at her.

"Look at this!" cried Rose.

"Whaa—?" moaned Violet, groggy and disoriented. She sat up and took hold of the paper Rose was thrusting at her.

"Read the headlines!"

Violet squinted through sleep-filled eyes. EARTHQUAKE! blared the black letters. BAY AREA ROCKS AND ROLLS. And then in smaller letters, farther down the page: GOLDEN GATE MIRACLE.

Jasmine tapped the page. "Read this, Vi."

"Yeah, and then tell us again how you didn't have a thing to do with it," Rose added softly.

Violet's heart began thumping harder as she read the article, but she tried not to let any expression in her face betray her.

GOLDEN GATE MIRACLE

During yesterday's earthquake a cable snapped on the Golden Gate Bridge, its entire length collapsing down onto the road's surface and smashing through the side railings on one section of the bridge. Saturday traffic is typically heavy with shoppers, tourists and families out for the day. Normally a hundred cars would be traveling the bridge at any one time. And yet yesterday, when the earthquake hit just after noon, the Golden Gate Bridge was entirely empty. It had been evacuated and closed down by police after they were notified of a bomb threat.

The bomb threat was called in to a 911 dispatcher at 10:34 A.M., police report. Police dispatcher Margaret Grady, who took the call, described the voice as that of "a young girl, perhaps in her teens. Her voice sounded scared, nervous. She said she'd overheard her brother and his friends making plans to bomb the bridge at noon on Saturday. I tried to get her to give me more details, but she cried out that I should get everyone off the bridge 'before it starts.' I thought that seemed odd, and she quickly corrected herself and said 'I mean before it blows up!' Then she hung up. Later I remembered what she'd said. It almost sounded as if she knew there would be a quake—not a bomb—but of course that's nonsense."

Nonsense or not, police hope to find the caller. Police Chief Parker is quick to assert that the caller will be hailed as a heroine. "There was no bomb," he says. "So whether she really believed there was or not is something we don't know. What we do know is that her phone call prompted us to close the bridge and ended up saving a hundred lives or more. We would like to thank her."

Anyone with information is requested to report to the San Francisco police.

Violet lowered the newspaper. "So?"

Rose grabbed the paper. " 'Anyone with information is requested to report to the San Francisco police.' "

"What? Do you have information?" asked Violet.

"Yes." Rose arched an eyebrow. "I have a sister who told us the bridge was going to fall in an earthquake at noon on Saturday. She wanted to close the bridge somehow but knew no one would take her seriously if she called the police to tell them a quake was on the way."

"That's not information," muttered Violet.

"It's logic," returned Rose. "And logic tells me that this sister of mine thought of another way to get the police to close the bridge."

Logic, thought Violet with an inward smile. She tapped the newspaper. "It couldn't be me," she said. "It says here the girl who called had a brother. *I* don't have a brother."

"Oh, Vi!" Jasmine bounced on the bed. "I can't believe you had the nerve to call 911. That's really illegal, you know—making a bomb threat! And now they're calling you a heroine!"

"They're not calling *me* anything," said Violet coolly. She would admit nothing. "Now get off the bed. You're sitting on my legs."

She couldn't tell them the truth, couldn't tell anyone. It had to remain her secret. It was better that way. Because how could she ever explain to people that what had led her to make the call in the first place were messages from the past?

How could she explain that screwing up her nerve to call had been less real courage and more newfound confidence in herself?

She still didn't know what had set everything in motion. Magic? A ghostly messenger? Or, possibly, the earth itself? She remembered the pamphlet from the street fair about the Gaian principles, about how disasters such as earthquakes were said to be no more than the earth's attempts to balance itself. Was a force of nature behind all that had happened?

She remembered Verity's dream, and Laela's, and her own. *The people! The earth will take care of itself, but who will help the people?*

The pattern was there, part of the earth's fabric, and it was nothing to do with coincidence: Two girls with sisters who looked alike. Two girls who suffered ill health. Two girls who were not fully in charge of their own lives. Two girls who lived in a place where the earth was unstable, where the cracks showed through.

The pattern was there, but it was not about Verity and not about Violet. Verity had died from her illness, but Violet's heart troubles were a thing of the past. Verity had died without ever becoming friends with her sisters, but Violet was finding her place in the Jackstone threesome and no longer felt so left out. Verity had trusted her companion to be her friend, but Laela couldn't be trusted. Violet, on the other hand, had trustworthy friends in both Beth and Sam.

Somewhere, sometime, there would be another girl, another combination of sisters and friends, illness and health, and shaking bridges and shifting ground. *"There's nothing new under the sun,"* Mr. Koch always said. *"It's the same old story."* And while there was some truth in those trite sayings, Violet now knew that her future—everyone's futures—was shaped by the past, but not *bound* by the past. She was looking forward to taking charge of her life.

"Was the man really afraid?" she asked on impulse. "The one not wearing the mask, I mean."

"What are you talking about?" asked Jasmine, darting a startled look at Rose.

"The man who was afraid to come home because of the man in the mask," repeated Violet patiently. "Was he really *afraid*?"

"Well, not exactly," said Jasmine. "Not really afraid. He was—"

"Sort of nervous," said Rose. "But you're just trying to change the subject, Baby. We solved this one already. Ages ago."

"*You* did, maybe. *I* didn't." Violet wanted very much to solve this puzzle as well.

"Okay," said Jasmine agreeably. "He wasn't afraid. Not really. Take it from there."

"So the mask wasn't really a mask and the home wasn't a house," Violet remembered. "And no one is really afraid. So what's the story?"

"You can do it," said Jasmine encouragingly.

Violet thought about why people wear masks. "Masks," she mused aloud. "People wear them to scare people. To hide behind. Maybe to protect themselves, like a surgeon's mask or a welder's mask or a...a catcher's mask."

"Bingo!" said Rose.

"And so the home isn't a house, it's home plate!" cried Violet. "And there's a player on third base afraid to run home because the catcher might put him out."

"There you go," applauded Rose. "It sounded so sinister, but it was just a simple game of baseball all the time."

"See how easy it was?" asked Jasmine. "Once the pieces fall into place?"

Violet knew all about pieces falling into place.

"Speaking of puzzles," began Rose slyly, "there's still this little matter of the mad bomber saving the day. I want to know where *that* piece fits into everything."

Violet shoved back the quilt and swung her legs over the side of the bed. "Speaking of puzzles, I've got a science paper to write today. And if I'm lucky, school will be closed tomorrow due to the quake and I'll get an extra day to work on it. I've got to make a *logical* story out of all this mess—somehow." First she would call Sam, though, and see how he was doing.

"But about the bridge—" Jasmine put her hand on Violet's quilt-covered knee.

Violet met her gaze unwaveringly.

"Oh, all right. But even if you *won't* admit anything, I just want you to know— Well, we won't tell anyone what you did. And we think you're pretty amazing."

"Yeah." Rose nodded. "We're proud of you, Baby."

Tears sprang to Violet's eyes. *They love me,* she realized. *But they're not sorry for me anymore.*

Maybe someday she would tell them everything—someday when the quake and the letters and the struggles of a left-out triplet fit like puzzle pieces into the past.

"Don't call me *Baby!*" was all she said for now, but she said it with a smile.

*A new time-travel mystery from
award-winning author Kathryn Reiss*

Paint by Magic

Something is terribly wrong with Connor's mom. Suddenly she is wearing old-fashioned clothes, cooking dinner from scratch, and she has removed all of the TVs from the house. What's even more troubling is her descent into increasingly disturbing trances. Connor suspects that an old art book full of paintings of a woman who looks *exactly* like his mom is the key to her strange behavior. But since the artist who created them died before she was even born, he's not sure what the connection could be.

When Connor is unexpectedly transported back in time to the 1920s, he realizes that it's up to him to solve the mystery—and to break the evil hold an obsessive artist has over his mom before it's too late.

Posing

When the wind finally stopped, I found myself lying all curled up, weak and tattered, like a piece of newspaper blown across the playground. It felt like I was waking up from a deep sleep. I wanted to stretch, but was too tired and too heavy to move a single muscle. All the energy had been blown right out of me. I lay completely limp, with a sort of sick feeling in my stomach. I felt the fuzz of rug scratch my cheek.

Then I smelled smoke.

Cautiously, I lifted my heavy head. My eyes smarted as smoke puffed right in my face.

"Hold it right there, boy!" a man's gruff voice roared at me. "Don't move a muscle!" His face loomed in front of me. My stomach clenched. As I drew in a smoky breath, I remembered *everything*: Mom's tortured face, Dad's panic, the sketch—

Had the wind knocked me unconscious? I could see I wasn't in my bedroom anymore. And who was this man—

maybe a doctor? But why would a doctor be puffing on a pipe? And where were Mom and Dad and Crystal?

I closed my eyes, dizzy again. My brain wasn't working right. In all that wind, my brain must have gotten rattled. Something had happened to me. But what?

I heard the man's voice in the fog. "That's good. Stay nice and still till I finish your face. Good, very good."

I opened my eyes again carefully. I could see that I was now lying on a brown rug in an atticlike room, with streams of soft afternoon sunlight glinting through the open window. A warm breeze touched my face, and I smelled flowers. The breeze fluttered the cloth that covered a large canvas propped on an easel by the opposite window.

"All righty then, boy, turn your face toward me, just a bit to the right. There—just there! Perfect. Now hold it just like that!"

I obeyed the voice slowly, fear pumping adrenaline through me. *Who is this man?* Mom's eternal warning seemed to echo in my ears: *Stay away from strangers.*

"Lift your chin, and turn toward me, for crying out loud!"

I lifted my chin and looked over, holding my breath. All I saw was a tall, skinny guy standing by an easel. He had gray hair all over the place like a mad scientist, but his face looked youngish—and he wore pants with red suspenders, and a white shirt with the sleeves rolled up. He was chewing on a pipe, puffing hard, and the smoke billowed around his head in a cloud. His face was creased with concentration, and he was dabbing at a canvas on his easel with a paintbrush.

"I've almost got it—just a little more blue right here," the painter said, and stabbed his brush into a jar of other brushes. "That's all for today." He clapped his hands at me. "All right, lad, get up and out of here—nap time's over! And next time you take it into your head to settle down for forty winks in my studio, let me know ahead of time so I can set up. It gave me a turn, I don't mind telling you, when I came in and saw you lying there like something the cat dragged in. I'd have preferred you to be over there on the sofa rather than beached like a dead fish on the floor—better lighting. And those clothes! I'd choose a different shirt." He frowned at me as I struggled to stand up. My legs felt as weak as if I had been scaling mountains.

"What's that mean, boy?" The man was scowling at my T-shirt. "'Rolling Stones Revival'—that some kind of revival meeting? Are you one of them religious fellows going door-to-door proclaiming the Lord cometh?"

I glanced down at my shirt. "It—it's just an old rock group." My voice came out hoarse and raspy, as if I'd been sleeping for a long time. "My dad got me the shirt—"

"Rocks? Your dad is a geologist, is he? You must belong to that family on the next block. Heard the fellow teaches at the college."

Now that the fog was clearing, fear made me feel razor sharp. My head pounded with questions.

What was going on?

I took a deep breath and tried to be calm. Okay. Okay—this guy didn't *look* like an alien. And *he* didn't seem to know what was going on any more than I did; that was clear. While he stood there looking at me, my mind was ticking ahead, trying to figure out what I needed to do. *Run!* screamed some part of me, the part that was pumping adrenaline into my blood. *Stay cool,* whispered another part. *Look around. Figure out what's happened.* How had I come to be here, when moments ago I was in my bedroom with Mom—poor Mom—and looking at that sketch? ...

The sketch! It wasn't in my hand any longer. Where was

it? I took a deep breath and looked around the studio—because that's what it was, an artist's studio. There were stacks of canvases along every wall, and shelves full of paints, jars of brushes, books and notebooks. A table in the center of the room held clusters of shells, pottery, a toy dump truck, a bowl of eggs, and lots of other stuff. The windows didn't have any curtains, and the sunlight was streaming in. There was a skylight in the ceiling that sent more light down, like a beacon, across the floor.

"Next time you need a nap," the artist guy was saying to me sternly, "you ought to knock properly on the door, not just walk right in. It's only good manners! Are you a friend of Homer Junior? You look to be right about his age."

Homer Junior?

The artist's voice turned gruffer. "Cat got your tongue? Legs don't work, my boy? Come on now, get your bones outta here! I'm a working man—or at least I'm trying to be."

I moved shakily toward the door. That's when I saw a calendar hanging from a nail on the wall near the sink. I edged toward it. It said MARCH 1926.

"'March 1926,'" I read, my voice still rusty, as if I hadn't spoken for years. I felt like you do after a bad bout of flu—sort of shaky and faraway.

"April, actually," said the man, reaching over and ripping the sheet for March right off. He balled it up and tossed it toward an overflowing tin wastebasket in the corner. "Always forget to change the dang thing."

Nineteen twenty-six, nineteen twenty-six. The number kept repeating in my head.

I heard footsteps tapping up the stairs somewhere nearby. The door to the studio opened, and an elderly woman stood there with a smile on her face and a dish towel in her hands.

"Hello, dear," she said in a surprised voice when she saw me. "Now, when did you come to call?"

"He just seems to have dropped in," replied the artist. "Chum of Homer's, no doubt. I wish you'd keep the children downstairs, Mother. How am I going to work with these disturbances?"

"I'm sorry, Fitz, dear," she replied. "But I see his appearance gave you something new to sketch. So that's good, isn't it?"

"I try to sketch whatever's to hand," he muttered. "Might as well. Now take him downstairs, would you?"

"Why don't you come down, too, dear? We're having lemonade on the porch." Then she turned to me. "I'm Mrs. Cotton. My grandchildren and I are down on the porch, and you're very welcome to join us—"

Cotton? Like the guy in Mom's art book? I turned to the man. "Are . . . are you that painter? I mean, Fitzgerald Cotton?" My voice sounded weird. I tried again in a firmer voice. "I mean, you're the famous artist?"

"Famous?" He looked gratified. "At your service, lad. And always in need of people to sit for me, even if they don't knock before coming in. I do portraits mostly."

I was still trying to understand what seemed to be happening here. "You mean"—it couldn't be so, but I had to ask it anyway—"You mean, you're the painter in the art book? The one with the muse?"

In a flash the seemingly mild man turned into a raging tiger. He lunged, toppling me back down onto the floor. *"Who told you about that?"* he roared. His eyes blazed down into mine with a fiery intensity. *"What do you know about her?"*

I struggled to get him off me, but he was much stronger. He pinned my arms above my head with one big hand. The other hand grabbed the neck of my T-shirt. I thought he was going to hit me—or strangle me.

"Fitzy!" I heard his mother shout over the roar in my head.

"Tell me, young scoundrel, before I thrash it out of you!" the man yelled at me. "What do you know of her? Where is she? Where is my Pamela? *Tell me!*" His voice rose with every word until he was shouting the house down. *"Tell me or I'll throttle you!"*

He knows Mom's name? I thought in terrrified amazement as I kicked him hard in the leg and heard him grunt with pain. But he didn't let me go. Then the woman, waving the dish towel over her head like a lasso, pushed herself between us.

"Fitzgerald!" she yelled. "Stop it this instant! My goodness gracious, what has gotten into you?" She pulled him away from me. Shakily, I got to my feet. The maniac just stood meekly aside as if he'd never done anything wrong in his whole life.

"Sorry, Mother," he said humbly. "I guess I just lost my temper."

"I guess so!" exclaimed the woman, dusting me off with her dish towel. "Now, are you all right, lad?"

"Not really," I said haltingly. *He knows Mom's name. He knows Mom's name!*

"He should be thoroughly ashamed of himself."

"I am ashamed, Mother. Indeed I am," said her son meekly. "The lad just—surprised me." Fitzgerald Cotton's words came out in a rush. "I thought he might know something about her. Or at least about a missing sketch of mine. One that is very dear to me. It's the one I did of Pamela—"

"I'm sure he wouldn't take any of your sketches," said Mrs. Cotton. "Would you, lad?" she asked me.

I shook my head. I was feeling dizzy again.

"Just a misunderstanding, then," the artist answered quickly in a mild, friendly voice. But the look he shot me was anything but mild or friendly. It was full of menace.

"He seems to be a good lad," continued Cotton in the same fake voice. "Just moved in around the block, you see.

Father's a geologist at the college . . . I'm hoping he'll come back and model for me. How about it, boy? Will you come back tomorrow and let me finish this sketch? Then I'll turn it into a portrait."

I didn't answer.

The woman looked at me with a frown. She started to say something, then thought better of it and pressed her lips together. She turned to her son. "Well, I hope you'll pay the lad for his time."

The man nodded his shaggy head. "Of course, Mother. I'll pay him handsomely! I'll pay him for his time today. A whole quarter. How about that, lad?" He fished in his pockets. His hands were trembling as he pressed a coin into my palm. "Now, you be back here tomorrow morning sharp on the dot of nine, and we'll finish up the painting."

I just stared at him and started backing toward the door. I couldn't get my mind around what seemed to have happened to me—and the fact that this man knew my mom. How could any of this be real? A calendar that said 1926? A man with the same name as the artist from the big art book—attacking me? And now, the guy calm again, trying to arrange to paint me?

None of this made sense, and yet a little niggling throbbing in my head was telling me it did make sense, if only I could believe it. I rubbed my eyes, hard.

"You're looking tired, lad," the artist said in his deep, kind voice that nonetheless held that hint of menace. "So we'll talk again tomorrow—about all manner of things. Things that interest us both, my boy. How about that?"

I hesitated, my heart still thumping hard. I wanted to mention Mom again, and the sketch of her that made the wind start blowing, but I was afraid of what he'd do. And if the calendar on the wall was right, and this was 1926 . . .

But of course it *couldn't* be. But what if it really was?

Time travel? A quick vision of Mom astride a brontosaurus flashed in front of my eyes.

So the crazy artist was right about one thing: We definitely *did* need to talk. I needed to find out what was going on—and how I would get home again.

He shot out his hand, grabbing my arm. "Tomorrow, boy. How about it?"

There was a curious pleading note in his voice. I glanced down at the coin in my hand. It was a quarter. Slowly I held it up, squinted at the year: 1924. It felt hard and cold in my hand, and as real as anything.

Proof that this wasn't all some fantastic dream?

"All right," I whispered.

"Well, if you've got that settled," said Mrs. Cotton, "then why not come downstairs with me for that glass of lemonade?" She smiled kindly at me and tucked a long gray strand of hair back into the bun at the nape of her neck. "The children will want to meet you. If you've just moved here, you've probably not met many playmates, I'll be bound."

"Thanks," I murmured, "ma'am." I don't think I'd ever said the word *ma'am* in my life, but it seemed to come naturally now.

Then she spoke to her son. "You come on down and have a glass, too, Fitz."

He shook his shaggy head. "No, Mother. Not me." Then he looked straight at me. "Nine o'clock sharp?"

Without a word I sidled past him, out of the room. He didn't stop me.

As I started down the steep stairs, following Mrs. Cotton, I glanced back. Fitzgerald Cotton was still standing in the doorway of his studio, looking after me with hard, glittering eyes. I stared back at him, my eyes just as hard.

I felt baffled and threatened at the same time, but I would be back. And I wanted answers.

Other Books by Kathryn Reiss

TIME WINDOWS

"Deft, entertaining and inventive."
—*Publishers Weekly*
An ALA Best Book for Young Adults
An Iowa Teen Award Winner
A YALSA Popular Paperback for Young Adults

DREADFUL SORRY

★"With its skillful plot twists, the book will have
readers anxious to solve the mystery. Reiss has crafted
a fine tale of psychological time travel."
—*School Library Journal* (starred review)
An IRA Young Adults' Choice

PALE PHOENIX

"A book with everything a reader wants."
—*VOYA*
A New York Public Library Book for the Teen Age
An Edgar Allan Poe Award Finalist

THE GLASS HOUSE PEOPLE

"The steamy summer heat, the atmosphere of tension
in the house, and the family dynamics are well-portrayed."
—*School Library Journal*

Kathryn Reiss is the author of many acclaimed time travel mystery novels for teens, including *Paint by Magic*, *Time Windows*, *The Glass House People*, *Dreadful Sorry*, and *Pale Phoenix*. She says of her work: "Much of my writing touches on various notions of time—memory, perception, history, time travel . . . It is probably because I haven't (yet) stumbled upon the key to time travel myself that I am compelled to invent characters who do! My writing has become my time machine."

Ms. Reiss lives with her family in northern California, where she teaches creative writing—and dreams of earthquakes with frightening regularity.